GW00382085

Published by G W Hartley

© 2020 United Kingdom

5th Edition

All rights reserved. No part of this book may be reproduced or modified in any form, including photocopying, recording, or by any information storage and retrieval system, without permission in writing from the publisher.

1

ONE

Kisule. 16 June 1962

Alice Mtale

The phone startled her, and she seized it without switching the light on.
'Jambo Bwana,' she said.

But it was not Bwana; she recognised the voice of the lady from Galloway Farm.

'Alice here speaking, madam. How are you?' she said in English.

'No, Mrs McCullagh, not yet. I begin to worry and ...'

'I know, ma'am, but Bwana said if they set off late and they stay tonight in Naivasha, he would ring the telephone for me but he ...'

'Yes, they might. I will send Simeon to see if Bwana's car is at the club, but I think Miss Barbara she would want to come straight ...'

'No, ma'am, I do not know why they bring her home, maybe she not well. Mrs Polly she said that's why they were going to Nairobi; to bring her back.'

'All right, I will tell Polly soon she comes back. What time is the meeting tomorrow?'

'Yes, I will tell her --- and thank you. You make me feel better. I will send Simeon to the club. Goodnight madam.' She opened the patio door. Ezekiel, the watchman, was asleep on the porch. The telephone had not wakened him, but there was no time to upbraid him. She sent him to the servants' quarters to ask Simeon to go to the club and see if Bwana's car was parked

2

there.

She switched on the light and went to the kitchen. The clock stood at ten past eight, which meant she must have been sleeping in the chair by the telephone for almost two hours. It was time to spray the bedrooms, but first she went to the cooker, where the casserole had been simmering since before six. She switched off the stove, used a spoon to lift one of the chicken pieces and was relieved to see that it was not ragged.

Simeon returned from the club; the Zephyr was not there. She made a pot of tea and Ezekiel joined them. When the men left, she went back to her chair by the telephone and resumed her knitting. The wool was soon finished but she could not risk going home for another ball.

About 10.30 she returned to the kitchen. The casserole was cold enough, so she found two plastic boxes, carefully spooned in the chicken, and reorganised the refrigerator to make room.

Then she remembered she had not pulled down the mosquito nets or sprayed the bedrooms. She went first into Barbara's room. Before lowering the net, she opened the wardrobe and brought over a chair so she could reach the top shelf and found the cloth lion she had made for her on her second birthday. She put this on Barbara's pillow, tucked in the net, sprayed the room, and held her breath while she closed the bedroom door.

When she had prepared the big bedroom, she turned out all the lights, locked up and went home.

Lying in bed, unable to sleep, Alice suddenly found the solution to her problem. She remembered the number. Tomorrow she would call him on the telephone.

Bwana Finnigan would know what to do.

Relieved, she turned over and at last went to sleep.

*

3

Kisule, 1982

Harry Paine

I had expected a headstone, not this tiny faux-marble urn.

PAINE FAMILY
16 JUNE 1962
EVER REMEMBERED

Not even enough space for their names. At least the grass around the graves was kept tidy and I turned to thank the vicar for that. He was standing behind me in the shade of a flamboyant tree. A tall Kikuyu not much older than me, early thirties probably. The other plots in this European part of the cemetery had headstones, many resembling those on war graves. My family remain segregated, even in death.

Anger did not quite overcome my feeling of guilt. This is where I should have started this visit to Kisule, but now it was almost time for me to leave. I had persuaded myself not to visit this graveyard until I had answers to the questions which brought me to the place. But, in my heart, I knew that it was fear of pain that kept me away. I was more disappointed than angry. The pathetic little urn summed up everything that had gone wrong with this visit. *Ever remembered!*

By whom? Who is left to remember them now but me and Grandpa? Yet, what right have I to expect a headstone? Who would have paid for it? Should I stop over for an extra day in Nairobi and try to organise one? Why, after all these years? Nobody else will ever come to see it. A donation will be better: this little church looks as though a bit of cash wouldn't go amiss.

It must be poor sort of life for such an intelligent chap to be stuck in a backwater like this. I doubt he has many Anglicans

4

left around here: locals will want something a bit more exciting for their Sunday worship, and who can blame them? Farming this top end of the Rift must still be hard work, and unrewarding; Dad certainly didn't make much out of it. There was no legacy, only the few personal possessions and photographs that Auntie Annie gave me when she felt I was old enough. Folk nowadays won't want to tramp all this way up the hill on their day off. They'll feel they've done their penance before they even step through the church door.

That's what I'll do, give a donation.

It had been a steep climb from the vicarage. 'Halfway to heaven', the vicar had joked, but this view rewarded the effort. Below us lay the township, with its only tarmac street now full of potholes. A laterite surface takes over when the buildings dwindle out. Then the road narrows for about ten miles, before joining the highway between Kitale and Eldoret.

Rising above the town, up towards Molson's Peak, were the farmsteads, each roofed with galvanised sheets, looking from here like the models in the toy-town village that Barbara and I were once given as our joint Christmas present.

Matlock Farm was tucked behind the hill we had just climbed. Our farmhouse was not visible from where I was standing, but I could make out the meadow where we had spent hours vainly trying to get our ponies to perform dressage routines, which Barbara was studying from the book a neighbour had bought her. The meadow was now given over to maize, a crop my father would never have considered, but which, I now knew, would have brought us a better living than did coffee.

Yes, this view was well worth the climb. Today, the mountains formed a hazy grey curtain, draped behind the scattered farmsteads. The Karamojas dominate the tiny settlement and put it into its proper perspective --- a mere speck on the canvas of this great continent of Africa.

To my left, beyond where Matlock Farm lies, I saw the old road, rising in a series of hairpin bends to the highest point in the area, what used to be called Molson's Peak (they would surely have changed the name by now). Though tortuous, this road looked to have a better surface than that on which we had reached the township and would be a shorter way to join the highway, despite its gradients. I decided that would be our route back.

My mind was drawn back to the last time I had been up that road; one of my earliest memories. Almost the whole of the European population of the district assembled after a party at the club, and we took off about an hour before midnight on New Year's Eve, children included, to 'see in' 1955. We held a picnic by the light of a score of storm lamps. This was a gesture of defiance. The land is still ours, we were saying, despite the celebrations having to be protected by a rota of armed farmers, taking turns to leave the party to stand guard.

I noticed that the hire car had returned from the filling station and was parked at the lych gate. The driver saw me looking and gave a short peep of the horn as a signal that we ought to be on our way.

Walking up with the vicar I had passed a brick cottage I remembered from my childhood. I used to see it on my family's rare visits to the church. It still bore the name *Avonwick* on the little gate; its owners had come out here from Devon.

In the garden now were orderly rows of vegetables, but the verge was a mass of zinnias, now grown wild. My memory took me back to how it had been twenty years or so earlier. An English flower garden, quite out of place in this hot dry country. A suntanned Englishwoman watered and weeded that same plot, no doubt daydreaming of a home she left behind in the South Hams, of which this was a replica.

On the way up I had gathered a handful of the zinnias, which I now placed into the little flower holder on my family's grave. Seeing me do this, the vicar went to fetch water from a tin drum beside the church door and returned with a jam jar full. His kind gesture drew tears to my eyes: a pathetic gesture, for I knew that within a few days these flowers would wilt in the sun and die, never to be replaced. I shook the vicar's hand and could not conceal a tremor in my voice.

'It has been most kind of you Reverend, sparing so much time, especially this morning when you were probably busy.' I handed him a donation of two hundred US dollars, which was accepted with feigned reluctance.

'You will be remembered in our prayers, Mr Paine. As for my time, there are few demands on it these days. We are told there are many ways to do the Lord's work, but my way is not chosen by most of my fellow countrymen in this parish. I am sorry we had so little success.'

He had spent most of Friday afternoon and Saturday going around Kisule with me. He and his wife had provided me and the driver with beds at their house since there was no hotel in the town. Surely there used to be, but a twelve-year old boy's memory cannot be relied on.

The man at Matlock Farm had met us with suspicion, perhaps thinking I was here to reclaim my inheritance. No, he had not known Bwana Paine: the place was allocated to him by the District Commissioner, he said. There were no white people around here any longer.

Did he know Alice Mtale?

Yes, she was a distant relative and he had gone to her funeral.

We moved on to what was once the club, the centre of social life among our small European community. Barbara and I spent many hours there, waiting for our parents to finish their sundowners. Now it was the local office of the Kenya Farmers' Cooperative

There was no more success at the general store, which I recalled having been run by an Indian gentleman. It had been my 'box of delights', the first shop I ever knew. It stocked the British comics, *Beano* and *Dandy*, which I used to buy with my weekly pocket money. Toys were kept in a glass case, away from inquisitive small hands. It seemed a miracle when some of them were in my Christmas stocking. The present owner said he had been the cashier under Mr Patel, but he claimed to have no recollection of a Paine family.

It was as if there was a conspiracy throughout the little town to hide the fact that this had once been a European settlement. Within ten years, Africa had erased all traces, not only of the Paines but of all the other Europeans who came here with such high hopes and had departed in defeat.

*

Pure impulse led me to make this visit to Kisule and the grave. I had been working in the Bandari Republic for almost two years. There had been many occasions when I could have come up to Kenya, but something at the back of my mind told me this would be a painful experience. It was only now, when my contract was almost at an end, that I decided to undertake this pilgrimage.

We crossed into Tanzania with no problem but in Arusha George discovered that we would not be allowed to take the UN Land Rover into Kenya, so he set off back to Karibune with the last of the soil samples and most of my gear. Then came another problem. The self-drive people told me I could not hire without an international driving licence, which was why I came to be driven by the unsuitably named Goodwill. He was a Chagga from the foothills of Kilimanjaro.

Goodwill had been uncommunicative on the way North, but now he was silent, almost to the point of insolence. He was unlike the friendly Chaggas I met on my soil investigations along the Tanzania border. He objected when I told him to take the peak road (*Mlimajuu* the sign now read) but after a mile or so I could tell he was enjoying battling with the bends.

At the summit we got out and walked to the edge of the escarpment, to look out over an unbroken vista, stretching as far as
the plains of Somalia.
I told him about poor old Molson, one of the original settlers in
Kisule. The story retailed among the settlers' children with the
power of ancient legend, though the event had taken place
within the lifetime of most of our parents. Molson had driven
up there one night from the club, a few weeks after his wife left
him. His body was found over three weeks later, impaled on a
sharp crag, two-hundred feet below the peak. At least, it was
assumed to be him. The jackals got there first.

On a clear day you could look in the other direction and catch a
glimpse of Lake Victoria, but today there was cloud over the
Serengeti. The air was fresh at the top of the escarpment, a relief after the dry heat of the valley, but, as I looked down on the
arid waste below, I was reminded that this was a land in which I
and my dead family had no place. It had been a worthwhile di-
version, but when we set off again Goodwill still had nothing to
say to me.

The silence in the car allowed me to take stock of the disap-
pointments of the visit I now wished I had never begun. In my
mind had been a clear picture of the little town, of the farm and
of the parents and sister I had lost. Yet the reality was altogether different. If these recollections of the town were mistaken, were memories of my family also false? Could it be that
the mother and father I thought I remembered were characters
I had created, moving pictures extrapolated from the faded photographs I carry in my wallet?

Of Barbara I was sure.   She was as real to me now as if she were
still alive, still sixteen and ever to remain so, a tall, slim tomboy,
whose soft light brown curls tossed in the wind as she raced
ahead of me from the stables to the farmhouse; my sister and
my closest companion. Often, when I thought of what had
happened, it was not with sorrow for my parents but with anger. That they had caused Barbara's death.

The other character whose reality I did not doubt was Alice, whom I had loved as one loves a mother; perhaps, I now admitted with a sense of guilt, more than my real mother. Alice Mtale came to us as nursemaid but became the formative influence in my young life. She was the source of all wisdom in those matters most important to a boy in Africa. She knew where to find hyrax, where the snakes lived, and which leaf would clear the venom of a spitting cobra. She taught me to recognise the berries which would sustain me should I be lost in the forest. It was Alice who had kissed me goodnight and tucked in the mosquito net as I settled down to sleep, while our parents sat on the veranda outside the dining room and talked late into the night, their conversation often ending in a quarrel which disturbed my sleep. Now Alice too was gone. It was as if every trace of my life in Kenya had been deliberately erased.

We stopped for petrol at Naivasha and had soup and sandwiches on the hotel lawn. Crested cranes strutted around as though they owned the place. The lake was pink with flamingos, which Goodwill had never seen before, and for a brief time he was elated, laughing excitedly at the cheeky monkeys who came to steal sugar lumps and the remnants of our sandwiches. We had our first real conversation. At last he revealed why he had been unwilling to undertake this trip. It meant he had missed a cousin's wedding. More importantly, he said he could not stand Kikuyu people. But once we were back in the car he reverted to silence. The dry, empty plain rolled by on either side. By the time we reached Nairobi I found I had been asleep for two hours.

TWO

I was born at Eldoret in Kenya, where my parents emigrated soon after the Second World War ended. Dad went out to take a partnership in a farm with another ex-service officer called Arthur Finnigan, who had served with them in Malta. But not long after I was born, Dad had a serious quarrel with Mr Finnigan and we moved up to Kisule. Barbara remembered him. 'Uncle Arthur' he had been, to her. In Kisule he was never mentioned, and the cause of the quarrel was a mystery to us children.

You won't find Kisule on many maps. There had been a Kikuyu village of that name for many years before white settlers started to arrive, soon after the Great War. Most were ex-soldiers who had served in East Africa, but they were followed by younger sons of farmers from further down the Rift valley, men wanting to set up on their own where cheap land was available. Many drifted back to their families when they found how difficult it was to farm the poor dry soil.

Then came what proved to be the final influx; ex-servicemen from the Second World War, lured by the British government's campaign to create a new generation of settlers, with a view to easing post-war unemployment in Britain. Kisule never became the town that its original founders intended. I suppose there were never more than eight hundred Europeans and maybe a hundred or so people of Asian descent, such as follow where settlers lead.

There was a small school in the town, run by the Anglican vicar's wife, a Mrs Taylor. She took children to the age of ten, but we had no secondary school in Kisule. Barbara went as a boarder to a Roman Catholic convent school in Nairobi, though both our parents had been brought up in the Church of England. When I was old enough, I was also sent to board in Nairobi at an Anglican preparatory school called St Mark's.

I have since realised why our parents took the uncharacteristic step of choosing a convent school for Barbara. In Kisule she was undisputed leader of our gang. She was a fearless tree

11

climber, could hold her own in a wrestling contest, play football with the boys, and at cricket she batted well and bowled a cunning leg break.

As I recall, there were not many girls in the European community; the settlers' wives seemed to know what was expected of them and produced predominantly male offspring. Certainly, none of the girls could challenge Barbara's dominance of the group that sprang up around her of which I was an honorary member.

Yes, I now have no doubt that the nuns of the Holy Martyrs convent were expected to make a lady out of my tomboy sister.

It was always intended that I would go to Castleberg, my father's old school in Yorkshire. Having been at the prep school in Nairobi, it was not a great break when the time came for me to say goodbye to Kisule.

I would be seeing everybody in the long summer vacations, but it was a sad parting from Alice Mtale. To me she seemed old and could possibly die before I returned, though I suppose she was probably only in her late forties at the time. As I left the farm with Mum and Barbara, my main concern was whether I would see my beloved Alice again.

*

We reached Castleberg soon after lunch, having been driven up in Grandfather Paine's Bentley by a man from a Matlock taxi firm. I had difficulty understanding some of what he said. Mum later explained that he had a Derbyshire accent. She warned me that my Kenya accent would be unfamiliar, so I must not be upset if boys made fun of me at first.

The headmaster seemed to be a nice man. He gave us tea and cakes in his study, though it was a little early in the day for that sort of thing. My sister and I followed, as he walked by Mum's side and led us to the main school building. Barbara tried to take hold of my hand, but I told her better not.

12

I was arriving a term late, something to do with a delay in them getting my results in the Common Entrance examination. As we entered the school yard I heard my mother express concern about my being behind the rest of the class.

'Don't worry, Mrs Paine. Although Henry should have been with us in September, he should have no problem catching up. His results were excellent. Allow me, this is rather heavy.' He opened a large wooden door and we entered a quadrangle.

Boys leaned out of windows to watch us walk through. There was a loud wolf-whistle from one of the upper floors. The head-master wheeled round to glare in the direction whence it came, but windows were suddenly deserted. Barbara looked rather pleased.

The headmaster opened a less heavy door. 'Right, here we are. This is your House, Henry. Mr Hollick is expecting us.'

It was a cold blustery North Yorkshire day and my slight trepid-ation at entering this new environment was overcome by a de-sire to get into some warm building as quickly as possible.

Barbara cried before they went and Mum ruined my day by kissing me as we said goodbye at the main gate, in full view of boys walking to lessons across the front quad. I had no inten-tion of allowing tears. My years at St Mark's had prepared me for such leave-takings and, after all, the only difference between this school and the other was a mere matter of around four thousand miles. My trunk and tuck box had preceded me. Two study mates helped me unpack and by supper time Harry Paine was an established Castlebergian.

THREE

At Castleberg sport was a major concern. Back home in Kenya what my sister and I most enjoyed was riding our ponies. When I got to prep school there were casual games of football and

13

cricket. They also had squash courts and I became quite good at the game, but I felt more at home in the classroom. Here in Yorkshire I found that St Mark's had indeed prepared me well. When Auntie Annie came to pick me up at the end of my first term I was able to tell her I had come top of the class.

I found it hard to like my Aunt. She was my father's elder sister and had to give up her job in Derby to come back home and look after Grandpa when their mother died. As I grew up I suspected she did not appreciate being given responsibility for the son of a brother who had estranged himself and gone off to foreign parts. In fact, I doubt whether she liked children as a species. But I loved my grandfather from the start.

They lived at Matlock in Derbyshire, in a rambling house that had been a farm. Grandpa sold off most of the land at the beginning of the Second World War, though he kept enough to graze his shire horses. They were his consuming passion and regularly won prizes at the county show. He was also fond of Mackeson stout. When I arrived back at Brough Farm for my first holiday from Castleberg, Grandpa gave me a small glass of stout at dinner, saying that it was 'Good for a growing lad,' but Auntie protested and removed the glass after I had taken a couple of sips. I was relieved, because to me it tasted like medicine, but I was nevertheless grateful that it had been offered.

Among my friends at Castleberg any interest in sport or lessons ranked well below our all-consuming obsession with girls. What motivated the opposite sex? For us 'opposite' meant 'opposition'. There were fifth and sixth formers who appeared to be men of the world, no doubt as knowledgeable about girls as they were about motor-bikes, but these boys would not dream of sharing such valuable information with measly third formers.

A boy in our form called Jackson claimed that, at a Christmas party, he had not only kissed a girl but had, to use his own phrase, 'taken things further'. He declined to give details, but he said the girl had co-operated. We knew this could not be true. Females needed to be cajoled or plied with gin. Those of us who had sisters confirmed it was unthinkable that girls had anything like the urge which motivated us. Barbara's attitude to boys was one of disdain.

To further our research into this fascinating subject, a project was planned for the long summer vacation. Each boy was given a task. Some were allocated a list of books to be perused at their local library (boys of our age would not be allowed to borrow them). Those with sisters were called upon, not exactly to spy (for that would not be gentlemanly) but to question the girls tactfully and try to obtain certain facts from a list which was carefully drawn up by the committee. A report would be given at the start of the following term.

My task was at a much more basic level. Since it was known that my grandfather kept horses, I was to report on how such matters were dealt with in the animal kingdom.

Grandpa was one of the last farmers in the district to plough with horses and when he finally got a tractor, he had not felt able to part with them. Of course, the original horses were long gone, but he continued to keep Shires as a hobby, which eventually turned into a business. He had two males, which had been gelded and were hired out for fetes and advertising functions. A decorated dray was kept in one of the barns, along with a pony trap and the Bentley. The mares were kept for breeding. The horses scared me at first, but Jimmy, who came in three times a week to help, taught me how to groom them, so I soon became accustomed to the huge beasts.

Just before Easter Jimmy told me one of the mares was 'coming on heat' and that a stallion was to be brought over from Ashbourne to 'serve' her; exactly what my committee wanted to know about.   I took the precaution of getting Grandpa's permission to watch the encounter, but the next day I heard Auntie discussing it with him. After lunch I had gone to what was still called the farm office but was now used as a storeroom. This was where I built my model aircraft. It was across a narrow passage from the main house and the side window of the kitchen was open.

'I still think it's not suitable, him being there when it happens,' she was saying. 'Boys are very impressionable at that age. You should sit him down instead and talk to him about that sort of thing. I'll take him on the bus down to Matlock when they come.'

'It's his dad as ought to have told him,' said Grandpa. 'There's nothing wrong with watching nature at work. Anyway, I'll bet the lads at that school of his know more than you do about 'that sort of thing', as you call it.

*

When the big day arrived, Grandpa and I were still having breakfast. It was around half past seven and Jimmy was already in the yard, waiting for the visitors to come. When we heard the truck turning into the drive we quickly finished our tea and were out before the Bedford had finished parking.

The horse box must have been made to order: it was a good deal taller than either of Grandpa's. I could hear the horse moving about in its box, but it was not released until the owner had come into the house to receive Grandpa's cheque. They were old adversaries from the show ring.

The stallion was a Suffolk Punch called Samson and his 'intended' was Millicent, one of our Yorkshire greys. I was told to keep well back while the animal was unloaded, but as it came down the ramp it seemed quite a docile creature. What struck me most was the delicacy of its movements, more noticeable than in our own horses. Its huge feathery feet were placed so gently that it appeared the horse wished to do no harm to the ground it trod upon, and it was a surprise to see hoof prints etched two or three inches deep in the ground when it had moved on.

Samson's owner took his stallion by its lead. 'Right then, Mr Paine, where is it to be?'

Jimmy guided them to the small back meadow where Millicent

awaited her intended. Grandpa and I followed. The four of us gathered by the fence, eagerly awaiting the start of the performance. Nothing happened. The two horses took up positions at either end of the field, grazing contentedly, completely ignoring each other.

Lunch was taken in a rota, then afternoon tea. As darkness gathered, the two settled down for the night, still with the length of the meadow between them. The owner insisted that his champion should be stabled overnight. He too was invited to stay and drank several Mackesons with Grandpa after dinner.

Soon after eight the next morning Samson was led from his stall, back to the meadow where Millicent awaited him, and we three observers resumed our posts. It was Jimmy's day off, but he appeared around nine o'clock to see if any progress had been made. He kept watch while we took coffee in the kitchen. When we returned, the show was already underway.

I had the evidence which the committee would require when I returned to Castleberg.

I was amazed that it had taken so long for the action to start. I wondered whether humans had the same problem: my personal experience made me doubt it.

*

When I was not needed with the horses, I walked across the fields to Bill Palmer's farm, to see if there were any jobs I could do. (It was to Bill's father that Grandpa had sold the land during the war). He was always glad of help. Occasionally it was something exciting, like sheep dipping, but more often it was planting or picking vegetables --- potatoes, turnips and sugar beet.

Although I was not keen on vegetable-picking I was always pleased to do so when I knew Bill's daughter, Kitty, would be there. She had left school and was attending a place called Lucy Clayton's Academy in Manchester, with a view to taking up modelling --- 'until the right man came along', Jimmy told me. I was not altogether sure what 'modelling' involved but, to me, it sounded erotic. Nor could I imagine that it would take long for the right man to come along to claim Kitty as his own, since she was the most desirable woman in the whole world. I found disbelief among my friends when I told them that Kitty's bottom was much superior to Marilyn Monroe's. Of course, my cause was hopeless, for she was four years older than me. Four years is an eternity.

Kitty loved riding and had won prizes for show jumping. Seeing her in tight breeches had helped me work out the differences in the anatomy of the two sexes, and my idea of bliss was to follow her up a row of vegetables. But it was then that my problem arose; a bulge appeared which was impossible to hide. I wondered how she could fail to notice. Then one day, in the turnip field, I became convinced that she *had* noticed, for she gave me a special little smile which suffused my whole body with joy; a joy centred in that area where the problem arose.

I looked forward to reporting these matters to the committee when I got back to school. I was sure they would agree that the performance of sex should present us with few problems. But when would we have the chance of putting theory into practice? Now, *there* was an intriguing question.

FOUR

I couldn't go home to Kenya for the Spring holiday. Dad wrote to say that 'funds were a bit strained' but that Mum and Barbara would be coming over during the next long vacation. I returned for my second summer at Castleberg happy in the knowledge that I would be seeing them in July, but disappointed that Dad could not leave our farm to come with them.

Grandpa and Auntie Annie never mentioned Barbara. I knew they had only met her once, but I hoped that during the coming visit they would get to know her properly. Barbara and I would be with them at Brough Farm for two weeks while Mum was visiting a wartime friend in Malta and I was confident that during this time Grandpa and Auntie would come to love Barbara as I did.

I wrote home every Sunday and got regular replies from Dad, usually with a footnote from Mother. What I read in the news-papers about independence talks in Kenya worried me, but Dad assured me that this meant that 'the Mau-Mau nonsense' would soon be a thing of the past.

Just before Speech Day, I proudly wrote to tell them I had been awarded the Fourth Form science prize. In the same letter I an-nounced my intention of following in the footsteps of Dad and Grandpa, by becoming a farmer. Despite the way that Dad used to talk about 'Britain letting down the settlers', he made it clear that he intended to stay on in Kisule after Independence.

Almost every week I wrote to Barbara at the convent school. Her replies made her school life seem much more interesting than mine. She gave me accounts of strategies to outwit the nuns, which I used to read out to my pals. Sometimes I wrote to Alice, knowing that the letters would have to be read to her and that she could not write a reply. I gave her descriptions of walks in the dales, tickling for trout in the fell streams and of the birds and small animals we spotted on outings with our housemaster. For me this was a connection to those happy days we spent together in the Bush.

*

About six weeks before the end of term I was lying in the sun on a grass bank alongside the cricket field, revising from Kennedy's Latin primer.

Towns, small islands, domus and rus, I repeated to myself.

This was a practice for the Colts team. My side was batting and I would not be going in until number eight.
A dative put, remember pray, after envy, spare, obey . . .

Then I heard the voice of Forrester, my House Captain. 'Drop that book, Paine. Come along with me. The Head wants to see you.'

On the way down I tried to think what misdemeanour might account for such a summons and, as we turned in through the school gates, my heart started to pound. When we reached the drive to the Headmaster's house I was amazed to see our Bentley parked outside. Forrester pressed the bell but immediately turned back down the drive, leaving me staring at the door in a state of panic.

It seemed ages before anyone came, but when at last the door did open I was pleased to see Mrs Hollick, my housemaster's wife. She took my hand and led me to the headmaster's study, the only time I had been there since that first day at school.

The Head was at his desk with Mr Hollick standing beside him. Auntie Annie sat in a leather armchair, looking uncomfortable. I was placed onto a settee and my aunt came to sit beside me, put her arms around me and gave me a hug. She had never done that before. I was surprised to see Bill Palmer standing by the fireplace.

'You are going to have to be a brave chap, Paine,' said the headmaster. 'I'm afraid your aunt has brought us some dreadful news.'

Lingering fears of the Mau Mau became reality; I found myself short of breath. I heard the headmaster's voice, but through a fog.

'I'm sorry to have to tell you outright like this, Paine, but I know you're a sensible and . . . um . . . a brave young fellow. It seems your parents were driving your sister back home from school when their car crashed. I can't tell you exactly how it happened, but they were all killed.'

'Excuse me, Sir,' I said, 'that can't be correct. You see it's only just past Barbara's half-term. They would never bring her back in the middle of term.'

Bill Palmer extinguished this ray of hope. 'I'm sorry lad, but it's correct what the gentleman says. I phoned your sister's, what do they call her Annie?'

'Mother Superior.'

'That's it, her Mother Superior; she's what we would call Head-mistress. It happened last week but it was only yesterday that the school got the news. They're having what they term a requiem mass for her today.'

Mrs Hollick came over and raised me to my feet. I liked her.

'Now, Henry', she said, 'Mr Palmer has kindly driven your aunt up, but he needs to get back tonight. She is staying with us and we want you to come over too. You must think things over, then you can decide what you want to do; either go back on the train with your aunt tomorrow or carry on for the rest of term. Don't decide now, but . . .Excuse me but I know what I want to do. To carry on here --- that's best, I think. There is one thing, though.'

'What is that dear?' said Mrs Hollick.

'May I go back first to collect my bat and my Latin primer from the cricket field?'

I had deceived them. My bat was drying in the study after being treated with linseed oil. I was borrowing Thompson's bat that day and I had left my Latin primer with him. But I needed to be alone for a little while.

I walked back up the hill, past the cricket field and on beyond the chapel, down a track that led to a field surrounded by a dry-stone wall. There were some Friesian cows in the field, my favourite breed. I opened the gate and carefully closed it behind me, then sat down behind the wall. Only now did the tears come.

Three cows came over to see what I was doing. They had sympathetic faces and seemed to sense my sorrow, so I explained to them what had happened. Sharing the news made me feel a bit better. I had forgotten to put a handkerchief into the pocket of my cricket flannels and the front of my shirt became wet with the tears. After a little while I got up, wiped my eyes with the sleeve of my shirt and set off down to shower and change before I went to the Hollicks' house.

*

I never thought of myself as an orphan. When I came across that word in novels it did not seem to cover my situation. Perhaps that was because my day-to-day life in England had not changed. I had friends around me at boarding school and Grandpa and Auntie Annie were down there in Matlock, just as they had been before the accident. The fact that I would never see my parents again did not emerge as a reality, more a dull ache nagging at my subconscious. Sometimes, in the night, there would be that horrible dream (always the same one), but next morning I awoke to the routines of school life and would shake off the nightmare as one discards a troublesome pest. Only occasionally was the truth brought home to me.

My best friend, Thompson, owned a pair of binoculars and we often sneaked off into a field beyond the chapel, which was out of bounds. If we were ever caught we would say we were 'bird watching', which would have been a version of the truth, since through the binoculars we could look down onto the sports ground of the girls' high school in the town below. At that distance, one of the girls was the living image of my sister Barbara. I never told Thompson about this, but when I saw her my body was seized by a sharp spasm, like a sudden attack of toothache.

Auntie Annie could not drive, so I did not see her on school on visiting weekends. Grandpa hardly ever left home these days. I used to be invited out by parents of my school friends and it was sometimes comfortable to have a fuss made of me by the boys' mothers. I would never have had such treatment from my aunt. However, I regarded this as weakness, exploiting their

22

kindness to 'poor Harry.'

After a while it occurred to me that I might find out more about what had happened by writing to Alice. My previous letters would have been read to her by my father, but now she may not have access to anyone who could read English, so I wrote to her in Kiswahili. This was a difficult task, for although I spoke the language fluently, I had never had occasion to write it. I did my best to form words from my phonetic understanding and I addressed the letter to our old PO Box number.

Over a month later it arrived back, marked *Not known at this address*. Now I would never discover how they had died. It was not grief that was uppermost, more curiosity. There were questions I would have liked to ask which now could never be answered. I still could not consider myself an orphan. *Orphan* was a word that applied to Dickens' characters like Oliver Twist or David Copperfield, not to me.

FIVE

I first came across her at the Amateur Dramatic Club auditions. We were both eighteen and fresh up to Cambridge. In my final holiday from Castleberg, the school took a production of *Saint Joan* round several West Riding towns. The title role was played by Mrs Hollick, who had been at RADA, and I had good reviews for my part as the Inquisitor. I thought I would try my luck at the Freshers' auditions at the ADC.

The lovely brunette stood out from among the other women auditioning. She appeared to ooze confidence, during a fine reading of Juliet's difficult *Mask of night* speech, and I thought she made my excerpt from *Saint Joan* seem mannered. It was a surprise when she stopped me on the way back to my seat. 'I enjoyed that,' she said. 'you act with maturity.'

A pretentious remark I thought but I was pleased that she had spoken. Everyone stayed to hear the result of the auditions. I was delighted to find that she and I had won parts in the Freshers production. As people left I caught up with her and her two friends and saw them to their bicycles. When they reached the corner of Park Street, she stopped and waved goodbye.

Her name was Gaynor Davies.

Male undergraduates far outnumbered women. In the confined world of the Cambridge colleges it was easy for someone with Gaynor's looks and personality to be a celebrity. She became one of the talked-about Freshers of our year and her photograph appeared in the student newspaper *Varsity*.

After our well-received performances in *The Cherry Orchard* I was asked by my college drama group to ask Gaynor to take part in a production of Coward's *Private Lives*.

This was the era of 'les evènements' in Paris. A group of undergraduates calling themselves *Les amis de Danny*, had taken up the anarchist cause, with Daniel Cohn-Bendit as their exemplar. They planned to be the future custodians of British culture.

Private Lives typified what they abhorred in the society they had chosen to reject.

Undergraduates tend to play out a fantasy of what they hope to become in later life. My college was no exception. Making a speech at the Union was the first rung on the ladder to parliament. Others strummed a guitar, with dreams of being the next recording star, secretly knowing that industry or the civil service was a more likely career for them. But a few had carefully mapped out the route to their chosen place in the real world. My friend Michael Wise was one of the latter. He later became a major figure in public relations.

Mike was secretary of Erasmus College dramatic society. He found a way to exploit the situation to his benefit. In Gaynor and me he had the ideal material. She was the daughter of a successful Welsh dentist and had won a scholarship to Wycombe Abbey School, emerging with a veneer of self-confident breeding guaranteed to antagonise the militants. In the scenario devised by Wise, Gaynor was the spoilt darling of a scion of the aristocracy, while I was built up into a hate figure, son of colonial exploiters who fled with their spoils when Kenya won its hard-fought battle for independence.

These bogus backgrounds were leaked to 'les amis', who in turn obligingly leaked to the newspapers. A short paragraph in the *Daily Express* was taken up by the *Daily Mirror*, which printed photographs of us under the headline **Young actors in anarchy drama**, alongside a vitriolic statement by the leader of 'les amis' (himself a product of one of Britain's more expensive public schools.)

Advance ticket sales for *Private Lives* soared and it was decided that an extra week should be added. 'Les amis' responded by hiring a lorry one afternoon and erecting a brushwood barricade outside the college, as a symbolic gesture to deter those wishing to buy tickets for the play at the college box office. Three Fleet Street photographers 'just happened' to witness the igniting of the barricade and the arrest of the ringleaders.

The farrago might have passed off as undergraduate posturing, but it struck a chord with the public; that intelligent young people were being seduced into political activities that could strike at the foundations of society. The college authorities became concerned that problems might arise from presenting the play on their premises and invited Wise for sherry and a 'friendly chat' with the Dean and Bursar.

He gleefully reported the conversation to a cast meeting when he got back.
-- Was *Private Lives* possibly not an entirely suitable choice?

–Perhaps the production could be delayed until the dust settled a bit?
–It would, of course, be unwarranted for the College to intervene in any way, but have you considered *Mother Courage*? An excellent play, don't you think? A stimulating challenge.

–Do have another sherry, Wise. We know that South African is no longer quite the thing, but one cannot renege on one's opposition to Franco, can one?

Two days later Fleet Street had an even better headline,

College heads censor Coward.

As a compromise, it was decided to move the venue to the city's Corn Exchange and the long-suffering Cambridge Police liaised with a delighted Michael Wise to try to ensure orderly performances. On the new opening night several London theatre critics were on hand, in some cases accompanied by colleagues from the news desks. Demonstrators picketed the hall, but their paltry numbers revealed that this was a small storm in a tiny teacup.

The show itself was a resounding critical success and Gaynor and I were interviewed on Anglia Television, with extracts from the interview appearing in the early evening editions of the national news. The citizens of Cambridge were eventually able to reclaim their town and life in and out of the colleges returned to normal.

When it was all over, we discovered we were in love

Gaynor had rooms in college, but the long cycle ride to Girton meant it was more convenient for her to use my bedsit between lectures or the laboratory. She had won an exhibition to study biochemistry and I was reading agriculture.

For my second year I declined the offer of a set of rooms in college and Mrs Miller's house in Arlington Passage became like home to the two of us. We continued to act, rationing ourselves to one play a term, and we tried to find productions with parts for both of us. I cannot remember whether we ever agreed we would not sleep together until we graduated but both of us accepted it would not happen. It would have made it hard to concentrate on work, as we needed to. The visit to Matlock changed everything.

SEVENTEEN

Auntie Annie went suddenly --- a heart attack. It had been my worst fear that she might go before Grandpa, who was weakening and becoming forgetful. Gaynor decided to go up to Matlock with me. Richard Butterworth, the family solicitor, invited us to stay.

When we arrived at their house, we found that Mrs Butterworth had made a wrong assumption about our relationship and put us together in a twin-bedded room. We did not embarrass her by asking to change.

The day of the funeral was cold and wet. I was surprised to find so many attending; Annie had seemed a withdrawn sort of person. The Palmers were there, of course. Bill read one of the lessons and I the other. There were forty or fifty people in church. At the graveside I recognised many of the ladies as her friends from the Women's Institute but there were several people I did not know. Some introduced themselves as having known her

27

during her days in Derby before she returned to join Grandpa at Brough Farm. She had been a librarian then.

The reception was held at the farm. As we walked to the taxi, Gaynor asked me, 'Who was the good-looking woman you were talking to, the slim one with the hat?'

'You mean Kitty, she's Bill Palmer's daughter. He read the first lesson, I introduced you to him.'

'I notice you didn't introduce *her*. Is she married? I couldn't tell with her wearing those fancy gloves, she certainly made a great fuss of you.'

'We're friends from childhood. She's married to a man at Granada Television. I didn't notice any 'fuss', as you call it.'

'Then it's time you did notice such things,' she said.

The depressing weather was in keeping with my mood. A conviction that I had never been kind enough to Auntie Annie coloured the proceedings and was enhanced by the nice things people said about her, remarks that did not seem contrived. Grandpa kept by my side throughout the reception and Gaynor was on hand to help with small talk, to divert attention from some of the old man's often illogical remarks. Gaynor and Kitty seemed to get on well and I heard laughter, which I guessed may be at my expense.

It was a relief when the last guests drifted home and Mrs Pollock came to take Grandpa up to his room. She had been parlour maid in the days when it was a working farm and had readily agreed to come back temporarily to look after him, but she had an old mother whom she could not leave. It was clear that some permanent arrangement would have to be made. Grandfather's condition further depressed me.

Elizabeth Butterworth had drunk rather a lot of sherry at the reception, and in the car on the way back to their house she was rather obvious in her matchmaking. 'You know what they say where I come from in Lancashire, Gaynor? Nowt beats a good funeral, nobbut a happy wedding.'

Richard said, 'Do shut up, Betty.'

Gaynor slid closer to me in the back seat and squeezed my hand. I hoped that, like me, she was thinking about the twin bedroom which awaited us.

By the time we reached the Butterworth's house the weather had cleared, though it was still cold. We borrowed scarves and wellington boots and walked across the fields, up to the foot of the High Tor. In the distance we could see Brough Farm.

'Do you realise that's yours?' she said. 'At least, half yours until the old man goes.'

I was somewhat shocked by her candour but of course she was right: I had been thinking of the responsibilities not the bene-fits.

By the time we got back it was already dark and the rain had re-turned in earnest, leaving us drenched.

'Poor dears, you must be soaked to the skin', said Elizabeth. 'A hot bath is what you need.   Hot baths, I mean . . . I mean . . . oh dear, I can't seem to say the right thing today.'

'Leave it to them, dear', said Richard

On the way upstairs I suggested, 'It does seem a pity to waste hot water.'

By the time we finished our bath and were drying ourselves in the bedroom, my excitement was all too obvious. Gaynor said, 'We really will have to do something about that, or you won't be able to get your trousers on. But put your dressing gown over the bed just in case, it's my first time.'

'Mine too,' I said. 'Be gentle with me.'

I wondered how many other members of the 'committee' at Castleberg had waited so long.

*

Richard was most helpful with the arrangements that had to be made. Grandpa could not possibly look after himself so, the following day, accompanied by Gaynor, we took the old man to see a residential home in Matlock Bath, which he immediately took to. He moved there the following week. He was still a handsome fellow, with an eye for the ladies. From the start he became a favourite with both residents and staff.

It was only now that I learned that Grandpa paid my fees through school, having taken out a covenant when I was born. Auntie had covered my expenses at Cambridge on the understanding that I would repay her when I started work. Now I was her sole beneficiary that debt was annulled.

Within a month Richard had arranged the sale of the shire horses and rented out Brough Farm. The tenants were none other than Kitty and her husband, David Masters. She wanted to start a riding school and livery stable. It gave me pleasure to think my boyhood love was living under my roof, albeit with a man I had come to envy.

EIGHT

Returning to East Africa in 1972 seemed like a new experience. Only the heat was familiar; in other ways I felt no different from those of my fellow passengers setting foot on African soil for the first time. The humidity struck me on the steps down from the VC 10. I removed my linen jacket as soon as my feet touched the tarmac of Karibune airport. It struck me that taking on this contract might have been a dreadful mistake. The tedious formalities of Immigration and Customs heightened the gloom.

As I entered the arrivals hall two scruffy men seized one suitcase each and disappeared through the exit doors towards a line of battered taxis. A short stocky man in a pale blue uniform stood among a line of waiting locals, holding a hand-printed card bearing my name.

'That's me --- Harry Paine' I shouted. 'Hold on a minute'. I ran off in pursuit of the two taxi drivers and found them arguing on the pavement outside the terminal.

'I'll have that back if you don't mind,' I said to the man who had taken the second bag.

Surprised at being addressed in fluent Kiswahili by a pale *msungu,* he abandoned it without a struggle. The other man, scenting victory, came over to grab it, but was equally taken aback when I took the other case and carried both back into the terminal.   The man in the blue uniform, who observed the performance from just inside the terminal doors, had a broad smile on his face.

'Welcome to Bandari, Mr Paine,' he said in English as he took one of the cases and walked ahead of me towards a smart Toyota, painted the same blue as his uniform. The words *Banzam Taxis* were inscribed on its door. 'I'm George Bwalya.' He presented a business card. 'I said welcome but should have said karibu; that Swahili wasn't learnt from a textbook was it?'

'I was born in Kenya, though I haven't been in East Africa since 1961. I'm starting a contract with WAFCO. Have you heard of them?'

'Who hasn't? World Agriculture and Food Commission. I tried to get a job with them last year.' He opened the door of his smart taxi.

Near the turn-off onto the main road we were brought to a halt by a stationary line of cars. 'Oh no! It's those bloody Russians again,' said George. 'Better make yourself comfortable.'

It took more than five minutes for us to join the main road, and then the Toyota inched forward, in a journey that took almost an hour. About a mile outside the city limits we passed the two Russian construction vehicles responsible for the delay. By then I knew most of George's life story and George knew a good deal about me. By the time we reached the New Bandari Hotel I believed I had found a friend.

A small boy, no more than twelve years old, ran out from the hotel, wearing a bright red uniform and blue solar-topee. He was darker than most Bandarians I had seen so far, with a skin like polished ebony setting off the flashing white teeth of a permanent grin. He attempted to lift both suitcases.

'Leave that heavy one to me.' My Swahili caused the grin to grow wider. 'Thank you, bwana. My name is Oscar. Today many guests are staying inside this place, but I will make sure Euphemia finds a room for you. Follow me, please.'

We negotiated a passage through a crowd of tourists.

Euphemia was beautiful.

'Hello, I'm Harry Paine. I was told to come here but I'm afraid I didn't make a reservation. You seem to be busy.'

'We are, but you are lucky. Miss Costas booked you in.'

She gave me a registration form. 'I just your need passport number and signature. I will do the rest.' She gave the key to Oscar and handed me an unstamped envelope with a crest on the back.

'This came yesterday, delivered from your Embassy. Dinner starts at seven.'

We were on the way to the elevator when I heard Euphemia shouting my name, which momentarily hushed the noisy crowd. I returned to the reception desk.

'I almost forgot to tell you. Mary Costas said will you please call at her office at eight in the morning --- we start early here. It's just round the corner but find Oscar before you set off. He will explain the way.'

Seeing Euphemia cheered me immensely; perhaps the Bandari Republic was not such a bad place after all? Then I thought of Gaynor, alone in Cambridge, and felt guilty.

Having delivered me to Room 303, Oscar stood grinning in the doorway.
At the briefing in Rome I had been told that tipping was frowned upon in Bandari, so I decided to give something in kind, the Isaac Asimov novel I had just finished. The boy appeared delighted, though I wondered what he would make of science fiction.

'Thank you very much, bwana. I can sell this to the bookshop next door. Whenever bwana is in the New Bandari I will be his personal boy.'

The grin had reached to his ears as he left the room.

The letter from the Embassy requested me to call on Terry Canham, First Secretary (Aid) at eight-thirty the next morning. Already things were going wrong. I phoned through to reception.

'Sorry to bother you so soon. Is there any way I can get in touch with Miss Costas? I only have her office number. Oh, sorry; I should have said; this is Harry Paine.'

'I think I know where she will be. Hold on.' After just over a minute a male voice said, 'Lucky speaking, Kiboko Roof Bar. Mary is coming, I just called her.'

She sounded posh --- one of those cut-glass accents you only found these days among people educated outside Britain.

'Hello. Welcome to Bandari, Mr Paine. Just a minute, it's a bit noisy here at the bar. I'll get Lucky to put me through in the cubicle.' A moment later she was back on the phone. 'OK. You have a problem?'

'I'm supposed to go to the British Embassy half an hour after you want to see me. Should I put them off? It's someone called Terry Canham, could be male or female.'

'Definitely male,' she replied. 'A bit hirsute for one of us. He's important. Better see him first and call at my office when you've finished. Euphie will tell you where to go. By the way, I'm only just up the road now. Can you come here for a quick one or are you jet-shagged?' I wondered if I had heard correctly.

'Do you mind if I don't. My body tells me it's two o'clock in the morning.'

'Goodnight, then. See you tomorrow. Sweet dreams.'

NINE

I had been fortunate to get this job at my age. After the degree in Agriculture at Cambridge I took a Masters at Wye College, specialising in soil science, so I had the relevant qualifications, but at the age of twenty-four I would normally have been considered young for carrying out the project alone. My having been born in East Africa helped, though the fact that I had not been there since childhood seemed to have been overlooked. What probably worked most in my favour was that I had done the groundwork for the presentation which won the contract with WAFCO.

The Haskins and Ede consultancy firm was set up by one of my former tutors at Erasmus College and another don from Trinity Hall. Getting a job with them when I left Wye meant I did not have to leave Cambridge and could stay on at Mrs Miller's place. More importantly, I could still be with Gaynor.

I was more dogsbody than consultant at first, but I persuaded Sylvester Ede that I was the man they needed to prepare the tender for a UN study which might lead to an aid package of several million dollars for Bandari.

When I went to Rome with Sylvester it was WAFCO who asked if I could head the project.

*

Terry Canham had one of those beards that look as though the wearer has a point to make; dark and apparently untrimmed. He had a very 1970s hairstyle to match. This Rasputin figure was not the diplomatic type I'd expected. He was a bit shorter than me, probably five ten. He wore a grey safari suit.

'Take that tie off. Informality reigns in this socialist paradise. Please call me Terry. Good of you to call.'

'Mary Costas said you were important.'

'What a little joker she is,' he said, but he looked pleased. 'By the way, you and I have something in common --- Erasmus. I was in the same year as Sylvester Ede, so I took the liberty of asking him if you might help us with a little job.'

I thought I should establish the ground rules. 'I'm sorry, Terry, despite what Sylvester may have said, it's WAFCO I'm working for now. If you have in mind anything outside my remit for them, the local UN rep should be consulted.'

'No, it's not a job as such, just that we'd like you keep your eyes open. Quite frankly, we have never had a Brit out here with such scope to travel all over Bandari. All I ask is that you let us know how certain matters are viewed in the countryside.'

'You make it sound a bit 'cloak and dagger'.

'In a sense it is. I do realise that you aren't under HMG's wing on this contract, but people that you might call more *important* than I am have taken an interest in you. I wanted a chat before you get started with Mary, and I guess you will soon be seeing

Festus Kasonde.'

'Yes, I have a letter of introduction.'

'OK, let me tell you a little about him. He's one of Moscow's men or, at least, he has been heavily exposed to the Soviet system.'

'I'm sorry. I really don't want to get involved in this sort of thing.'

'Purely background, dear boy. Just listen for a minute or two. I might save you a lot of delving.' He chuckled. 'That's an appropriate word, in your case, isn't it?'

As I later discovered, Canham's briefing was remarkably accurate. Festus Kasonde was at that time the Deputy Permanent Secretary of the Ministry of Natural Resources. The Permanent Secretary was a pleasant elderly farmer who had been a founding member of the ruling party during British colonial rule, but any important decisions were made by Kasonde. A product of Moscow University with degrees in Agriculture and Economics, he was a rising star in the party.

'So, all we want you to do is to look and listen,' Canham continued. 'Let me know how the new village schemes are being accepted in the countryside. You will have been briefed on the kiwanja villages I trust.'

The Bandari government's rural development schemes were known as kiwanja villages. This policy was a major topic at my briefing in Rome. Unemployed people in the towns were regularly rounded up and transferred to these agricultural projects, spread throughout the countryside, often in places not well suited to farming. Just as conscripts are seldom keen soldiers, these urban people were no doubt unhappy at being enlisted as peasants.

Canham and his bosses thought there was a danger of Bandari going the same way as Idi Amin's Uganda. Already the increasing nationalisation of wholesale trade had put the Asian community under pressure and there was mounting opposition to this rural relocation programme. I was asked to listen out in the villages, to see if there were signs of serious unrest. China was already deeply involved with Tanzania and Zambia, and any unrest could be seized upon by the Soviet Union to increase its influence in Bandari. It was put to me that it was my duty as a loyal Briton to help counter what could become an expansion of the Soviet empire.

'As you see,' said Canham, 'this is not a job; it's just that I'll always be pleased to see you for a little chat whenever you are in town. Anything you may hear will be of interest. But there's no compulsion, none at all dear chap. There is, however, one proviso --- not a word to Mary Costas about this. You'll understand why in due course. By the way, you look like you may be a recruit for her beach party set.'

I left the Embassy bearing a permit to buy duty-free liquor at their commissary; not a particularly rich reward for a potential 'spy'.

*

Mary Costas put me under pressure as soon as I entered her office.

'So, what did Terry want?'

'Complete waste of time,' I lied. 'He wanted to tell me that he was at my old college. They must already have a file on me.'

'It's an obsession here. There will be a few of your files around. See, I have one too.' She held up a manilla folder marked *Paine, H.A. -- WAFCO*. 'You must be careful not to let your people use you. They haven't got over the fact that Bandari never joined the Commonwealth and now they think we're getting into bed with the Soviets.'

'I'm a citizen of the world on this contract, but thanks for the advice.'

37

She was about thirty. A nice mouth, big owl-like spectacles. The aquiline nose was no doubt a bequest from Greek forbears. She wore a loose Mao-style khaki uniform, but she probably had a good figure. Her most striking feature was beautiful red hair, loosely waved, not at all Greek. I found it hard to establish eye contact with her. She appeared embarrassed, shy even.

'OK let's start,' she said. 'First of all, it's my job to sort out any problems you may have. IALO stands for International Aid Liaison Office. Sounds impressive I know, but it's just the two of us, me and Poonam. We have a lot of helpless people on our books, so I'm trusting you know how things work in this sort of country and will keep out of trouble.'

'I've been around East Africa before, as I gather you know. I was just a kid then but I'm sure it will all come back. Just one question and then I'll let you get on with your work. I'm picking up a Land Rover from the UN office this afternoon. They don't provide a driver. Can you recommend someone?'

'Possibly the man who picked you up yesterday will be interested. I know that George is keen to learn about farming. He has his own business, but he told me he's fed up with driving taxis. I'll find you his card.'

'As a matter of fact he gave me one.'

'Better make it after seven tonight, at his home number. He often phones me, though. If he does, I'll tell him to get in touch.'

'OK, thanks. I'll be off then.'

'No, hold on. I have found you somewhere to live, if you agree. WAFCO said you were hoping to set up base in Malua, so I looked up some possible properties.' She handed me a typed sheet listing four addresses, with the number of rooms available and rent required. One was marked in blue highlight.

'The one I've picked out is owned by the local chemist. He's an old friend of my father.'

'That's a wonderful help. Thank you, ma'am.'

For the first time, she looked me in the eye and smiled. The smile transformed her. Then I remembered the letter that Sylvester Ede had given me.

'Sorry, there is something else. I was given a letter of introduction to a Mr Kasonde at the Ministry of Natural Resources. How might I get in touch with him.'

'Let's try him now.' She picked up her phone and dialled a number from memory.
' Hi Festus, how's you?' she said, in English. 'Myra OK? . . . Good, give her my love. Sorry to disturb you but I have Mr Paine with me, fresh off the plane from England. Can he have an appointment? . . . Really? I'll ask him.'

She covered the mouthpiece. 'He says he'll see you now. OK?' I nodded.

'Right,' she said into the phone, 'he's on the way.'

That's how I met Mary. I'll tell you later about Festus.

*

George accepted my offer of a job.

Since then, we had been in each other's company for the best part of two years, sleeping in doubtful hotels, often under canvas, even in the back of the Land Rover. From time to time I called in to talk to Terry Canham, but I doubt that what I reported was news to him. In fact I believe I had the better part of the bargain; being able to take a bottle of duty-free whisky into a kiwanja village proved an invaluable introduction.

Now my contract was drawing to its close. I had gathered comprehensive data on the soils and water quality of most of the arable areas of Bandari, I would be able to make recommendations for improving rural infrastructure and for the distribution of cash crops throughout the regions. All that remained was to collate this information into a final report and put everything into a saleable package. For this I needed access to a mainframe computer. My old department at Cambridge had agreed to give me access to theirs and, if WAFCO would let me use the data, I also had enough material for a PhD thesis. I felt I had justified my appointment. In many ways I was sorry it was ending.

But I needed to be with Gaynor.

TEN

It was a relief to find George waiting at Karibune airport when I eventually reached there from my visit to Kinsule. The Monday plane from Nairobi was fully booked, as was the following morning's direct service, and I had to take the 'milk run', via Arusha and Mwanza, to reach Karibune on Tuesday. George was dressed in his Banzam taxi uniform and insisted on carrying my suitcase to his cab.

'What kept you? We expected you back yesterday, and thre was no sign of you on this morning's Nairobi plane.'

'It's a long story,' I said. 'But why the uniform? I thought you still worked for *me*.'

'Can I afford a day off? Can I keep a wife and two hungry girls on what you pay me? And listen, bwana. Mercy says on no account can you leave Bandari before the second Friday of next month. That's our anniversary party. You are guest of honour. She and her cousin are going to make a special brew of pombe --- it will knock your head off.'

'That's another five weeks. Sorry George, out of the question I'm afraid. I must get back to Cambridge to put my report onto the computer, and Gaynor is going to kill me if I am away any longer than I promised her.'

This time the road into town was clear. George had met every plane from Nairobi and Arusha for the past two days and had dug out his driver's uniform so that, if I was not on the plane, he could get fares to compensate for his waiting time. It was clear why Banzam Taxis had become so successful.

'All right how was the old home-town,' he said, 'Tell me all about it. By the way I didn't like the look of that young Chagga driver they gave you.'

'Before I start, George, could we call at the IALO office on the way to the hotel? Mary might still be there and I'd like to collect my mail.'

'Look in the glove compartment.'

I was delighted to see that George had already collected my mail, and there were three letters from Gaynor.

'And you won't find Mary working overtime. There's a new girl-friend.'

'Anyone I know?'

'No. A Scandinavian kid who came up from Tanzania. You know I don't generally go for white women, but this one, bwana! Wait till you see her! She's like that actress who married the prince. What a waste to make a girl like that lebanese.'

'You're wrong, George. About Mary, I mean. She just likes having new people around her, I'm sure that's all there is to it.'

'Oh yes? So, what does Mary buy for this new friend's birthday? A box of chocolates? Lacy undies? No, bwana --- a motor bi-cycle, that's what she buys her. That is the sort of friend I'd like to be, let me tell you. Lebanese is what they are. Definite.'

'You're an old gossip, George, do you know that? I can't imagine why a nice woman like Mercy ever fell for you.'

'I told you not to use words I don't understand'

'Gossip means you talk too much. And 'lebanese' is not the word you want.'

'OK then. I bet you one hundred shillings that even *you* won't get anywhere with that blonde lady. I'd make it a thousand shillings except I don't like robbing you.'

I gave up and began to tell him about Kisule.

*

Oscar must have seen us arrive. He was there to open the cab door even before I said goodbye to George. The lobby was crowded with smartly dressed people of all nationalities, greeting each other, raising the decibel rate to an impossible level. I never bothered to book in advance and had always been found a room but now I was worried. I excused my way through the crowd and reached the reception desk, where Euphemia was again on duty.

'Go away,' she shouted. 'We do not have room for people of your sort. See, we have doctors and professors, respectable types of person. We don't want Englishmen who spend their time digging up soil in the bush.' She pointed to a banner strung over the stairs,

WELCOME WORLD HEALTH ORGANISATION

'If you want a room here tonight you will have to sleep with me --- and stop grinning, Oscar.'

'Seriously, Euphie, are you really full?'

'Yes, but I kept a room for you, although you will have to pay for last night. Mary booked you in, but she told us you would be here yesterday. She said she will be in the roof bar at the Kiboko at six, as usual.'

On the way up in the elevator I speculated as to whether the offer of her bed might be serious.

Before opening my suitcase, or even sitting down, I took out
Gaynor's letters from my airline bag. I cheated, by finding the
latest one to read first. The others were thicker letters which
could be read at leisure. This was an air-letter form.

Dearest Harry,

*I have made so many attempts to write this that I decided to use
an aerogramme, so I would not tear it up as I have destroyed all
the others. As I said in my last letter, Hans Morgenthau has been
over again to see the people at the Molecular Biology Unit and he
had read my last article in 'Nature.' We met for tea at the Bull
and I was quite flabbergasted when he asked me if I would like to
take a Visiting Professorship at Berkeley. It would be for two
years and frankly darling I really can't refuse. He is working on
industrial applications of microbiology, what they are now calling 'biotechnology', and this is exactly what I want to do. If I can
get some good work behind me at Berkeley I would stand a good
chance of getting into the MBU when I come back. Now, this is the
hard part. Your letters from Bandari have shown me just how
much you enjoy the life in Africa, and I know that that sort of
work is what you should be doing. But where would this leave us?*

*I have been so lonely without you, dearest. Sometimes I have
wondered if this were to be the pattern for the rest of our lives. I
can't be just the 'little woman' waiting at home for the white
hunter to come home with the spoils! I know that's a bit below
the belt, but, for both our sakes, I think we ought to let a bit of
time go by, until our careers have sorted themselves out. I love
you very much and I think I always will, but I've persuaded myself
that I should take this Berkeley job, and that we should both feel
free to take up another relationship, should one develop. But
don't go thinking I have fallen for Hans. He's a happily married
man with two children and I'm not a husband stealer. Dearest
Harry, I hope I do not make you unhappy. It is my fondest wish
that when I come back from the United States we shall take up*

where we left off. I shall not blame you if you never write again, but I hope and pray that, if you are able to sit back and look at our situation dispassionately, you will feel as I do.

The rent here is paid up to the end of March and I have told Mrs Miller that you should be back within a month and would let her know if you wanted to keep it on. Just in case you don't, she has asked me to remove the suitcase and the tennis racket you left here, so I am going to take them over to Professor Beeson at Erasmus to keep for you. I met him in King's Parade on Tuesday, and he said he won't mind. In fact, he wants to see you when you get back. He is very keen that you should take your PhD. and he says he can get you a research studentship if you put in an application before July. Do think about it, dearest. I long for the day we can work together. After all, Cambridge is 'home', isn't it?

When I get settled in Berkeley I will send you my address (c/o Grandpa Paine). Please write, my darling. Try to understand, and keep on loving me, as I shall always love you.

Gay

ELEVEN

The Kiboko Hotel is a few minutes' walk along the seafront from the New Bandari and this evening the promenade was almost deserted. I leaned over the railing to talk to a group of Zanzibari seamen unloading a dhow on the shore below, by the light of storm lamps. They gave up what they were doing, and their curt replies gave the impression that they would rather I did not see what their cargo was, so I moved along to sit on a bench further up the promenade. I needed to do some thinking before I talked to Mary.
A couple on the next bench stopped their kissing and moved on.

Gaynor's letter entirely altered my plans. I meant to leave at the end of the month and arrange a stopover in Amsterdam, to buy an engagement ring to present to her at Heathrow. Now there was no reason to rush home.

Of course, she was right. How would our relationship withstand another long period of separation? My immediate reaction was to cancel everything and take the next plane home, before she left for America. But would this be fair to her? Her career plans excluded me, temporarily at least. Did she love me enough to drop what could be her big chance? Should I forgo another contract in Africa?

The questions I asked made me realise that my own happiness had been uppermost; not what was best for Gaynor.

I must accept her decision.

Plans were forming in my mind, which I wanted to discuss with Mary. Some of the survey results might need to be retested. The computer program I had designed might throw up errors in the correlation between the soil tests and my crop recommendations. Was there a suitable computer somewhere in Bandari? If so, there were advantages in staying here a bit longer, in case I needed to repeat a field visit. OK, I would sacrifice some terminal leave, but this was certainly not a bad place to take a holiday.

Mary usually had the answer to my problems, and I was looking forward to sounding her out.

The Kiboko was considered the country's prestige hotel but, despite its undoubted comforts, I had never really taken to it. For me it lacked the charm which the New Bandari had managed to retain. The original Bandari Hotel dated from when that part of East Africa was a German protectorate.

I could not remember having visited Karibune as a boy, but there was a photograph of me with my mother and Barbara, taken in the palm court of the original hotel. They must have come down here when I was about four years old. I wondered what my parents would make of this modern city.

The roof bar of the Kiboko had become a popular meeting place for younger expatriates and Mary Costas was regularly to be found there about this time of the evening.

Few people could understand why she had taken the job of Director of the International Aid Liaison Office, since her father was without doubt the richest man in Bandari and she was reputed to be enormously wealthy in her own right, but I understood. The desirable things which needed foreign exchange were beyond her reach. Her wealth was in Bandari shillings, which was like being the richest lioness in the cage. This job earned her some foreign exchange.

When a group of aid donors decided to set up a shared liaison office in Bandari, Mary had been an ideal choice to head it. She was a citizen --- her father was among the founding members of the ruling party --- she had an Economics degree from University College, Dublin. There was hardly anyone of influence in the country whom Mary did not know. More importantly she had a natural rapport with the expatriates, most of them young and well-qualified, who came to the country as sponsored researchers or technicians. She was ideally placed to act as 'fixer' for their myriad problems. She used to call us her 'economic mercenaries'. At first, I had been annoyed to be called that, but on reflection I had to agree it was not far from the truth. Without her it was doubtful if I could have completed the project on schedule.

As I entered the Kiboko the overseas newspapers had just arrived and were still being sorted. I should be able to get the previous day's *Daily Telegraph*. The palatial lobby was set out like an exhibition centre, with the display stands of several drug companies, two of the major aid charities and the local tourist organisation. But it was deserted. The air-conditioning cooled only me and the staff manning display booths. Rising above the muzak I could hear the amplified voice of a lecturer, emanating from the conference suite on the mezzanine floor. Displayed in huge coloured capitals above the elevators was this hotel's greeting its visitors.

KIBOKO WELCOMES WHO

This amused me. How many visitors knew that Kiboko was the Swahili for hippopotamus?

Having bought my paper I crossed to the elevator and pressed the ROOF button. Immediately I stepped out on the seventh floor I could hear Mary's voice through the swing-doors of the bar. I needed a serious talk with her and prayed she wasn't drunk. As a precaution, I peeped through the glass panel in one of the doors before going in. The bar was always kept quite dark and I had to adjust my vision to the gloom inside. This was 'happy hour', usually a scene of crowded activity, but tonight the bar was remarkably empty.

I could make out two people in a 'speakeasy' booth, Peter Larsen, a Danish volunteer teacher and Andreas Potgeiter, the South African political refugee. (Nobody called him Andreas, he was known as 'Potty'). Only two tables were occupied. At one, alongside the dance floor, were four tourists. I could tell at once they were American. The brand-new safari suits spoke un-mistakably of Saks Fifth Avenue or some similarly expensive outfitter.

I saw Mary sitting at the table nearest the balcony. Fortunately, she had her back to me. Opposite her was a blonde, doubtless the girl about whom George had enthused. I could not see the woman's face. She had turned her chair so to face the balcony, in what I assumed was an attempt to shield herself from Mary's tirade. Mary was normally the sweetest, charming, companion, but with too much drink inside her she could turn into a har-ridan, and her coarse language was accentuated by that posh voice. I crept in, to join Peter and Potty in their cubicle.

'Quite a battle going on,' I remarked. 'I could hear it when I stepped out of the lift. What's it all about?'

'Don't ask, man,' said Potty. 'Woman problems. Something to do with a hen party at the beach house last Sunday. Best keep out of it.'

47

*

Mary's beach house was unlike any of the others along Lundini Beach, most of which were ramshackle wooden structures, little more than changing rooms. Mary's had been built by her father in the 1950s. It resembled a desert fort of the French foreign legion. The designer was the same Greek architect who built John Costas's unusual house in the south of the city, which he had named 'Magoulas.'

Windowless high walls provided perfect security when it was not occupied, and passers-by would be unaware of what was going on inside when a party was in progress, which was sometimes just as well. The interior was in the style of a Spanish hacienda. An open courtyard was mostly taken up by the swimming pool, alongside which was a bar with a dance floor. On the other side were a kitchen and a dining area. Upstairs, behind the balcony overlooking the courtyard, were two bedrooms and a bathroom.

This was a weekend retreat for those lucky enough to be counted as friends of Mary Costas. She loved parties and being director of IALO gave her access to like-minded people, more than willing to let their hair down when the opportunity presented itself. You felt you were a member of a private club, except that members were selected by just one person. If Mary liked you, found you amusing or attractive (whichever your gender) you were 'in'. As Terry Canham had forecast, I became a member of this charmed circle from the first week I arrived.

We were all much of an age, few above thirty. Only occasionally would there be a Bandarian there. I am sure this was not colour prejudice on Mary's part. Black friends of other nationalities were regular members, but it was understood that this was a haven where expatriates could let their hair down and, if they felt like it, sound off about working in this tightly-controlled society.

I was there when Mary first announced one of her 'hen parties'. It was about three months after I had established myself in

Malua, and I came down to Karibune for a weekend break. Having a standing invitation, I joined the beach house party on the Sunday. I was sitting talking to Betsy from the American Embassy. There were about twenty-five or thirty people there and the pool became too full for me to swim in comfort, so Betsy suggested we go to the ocean.

She was the stronger swimmer and outpaced me to a point over a hundred yards north of where we set off. When we emerged from the water it was a good walk back to the beach house. We stopped on the way back to rest under a palm tree. The beach was empty, apart from a group of small boys playing by a breakwater, near where we had come ashore. There was a pleasant warm breeze. It was all rather romantic.

I did not quite know what to say to this attractive woman, whom I hardly knew but, to my surprise, she said, 'Do you kiss? You look like you might be a great kisser.'

I muttered something about being engaged, not wanting to get involved; in short, sounding a complete prig. Betsy laughed and held me by the shoulders.

'Look Buster, I just want to kiss you, not screw you. I've got a boyfriend back in Atlanta that I miss every bit as much as you miss your girl. Maybe you never heard of 'fun kissing'? We're at a party, right? At a party you eat, you drink, you dance, you kiss. No big deal. It don't mean a thing and its fun. Try it, you'll enjoy --- bet you never kissed a black woman before.'

I did enjoy the kiss but could not help feeling disloyal to Gaynor.

When we arrived back the party had fallen flat. Unattached men were talking sport or politics, one or two of the women were reading paperbacks. Mary stood on a chair and called for quiet.

'Listen everybody, this is boring. Having men around is the trouble, isn't that right girls? I've decided that next Sunday all you men are barred --- and that includes you two.' She pointed

49

to Tim and Craig, the gay Australians who were cooking hamburgers at the bar.

'I decree that next Sunday will be a 'hen party' --- strictly women only. Spread the message, ladies. Everyone is welcome provided they don't have those dangly bits. Eleven o'clock onwards, come and let your hair down; swimsuits optional.'

And why not? I thought.

TWELVE

Peter Larsen picked up my newspaper, which had a headline about that hotel break-in in the United States. I was rather out of touch with world events, having spent so much time away from the capital, but Peter thought this would lead to the collapse of the Nixon administration. He was in the middle of trying to explain why, when I saw Mary rise from her seat and walk towards us. She was not wearing her glasses, but that was not why she had difficulty steering a straight course.

'Paine, my darling', she said as she peered into our cubicle.' Her speech was slurred. 'Why are you lurking in the corner with these two reprobates? I'm cross with you. You were so long in Kenya I thought you'd bloody emigrated. Come and join us. I'm just off to powder my nose, so redeem yourself by getting us all drinks. You two as well. Over to my table and don't be so antisocial.'

Peter and Potty obediently walked across to Mary's table, while I went for the drinks. As I did so, one of the Americans also rose from his seat and joined me at the bar. Before I could order, the man said 'Pardon me, sir. You appear to be a friend of that red-haired young woman who just went out. It would oblige us greatly if you could persuade her and her friend to leave. We have just been subjected to a performance which would never be permitted in any respectable bar in the United States of America.'

50

As he warmed to his subject his politeness deserted him and he raised his voice. 'I would have thought that white folks living in a beautiful place like this would set a better example. The bar was full when those two came in, but they've managed to empty it. The rest of our party have quit, but we don't see why we should have the first night of our vacation ruined by a coupla goddam dykes! If you can't get her to go quietly I'm going to have to ask the bartender here to throw her out.'

He went back to his table and his wife gave me an angry scowl, as though I was responsible for their problem.

Lucky had heard the conversation. 'I wish you would try, Harry. I don't want to lose her custom but I really cannot serve her no more vodka. Her friend she's OK, she's on tonic water now. So, it's whatever you want and another for Potty, Pete and the young lady. Agreed? Oh, and sorry, it's just gone seven, so I have to charge you full price.'

I ordered myself a Tusker lager which was what the other two men were having, and tonics for Mary and the blonde. Mary was back in her seat by the time I reached the table. Her friend turned and looked up at me.

She was everything George had led me to expect. She attempted a smile. Her cheeks were flushed and she had obviously been crying, but the look in those deep grey eyes made me want to lift her up, to cradle her in my arms, to comfort her and dry away her tears.

Drunk as she was, Mary had noticed this. 'I suppose I shall have to introduce you. This beautiful creature is Harry Paine and this ungrateful person is called Inge Jensen. And you,' she said to the other woman, 'can keep your hands off this man. He is no-go territory, understand? He has a young lady in England wetting her knickers for him to get back into bed with her.'

'Really, Mary.' I tried to intervene, but she interrupted before I could finish.

'Sorry. Tell the truth I think I'm just a little bit pissed.' She looked at us, challengingly. 'OK, you all think so, do you? Maybe I am, but I know what I need to tell Harry. Listen darling, Festus Kasonde wants to see you at the Ministry at nine o'clock in the morning. I promised him you would be back to-night. There, you see, I can't be all that pissed. I remembered that, didn't I?' She hesitated, as though she needed to think what to say next.

'However, I do agree it's time I left. Bwana Potgeiter, I assume you have your motor bike with you. Would you be so kind as to take me home?'

She handed her car keys to me.

'You, dear boy, shall have the doubtful privilege of escorting Miss Jensen to her apartment. Don't worry, you are in no danger; she is what the girls at my convent school used to call a cock teaser. You'll find my car in the secure car park. Bring it back to the office tomorrow and come to see me after you leave Kasonde.'

It was Pete who took up the defence of Miss Jensen and I was shocked to find myself jealous that it was not me intervening on her behalf.

'Mary, before you go,' he said, 'you must apologise to Inge for the way you have treated her. Come on, let's hear it.'

'Why should I apologise? Shouldn't someone who walks out of my party without saying 'thank you', or even 'goodbye' --- shouldn't *she* apologise to *me*? Isn't that fair? But if it makes everyone feel better, I shall say sorry. *Sorry*. There now that's OK is it?'

She looked to Peter for approval. 'Harry understands me don't you, darling? I get upset when people treat me as though I have no feelings. Come on then Potty let me feel your throbbing mo-tor between my legs. Goodnight all, and flights of angels sing thee to thy rest.' She rose, with all the dignity she could muster, took Potty's arm and walked to the door. As she passed the Americans' table, she gave them a contemptuous curtsey.

Pete now said something in Danish which appeared to be an offer to take Inge home and I was pleased she appeared to turn him down. As she left for the washroom Pete prepared to go, not without first gulping down his lager.

He was angry. 'See here Bwana Paine, remember that Inge is new to this country and just twenty-two years old. Try something on with her and you will answer to me. Understood?'

'Calm down Peter,' I replied. The only reason I was chosen to take her home is because I walked here. So off you go. I'll see you at the beach house on Sunday.'

He had left by the time Inge returned, now looking more composed but no more cheerful than when she left. She said, 'If you please I think I would like to go now.'

This evening had all the makings of a disaster. Mary's condition had ruled out my plans to get her advice about staying on in Karibune. I hadn't even had time to drink my beer. I was damned if I was going to be hustled away to suit the whim of this stranger, beautiful though she may be.

'No, I am sorry, Miss Jensen,' I said, 'we are not going yet. In front of you is a glass of the most expensive tonic water in East Africa and I have not even started my drink. I intend to sip this and then maybe have another. It would be nice to have some conversation while I drink my beer, but if that's not possible I would still appreciate your company, in silence.

At last she smiled. 'It seems to be a lovely evening. Maybe we could go out onto the balcony. Those Americans make me a bit uncomfortable.'

I had never driven a Mercedes before, but the automatic gears made it simple. How ironic. Here I was, driving a fabulous sports car, with the waters of the Indian Ocean gently lapping the shore alongside us. Next to me sat the most beautiful woman I had met in years. And then what --- a polite handshake and 'Thank you, goodnight'?

I drove slowly, partly to be able to look at the ocean, but chiefly to enjoy the pleasure of sitting next to Inge. She was looking past me at the ocean. Once, when I glanced across towards her, she instantly turned away to look out of the other window. I suspected I was being appraised. She asked to borrow a handkerchief.

Conversation on the balcony had been sparse, nor did I learn much more about her while driving her home. Each question evoked a brief answer, the minimum response.

She came to Africa seven months ago. Though she was Danish, her grant was from the Swedish aid agency. It was for her to teach textile design in the new cotton mills. She had spent four months in Tanzania with NATEX the newly formed textile corporation and had just moved down to Bandari to the Russian-funded mill in Karibune. She lived in the suburb of Umoja, which was where we were headed. That was all I discovered. She did not ask about me, so I did not volunteer anything.

She directed me to her apartment. As we approached, I was surprised to find that this was one of the city's most prestigious blocks, not exactly the sort of place a young aid volunteer would normally afford. I would have asked how she came to be living here but she was already out of the car. My forecast was more-or-less correct. I got out, she gave back my handkerchief and we shook hands.

'Goodnight Mr Paine. I think you are a nice gentleman. Maybe we can be friends. Sometimes I drink tea at the New Bandari Hotel; can I see you there tomorrow at four o'clock?'

'That will be a pleasure. I'm staying there.'

When I held out my hand again, she leaned forward, kissed me briefly on the cheek and ran inside.

On the way home I pulled in at the Palm Court hotel, realising that I had not eaten since leaving the plane. Potty was in the bar, also having completed his transport duties and enjoying another beer. He was a good-looking man, below medium height but well-built and blond, and he had recently adopted a beard in the Boer fashion, with no moustache. This made him even more striking, for the beard was also blond. (Mary said a bottle of peroxide played some part in this).

I asked him to join me in spaghetti Bolognese. I was keen to learn more about Inge Jensen ahead of our teatime appointment and Potty was undoubtedly the best source of information about the expatriate community. He was the type that people instinctively trusted with their secrets, without the slightest justification, for he was as anxious to pass on gossip as he was to glean it. The fact that he was a South African automatically made him suspect in this town. He had started to broaden his South African accent as a gesture of defiance to local sensibilities, but with me he kept within the bounds of intelligibility.

'None of that spaghetti stuff for me if you don't mind, 'Arry. A man needs decent food at this time of the night.'

'Have whatever you like.'

Potty's idea of 'decent food' proved to be a cheeseburger and bacon, with two fried eggs, sausages, and a double portion of chips. We moved from the bar to a table and immediately he started talking about Inge.

'Well man, any luck with the blonde? Pete was just about ready to slit your throat back there, but I bet you got the cold shoulder. Am I right?'

'We did have a quiet time, but I got myself an invitation to tea.'

'Take care boy. It's Mary you will have to watch out for, more dangerous than our old friend Pete. Think about what you could lose with Mary before you get your teeth into the Danish pastry.'

'I see, so you think the rumours are true?'

'You know I don't spread gossip,' said Potty, and I tried to keep a straight face, 'but I wonder why Mary lets the kid live rent free in one of the most expensive apartments in town. Of course, it may be her motherly instincts coming out, but I just wonder. I owe Mary a lot, she has been very good to me, but all I can tell you is that I have had no joy when I tried to thank her in the way that many women would have been happy to accept. Do you get my meaning, man?'

It was true that Mary had been kind to Potty since he had got through his cash, but he was always good company, despite his habit of inventing stories about himself. During the eighteen months he had been in the country, he had earned himself the reputation of a 'character', due largely to the manner of his arrival.

In 1972 he had walked off a freighter from Lourenço Marques, dressed in the camouflage fatigues of a sergeant of the South African Defence Force, with no passport and carrying only a back-pack, reputed to have held just a change of underwear and several thousand Rand. He had, of course, been arrested on sight, but he must have told a convincing story to the authorities, for after about a month he emerged from prison with a year's residence permit and his money converted to Bandari shillings in the National Bank.

Since then he had tried several times to get himself recruited by the ANC or one of the Zimbabwe Guerilla movements, but these organisations did not respond as favourably as did the Bandari authorities who renewed his visa when it expired.

The authorised version of his story was that he had deserted from duty on the Mozambique border, having previously withdrawn his life savings, and had bribed his way through to the port and onto a Liberian tramp steamer. His revulsion against the regime in his home country seemed genuine, and there was a subsidiary plot that he had been thwarted in a love affair with a Cape Coloured woman, but the source of his funds was open to doubt.

During an evening of double brandies with Peter Larsen, who was his frequent boon companion, he indicated that the money came from sergeants' mess funds. Whatever may have been the source, the cash was now all but exhausted and Potty was reduced to living in one room near the railway station and sponging on Mary, until 'the boys in the bush' accepted him as one of their own, which was not a likely outcome.

But I needed to know more about Inge and Potty was my man.

'Pete does not accept that this kid is queer,' Potty said. 'He may be right I suppose. I'm not an expert on that sort of thing; myself I am a 'straight up the middle' sort of a guy, if you follow me --- but I think she must be. Gay, I mean. That's what they call it nowadays, yes? Otherwise I do not have a lot of time for her, because it would mean the kid is just using Mary.'

'That doesn't sound likely,' I said.

'I agree. I've never seen Mary quite so keen on anyone. When I took her home, she was crying like the great love of her life had just walked out on her. OK, so those were vodka tears, but you have to accept that dames like that feel just the same way you and me do. All I say to you, 'Arry my friend, is that if you take that pretty young woman away from Mary you will have made an enemy.'

It was time to get back to my hotel. I needed a good night's sleep.

THIRTEEN

Meeting Festus Kasonde was always a challenge. My monthly reports to Haskins and Ede not only provided data but made comments and recommendations. Although the Ministry of

57

Natural Resources was our client, I was not empowered to give them interim reports. Whenever I needed to see Kasonde there was a sparring match. Festus tried to elicit information and I put up my defences, hoping not to appear uncooperative.

After leaving Potty at the Palm Court I spent the rest of the evening rehearsing a summary of the last three months' work, which I could deliver to Kasonde without giving anything important away.

It was thus in some excitement that I entered the Natural Resources building on Mandela Front. During my two-year contract I had got to know several of the Ministry staff quite well so I was immediately asked to go up to the sixth floor.

'Do come in,' Kasonde said, as I opened the door of his office. 'You know Kenneth, of course'.

Seated alongside him, looking ill at ease, was Ken Pereira, the director of Langwa Experimental Farm. (It was always referred to as LEXFAR). Ken was a second generation Bandari citizen, of Goan extraction. He always looked uncomfortable when he was on Ministry territory.

Lexfar was an anomaly in this socialist state, in that it depended for most of its support costs on private funding. John Costas, Mary's father, met all its local expenses and it was housed in an old sisal estate that had been the original home of the Costas family. I knew that the Ministry resented not having Lexfar entirely under its control.

My personal file was on Kasonde's desk.

'Coffee, Mr Paine? Henry, isn't it? I feel that after all this time we should be on more familiar terms, don't you?

'Yes please, milk but no sugar --- and people call me Harry; one of our odd British customs.'

'Oh yes, I remember. Henry becomes Harry, John is Jack if I am correct and William . . . No, I forget that one.'

'Bill,' I said and wondered when the silly foreplay was going to end.

'Yes, of course, Bill. Well now, Harry, how have things been going since we last met? We would be most interested to know, wouldn't we Ken?'

Festus and Kenneth sat back in their chairs. Between sips of coffee, I launched into my prepared text. To a layman it may have sounded like a comprehensive summary, but it did not fool my audience. In fact, Ken was so appreciative of the performance that he gradually relaxed and a grin spread across his face. Only a quarter of the way through my prepared text Kasonde brought it to a halt. Even he betrayed some amusement.

'Thank you. That will suffice for the moment. I wonder if you ever considered a career in politics, Harry?'

'No, why do you ask?'

Kasonde had a twinkle in his eye. 'Because to say so little so convincingly is an art which many of my political colleagues would envy. You are telling us once more that we shall have to be patient and await news from WAFCO in due course. However, since you have been so kind as to spare us your time, there is one other little matter we might usefully discuss. Shall I continue, Ken, or would you rather put our suggestion to Harry?'

Pereira, who had said nothing so far, indicated that he should carry on, as Festus clearly intended.

'You will be aware, Harry, that we have some problems concerning the administration of Lexfar. At this stage I want what I say to remain confidential. If you feel that your friendship with Miss Costas would make this difficult, we shall fully understand but we would very much appreciate your views. In fact,' he added intriguingly, 'you personally would have a major role to play. How old are you now, Harry?'

'No doubt you have referred to my CV in the file you have on your desk,' I replied cheekily.

Kasonde registered a glimmer of annoyance at this response.

'Yes, of course; twenty-six I believe, which makes you just two years my junior. In many countries we would be considered mere beginners, but young nations need new ideas and it is we young people who can provide them --- properly qualified young people, I mean. I hope, with due humility, we can both claim that.'

I recognised a skilful softening-up process.

'Due largely to the sterling performance of Kenneth here, Lexfar has become one of the most respected institutions of its kind in East Africa, perhaps in the whole of Africa. It goes without saying that this success is also due to the extreme generosity of Mr John Costas. He has proved himself a worthy Bandarian.'

Good heavens, I thought. Festus might also have been burning the midnight oil in preparation for this interview. What he was saying certainly sounded suspiciously like a rehearsed text.

'However,' he went on, 'Some of us have begun to feel that it may now be time to relieve Mr Costas of the financial burden he has borne for so long. I must add that having a privately funded institution at the heart of our agricultural development programme is not entirely consistent with our progressive socialist ideals'.

I adopted my most attentive expression.

'What the Permanent Secretary has in mind is that we should take Lexfar fully under Government control and that it should become the basis of a new organisation, to develop our kiwanja villages into thriving production units.'

I spent a lot of time in these artificial 'villages' and found their inhabitants sometimes apathetic, sometimes hostile, to the life chosen for them. But like most expatriates working in Bandari, I accepted that building a prosperous nation with limited resources needed policies which might offend those born in places with a more viable economy. I made no comment and let Kasonde develop his theme.

'We intend to open depots throughout the country, with a view to replacing the marketing boards. An export department will . . .'

I could not let this one pass by. 'Sorry for interrupting, Festus, but surely Mr Costas isn't expected to finance all these developments.'

'Of course not, Harry. We intend to relieve him his responsibilities.'

'But can the State fund such a venture? I thought that until the new highway was completed you were . . .'

'Well done. You have reached the heart of the problem and the solution; which is that WAFCO will finance us.'

'Congratulations. That must be a major coup for you.'

'No, no. I don't appear to have made myself clear. What Kenneth and I are suggesting is that what I have just outlined would be a logical extension of the proposals you will be making to them in your report. I am sure that Britain would like to help, but your Mr Healey's present difficulties with the IMF may put further aid ventures on the back burner. We don't get on too well with the World Bank ourselves, of course.'

He allowed himself a quiet chuckle.

Bloody cheek! How do they know I am going to recommend any kind of investment, let alone a project like this, which could become a black hole for the most altruistic donor? But I didn't want to pour cold water until I knew what might be in it for me.

Festus appeared to read my mind.

'Now Harry, let us move to your part in our proposals or, I should say, to the part we would very much like you to play.'

It was neat. I would be Consultant Director of the new organisation, which would give me an extra incentive to sell the package to WAFCO. Ken would become Research Director, relieving him of the routine administration work which he found so uncongenial. The titular head of this grandiose project was to be none other than Kasonde's boss, the old Permanent Secretary, thus creating a convenient path for Festus to become acknowledged King of the department, rather than Crown Prince. Clearly his years in Moscow had not been wasted. In one fell swoop Festus cleared the final hurdle in his career, Ken kept control of research at his beloved Lexfar, I had a tempting bribe and the dear old Perm Sec moved from one sinecure to an even more comfortable one.

I resisted the temptation to say, 'bugger you'. Instead, I smiled and said, 'Thanks very much, let me think about it for a while?'

*

Mary looked awful. 'It *was* you I gave my car keys to last night, wasn't it?'

'Yes, it's parked round the back. How did you get in to work? I didn't see the Beetle in the car park.'

'I phoned Poonam to pick me up; didn't feel much like driving this morning. Was I rude to you last night? Go outside and ask her if she would bring us coffee, another black one for me. I'm just beginning to feel human again. You want some coffee do you, or have you been supping with the opposition?'

'To answer your questions in turn. No, you weren't rude to me, but I think Miss Jensen will need to be mollified, and no, I don't

62

want any more coffee. Finally, Festus is not 'the opposition' nor is Ken Pereira.' I realised I had made an error.

'Ken was there, was he? So, it was about Lexfar. Oh yes, I know what Festus and his pals are after; they can't stand the fact that the place couldn't run without Daddy's money. Millions of shillings he's poured into it and they resent every cent. They won't allow Ken a few measly dollars-worth of foreign exchange to buy so much as a test tube.'

'Come on Mary don't be paranoid. Festus told me how much they owed to your father. "A worthy Bandarian" he called him. I'm beginning to think it was a mistake for me to take citizenship. The young ones like Festus don't appreciate what people like Daddy gave up for this country. Anyway, it sounds as though *you* have been won over. What have they been using to bribe you?'

She was so near the truth that I hoped my face did not betray confusion. It was time to change the subject, before resorting to falsehoods.

'They wanted to know what I was going to put in my report, and I had to flannel as usual. By the way, you look awful --- I was surprised to see you here today. You really should take it easier Mary. Why don't you change to beer like me?'

'Listen, sonny, if I couldn't do my job with a hangover, I would have given up long ago. I'm perfectly capable. It's obvious from the look on your face that you have something you want to get off your chest. As from this afternoon I'm tied up for the rest of the week with this W.H.O. conference, so fire away.'

When I told her about Gaynor's letter, she took off her glasses and came round the desk to kiss me --- on the lips.

'What was that for?' I asked, in some surprise.

'That was a demonstration of sympathy. I know how much she means to you and how upset you must be, but I also wanted to show you that there are other fish in the sea . . . if I may describe myself as a fish.'

There was no reply to that, so I carried on. 'This means there's no need now for me to rush home, except that I need access to a mainframe computer.'

'The University has just got an IBM,' she said. 'An information technology expert has come from America to supervise the commissioning. Very nice chap called Wayne Marshall. I'm sure he can get you access, because they are running trials before they put the important stuff on. So that's settled; you stay in Karibune.'

'I still have to clear it with my firm.'

'Tell them straight away that you are staying on. Be firm, don't ask them, *tell* them! I'll draft a telex for you. Say you will need another two months. Oh, Harry, think what a good time we can have in two months.'

'There is one other thing,' I said. 'My expenses will only cover four more days in the hotel. I will need somewhere to live.'

'That's easy; go and see Wellington.'

She scribbled an address on her memo pad

FOURTEEN

I set out to find Wellington Stores as soon as I finished lunch at the hotel. The address Mary gave me was somewhere in a warren of narrow streets in the commercial quarter, quite near the hotel, but an area I had never entered before. All was remarkably quiet as I approached my destination, which led me to suspect that the shopkeepers took a siesta. Many of the stores appeared to be permanently closed and some were boarded up. This was the first evidence I had seen of the Asian trading community starting to leave the country.

Wellington Stores was a double-fronted shop, recently painted but with dirty net curtains at the windows. There was nothing on display. Potential customers must know what they were coming for. I peeped into the shop through a hole in one of the net curtains and could see a thin gentleman of Indian or Pakistani extraction, dressed in a white suit. He lay in a deck chair, apparently asleep, with a panama hat pulled down over his eyes. The hat was supported by an exceptionally large nose.

I debated whether to call again when the shop was open, but there was no indication of business hours. I tried the door as quietly as I could. It opened, causing a loud shop bell to tinkle.

The effect of the bell was like that on a contestant in a boxing match. He jumped from the deck chair, causing it to collapse, and his hat dropped to the floor. He sprang forward to shake my hand and rapidly produced a business card, which read,

WELLINGTON STORES
Ship's chandler and fancy goods
Prop. J. K. CHAUDHURI

The shop resembled an untidy Aladdin's cave. Cabin trunks were piled precariously on top of one another. There were boxes of fishing floats, plastic rope of various colours, camp beds, and several items which seemed to have no obvious connection with the rest of the stock, such as a row of wall barometers, old fashioned tennis racquets, a rack of track suits and display cabinets full of plastic dolls.

'I'm sorry to disturb you in your lunch hour,' I said.

'Mention not, young man,' said Mr Chaudhuri. 'This emporium does not close in the luncheon interval. I was taking advantage of a brief lull in the flow of customers to enjoy some few moments of relaxation. To see a person such as yourself walk through the door of my establishment is indeed a delight. No doubt it is an expedition of some kind you are planning or perhaps you wish to equip a boat?'

'I'm sorry but...'

'How pleasant it is to get out on the sea on these warm days. By the way, should you be needing to know where the best fishing is to be had, I am the person to advise you. In my younger days I was a fisherman of some renown, if I may say so with due modesty.'

'No, it's not...'

'In short, young man, be assured that you have chosen the ideal place to supply whatever you require. In the past we have given complete satisfaction to many famous travellers. Are you familiar with the works of Mr Eustace Prendergast?'

'No, but...

'You really should read his *Strolling through East Africa*. He expresses himself most satisfied with his purchases from this emporium, and we have had the honour to serve many other English gentlemen travellers --- you are English, am I not right in saying so?'

It was a relief to get a word in at last. This prologue had been delivered without so much as a pause for breath.

'I beg your pardon Mr Chaudhuri, but I should explain that it was about renting an apartment that I came to see you. Mary Costas said you may be able to help me.'

'Ah, it is I who should beg *your* pardon, young man. I have been under complete misapprehension. You are a friend of Mary, then?'

'Yes. So, I wonder...'

'I have known her since she was only a small tot. What a delightful and most intelligent young lady she has become, isn't it? Take this card.'

The new card read,

WELLINGTON K. COWDREY
Life President
MOONLIGHT PROPERTIES Inc.
Karibune and Auckland

'Please accept refreshment.' He went behind the counter and opened a small refrigerator. 'Now then, let me see. Lemonade or cola is available, or perhaps whisky you would prefer. I am not a partaker of strong beverages but everything of that nature is on hand in the storeroom.'

'Whatever you are having will . . .'

'Boy!' he suddenly shouted. A child about Oscar 's age appeared from behind bead curtains.

'*Lete cola mbili*,' he ordered. The boy went to the fridge and poured two drinks, picking up the collapsed deck chair and the Panama hat on his way out.

Was Mr Chaudhuri/Cowdrey serious? This performance may have amused European customers in colonial days.

'Cheerio,' he said.

'Cheers,' He took a large swig.

'Do I call you Mr Cowdrey?' I asked.

'A new name for a new life,' he replied, enigmatically. 'Please call me Wellington. It was Mr O'Connor, the excellent District Officer of Morogoro, who gave me that name --- now long deceased, I regret to tell you. He told me that I reminded him of your great Iron Duke, is it not so?'

He turned into full profile. The long-deceased excellent Mr O'Connor had a point. Probably Wellington had performed this

act so many times that he was not aware how much of a carica-
ture he had become.

'Well, now let us to our business', he continued, resuming his
rapid sales patter. 'Golden Bay is no doubt where you will be
wishing to reside and it so happens that three highly desirable
residences are recently available in that area, due to the temporary absence of local businessmen. Between ourselves',
lowering his voice he confided, 'absence may well be permanent. You will perhaps be aware of the difficulties my community is experiencing. Let us take keys and inspect.'

Mr Cowdrey stood up and yelled, '*Mafunguo*.' The child re-
appeared almost immediately, carrying an old Gladstone bag.
He must have been listening to our conversation.

I took advantage of the pause to interject, 'If I could just explain
what I want, please. Do you have something quiet and cheap
which I could take for only about two months? I don't want a
big place; it's only for me and I couldn't afford Golden Bay.
Somewhere around here would be fine.'

Mr Cowdrey seemed disappointed. He downed the remainder of
his drink in two gulps and placed the empty glass on the
counter. I felt I should do the same, as the young boy was staring expectantly at him. I got up to join them, already at the
door.

Wellington locked up and we set off on a tour of the local
streets. Every other shop seemed to have rooms available to
let. The boy found keys from the Gladstone bag with no difficulty, though some had no tags on them. At one address we
found a man in bed. He yelled a stream of protest in Bengali but
this did not deter Wellington.

'Maybe this one you would like?' he said. 'By the way, we did
not discuss price.'

'I thought about forty dollars a week,' I said hopefully. The
word dollars caused Cowdrey's face to brighten.

'You are referring to the currency of the United States of America?' A reverential tone entered his voice as he pronounced the name of the great power. When I confirmed this to be the case, he said,

'For a friend of Mary Costas, a special arrangement can be made. Could we talk in the region of one hundred dollars a month?'

'Sixty?'

'Let us return', said Mr Cowdrey.

When we got back to Wellington Stores, he led me through the bead curtains into a storeroom and up a flight of stairs with Axminster carpet.
He unlocked the door and we entered a sitting room. It had two windows, one overlooking the street from which I had entered the shop and the other giving onto an alley. The red flock wallpaper was not to my taste, but it was comfortably furnished; a three-piece suite upholstered in yellowish imitation leather. I was pleased to see a large desk under the alley window. This was far superior to anything I had seen on our expedition through the neighbourhood.

Chaudhuri opened a door to a galley kitchen, with plenty of cupboards but old-fashioned equipment. The other door from the sitting room led to a comfortable bedroom with a double bed. There was a bathroom through a narrow archway.

'Perhaps this would be suitable for your purpose', said Wellington. 'I saw that none of my clients' properties was what you required. This is where Mrs Chaudhuri and I lived before we built our house in Golden Bay. It has never been let. I have always felt it wise to keep it available, in case we ever needed to sell our property, but soon we shall be joining our eldest son in New Zealand. You are welcome to this for as long as you need, but I hope you will agree that one hundred dollars would be a fair rent.'

'Certainly,' I said, and thought myself lucky.

FIFTEEN

The New Bandari Hotel has a patio forecourt. Large umbrellas shade the tables and terracotta pots hold an assortment of tropical plants. It is more popular than the indoor area, frequented not only by tourists but by locals wishing to relax after a busy day, to trade gossip or to see who was new in town.

Knowing that the teashop would be busy, I rushed back from Wellington Stores, had a quick shower and change of clothes and was down by a quarter to four to claim a table. This had been a full and successful day, but always at the back of my mind had been this teatime appointment.

I received some disapproving stares after the rest of the tables had filled up, occupying one on my own, while groups of customers had to move indoors. I had been prepared for a long wait, so was pleasantly surprised to see her soon after four o'clock. She hesitated at the corner of the patio, then smiled as she recognised me, and moved across. All eyes moved with her. She was casually dressed, a plain white tee-shirt over blue cotton slacks, and she carried a motor-cycle helmet with the Danish flag on the front. I rose to draw out a chair for her and she placed her helmet on the other.

'Good afternoon,' she said. 'Please sit down. It is not usual for men to stand up for me. Now I can tell everybody that I have a friend who is an English gentleman. Am I late? I forgot to put my watch on this morning because I was in such a rush, and I have come straight from the factory. You are not cross with me?'

She ordered lemon tea, so I did too.

'Would you like cake?' I asked.

'Just a moment, I will see.' She got up and sat with a couple of Asian ladies at a neighbouring table.

'They say the cheesecake is very nice', she said when she returned. 'May I please have some of that?'

She had an attractive 'break' in her voice which on the previous evening I thought was due to her being upset, but it was her natural tone. The Scandinavian accented English made it a pleasure to listen to her, though we talked trivialities.

In contrast to last night's stilted conversation she now chatted easily and appeared relaxed. I was determined not to mention Mary or the scene at the Kiboko. Today would be a fresh start and I would keep the conversation in neutral territory. Unwittingly I failed, I should have remembered what Potty told me.

'I was impressed by your address. That must be one of the smartest apartment blocks in town. I can't imagine SIDA paying that sort of rent, are you a secret millionaire?'

Her smile vanished and there was a short silence. Eventually she said,

'It is hers, Mary's. She owns the block.'

Hoping to bring the conversation back to less dangerous ground, I ordered her another piece of cake. She smiled again. The next question took me by surprise.

'Do you love her?'

'Do I love who?'

'Mary.'

'Of course not. Well yes, I mean I like her very much but not *love*.'

'She is in love with you, she told me so. She wants to fuck you

71

before you go home.'

I looked quickly at the other tables to see if anyone had heard this. All continued as normal except I noticed two pretty Asian girls staring at us, but reckoned they must be out of earshot. Inge was laughing at my confusion.

'Sorry gentleman, I've said a rude word, haven't I? Honestly, I do try to behave like a lady but really I am just a Danish peasant. Now that I have met you I can understand why Mary loves you. You are a nice man and you *are* good looking. There I've said it.' She made a long face.

'Why do you look like this? Don't you like people to say nice things about you? If you don't believe what I say just look at those two young girls over there. They have been staring at you all the time we are talking. They want to eat you up like one of their cream cakes. Give them a smile and make them happy.' She gave the girls a friendly wave, embarrassing them and me equally.

'Do try to behave, Inge.'

'OK, but on condition that you tell me all about yourself. How do you
come to be so brown? Do you not know that too much sunshine is bad for you?'

She was easy to talk to. In the daylight I could see that her eyes were grey-green. They seemed to draw from me things I had mentioned to no one since I came to Bandari, not even to George. I told her about my school, about Cambridge, about Gaynor. When I came to the part about the death of my family, she reached across the table to take my hand in hers. I held it for longer than I should, a strong hand, with no jewellery. There were signs of paint in the cuticles. I could see I was embarrassing her by my inspection, but I wanted to remember everything about her, in case this were to be our last encounter.

I told her about my work in Bandari over the last two years and

some of my adventures with George, then I related that afternoon's encounter with Wellington, which made her laugh.
When the waiter came to clear the next table, I noticed with surprise that almost everybody else had left the patio. We had
been there for almost an hour.

'Poor Harry,' she said. 'Now I know all about you. Someday I
will tell you all about me, but not now.'

She stood up. 'Now I must go to powder my nose. That is such a
funny thing to say, isn't it? Very English. Mary told me what it
means. Noses have nothing to do with it, do they? Take care of
my helmet. When I come back I will show you my lovely new
motor bike.'

I signed the bill, picked up the helmet and waited for her outside the washrooms. The delegates to the health conference
were assembling in the lobby. Once more I noticed people
watching as I escorted her to the door and felt proud when she
linked her arm in mine.

Inge did not seem to notice the effect she made, she must be
used to being the centre of attention.

At the entrance to the car park, the askari saluted and raised the
barrier for us. Inge gave him a dazzling smile and tipped him a
coin. The size of her motor bike surprised me.

'Good heavens Inge, it's huge.'

Her reaction was alarming, a complete change of mood.

'You too!' she shouted. Because I'm a woman you think I should
have a tiny bike, all . . . what is it you say in English? Oh, I can't
remember the word because you make me so cross. You think a
weak young girl like me can't handle a proper machine, don't
you?'

Her anger only increased as I began laughing. 'No Inge, honestly, it's just that I didn't expect . . .'

73

'Just like Peter Larsen. He says I will kill myself, but I ride better than him. Get on! I'll show you.'

'But I don't have a helmet. It would be dangerous to . . .'

Before I could protest, she pushed her helmet over my head and bundled me onto the pillion. The car park attendant had lowered the barrier again during our fight and was only just in time to raise it, as she sped the bike towards the exit. We avoided decapitation by inches, or so it seemed to me.

She slowed to a reasonable speed to negotiate the narrow passage onto the main road, but once on the seafront she opened the throttle and roared along at what seemed a suicidal pace.

'All right, I believe you,' I shouted, but there was no indication she had heard.

Though I had driven a motor bike, I had never travelled as a passenger, but once the initial terror subsided, I began to like the experience. Inge's hair was blowing in the wind. The back of her neck looked so vulnerable that I longed to bend forward to kiss it. I put my hands on her hips, as though to steady myself, and she did not appear to object. I was enjoying this.

By now we had reached State House pier, but as we turned the corner onto Ocean Road, we met the procession. She shouted in Danish what I took to be an expletive and revved the engine in irritation, as she tucked in behind a Peugeot packed with about eight people. Ahead stretched a line of cars travelling at ten miles an hour. On the other side of the road a similar line of traffic moved at the same pace. This was the 'Asian crawl'. We were trapped.

It was a tradition that after the Indian and Pakistani office workers and shopkeepers left work they would drive their families along the sea shore to watch the fading sunlight and gaze towards the far distant lands they called home, but which few of them had ever seen. Despite what I heard about the departure

74

of the Asian community they were still out in force. This snail's pace progress would continue all the way back into town.

Inge turned around with a gleam in her eye. 'You wanted to see if I was a good driver so watch this, English gentleman.'

Panic hit me as she moved out from behind the Peugeot into a narrow corridor between the traffic on the opposite side of the road which only just allowed for the width of her Suzuki. She increased speed, running the gauntlet. Horns hooted, but many male drivers stuck their heads out of the car window and took the opportunity to ogle this mad blonde. I was grateful for the anonymity which the crash helmet gave me; at least I hoped it did. In a perverse way I wanted the police to appear, to prevent our imminent death. We both instinctively bent from side to side to avoid protruding wing mirrors, but after a time I abandoned the exercise, closed my eyes, and relied on prayer.

At last I experienced that she was slowing down. I opened my eyes to find with overwhelming relief that we were in the parking lot of the Palm Court Hotel. Halfway home and still alive. There is a God, after all.

'Now it is your turn to drive,' she said, and got off to replace me on the pillion. I rode three times round the car park for practice, then out into the road to re-join the stately procession. Some of the cars hooted disapproval as they recognised who we were, but I did not try to repeat Inge's heroics and kept the bike safely behind a Ford Cortina, whose rear-seat occupants turned to glare at us.

I had forgotten what fun it is to drive a motorcycle. As we reached a wider part of the road I started to overtake, albeit with more caution than she had displayed. The pleasure increased as I felt her arms encircle my waist, and she leaned forward to place her head against my left shoulder. I slowed down again, to prolong the pleasant sensation. She had proved so unpredictable that I feared this may be the last time we would be so close.

It was dark by the time we returned to the New Bandari hotel. I dismounted and removed the helmet, but Inge remained on the bike. She edged forward onto the driving seat, leaned across to pull me towards her, kissed me once on the lips, donned the helmet and drove away.

SIXTEEN

The Land Rover was garaged in the Banzam Taxis depot. It had to be handed back to the UN representative on Friday, so later that evening I phoned George. I asked if it was convenient to make a final visit to Lexfar the following day. I was tempted to tell him about my adventure with Inge, but could not think how I might answer the inevitable questions. How *did* I feel about her? It felt remarkably like love. So, I mentioned nothing of what was uppermost in my thoughts (and omitted to claim the hundred-shilling bet.) instead, I told George about my arrangement with Mr Chaudhuri.

'That man's an old fraud', was his comment. 'I suppose he gave you the comic act, did he? --- *Oh, my God, whatever will become of me*?'

George was an excellent mimic. 'Don't kid yourself Harry, he's a very clever fellow. Softens you up with his nonsense and then takes you to the cleaners. Mind you, he has done a lot of good for his community.'

'All I do know,' I said, 'is that I have found a decent place to stay for the next few weeks. Come and have a look when we get back from Langwa. As a matter of fact, I would appreciate your help in moving my gear.'

Most of my belongings were stored in the garage of George's bungalow, ready for packing.

When I woke next morning, I had to remind myself that the previous afternoon was not part of a beautiful dream.

We set off early. The road had been graded since the end of the heavy rains and we made good time. By nine-thirty we had reached the turn-off for Langwa. After less than a mile we followed the sign

LANGWA EXPERIMENTAL FARM. LEFT 800 YDS

I preferred to think of the place by the name it bore when Mary lived there as a young girl. As George slowed to turn into the entrance, I saw the familiar rusty metal gate supported by its two tall stone pillars. Atop each pillar is a figure of the German eagle, its bronze patina now turned a pleasant shade of green. A square brass plate is set into the right-hand pillar, with the inscription still decipherable.

P COSTAS
KNOSSOS
1920

Then follows more than a mile of dirt track, straight as a Roman road and lined with mature acacia trees. Behind the acacias, row after row of sisal bushes stretch into the distance on either side, no longer cultivated, forming a miniature forest from what must once have been an orderly estate.

The house was built to resemble a Bavarian hunting lodge. From a distance it appears impressive but, as one draws near, it betrays neglect. A block is missing from one end of the portico. Inside, only the quarters reserved for Mr Costas are properly maintained.

On a couple of occasions George and I had spent the night there. We had grown used to rough surroundings. For us, this was comparative luxury. Waking in the morning, it was difficult to realise that one was in the heart of East Africa.

We stopped at the old bungalow to say hello to Mrs Pereira. She ushered us inside. 'Lovely to see you again, Mr Paine. You

77

will find Kenneth in his lab but before you go over let me make you both some breakfast. You must have set off at crack of dawn.'

George accepted her offer but I excused myself and walked across to see Ken. His laboratory was in what had been the kitchens of the old house. He gave me the analysis of my final batch of soil samples and then we went together to the trial beds to inspect some of the maize varieties that he was growing for me.

I had not had an opportunity since our meeting with Kasonde to ask him what he really thought of Festus's plans for the future of Lexfar.

'I think he is genuine about this one,' said Ken. 'He's ambitious, I know, and a politician to his fingertips, but he really does believe this to be in the nation's best interests.'

Then he surprised me. 'Whatever happens I won't be part of it. We are off to Canada soon, to join my sister and her husband. They've started a pharmacy business in Vancouver, and she wants me to go in with them --- that's my background, pharmacy. There's no long-term future here for someone like me. John Costas agrees, by the way.'

Suddenly, my mind was being made up for me. Kasonde's project had been seeming attractive but it would lose a cornerstone without Ken in it.

'Please keep mum about what I just told you,' he continued. 'Getting away will be difficult. I need to pretend we are just going on holiday but I've been squirrelling foreign exchange away over the years. I hope you don't think I'm letting you down.'

'For goodness sake, Ken, of course not, but not having you on board makes a huge difference. Now Mr Costas knows about it, do you think he would see me? When George and I were up in Lassita I tried to speak to him, but got a clear brush-off. Maybe you could clear the way for me.'

Ken shook his head. 'Nobody gets to see him up there, he's like a hermit.
We keep a suite of rooms ready for him here. He turns up from time to time, but we never know when to expect him. Frankly, I wouldn't know how to arrange for you to meet him. Why not try Mary? Now that her father knows of the plan it needn't be a secret from her.'

It was a relief that I would be able to discuss the proposal with Mary, but I must choose the right moment. I could not forecast how she would react to my having kept this from her.

'You still ought to give serious consideration to Kasonde's plan,' Ken continued. 'If you can swing the aid package you could be onto a winner and, don't forget, you could influence policy. Festus has great respect for what you've done these last two years. George is one of your greatest fans.'

'What has George to do with this?'

'Oh, didn't you know? Kasonde married Mercy's cousin; there can't be much that George hasn't told him about you.'

SEVENTEEN

MERCY BWALYA

Mercy sat on the veranda with her crochet work, waiting for George to return from Langwa. His work had meant that long hours of her married life had been spent waiting like this.

When they first met, he had been a lorry driver and she still a schoolgirl. She used to help in her parents' restaurant after school until the regular waitress came on duty at six o'clock. It was always quiet at that time of day, but this man used to come in around five with his friend. She found out that the man was called George and the friend was Wilbert. She knew they were not Bandarian but the shorter man spoke beautiful Swahili, bet-

79

ter than most Bandarians; just like announcers on the radio.

She normally kept her blue school uniform on when she was serving, but after he had been visiting for some time, she used to change into a khanga before she went into the restaurant. She was nearly eighteen and didn't want him to think she was a child.

Then she used to see him in church. He was a Lutheran, as were her family, and she heard him singing in a lovely deep bass voice. It was his voice she first fell in love with, and the way he walked.

After about six months he started coming in on his own, much better dressed. He now wore a pale blue uniform, just the colour of her school outfit, and his Toyota taxi was painted the same shade of blue. It was often about seven when he came for his meal and she asked Miriam, the waitress, if she would be sure always to let her serve him.

Miriam warned her. 'Yes, he is very nice but take care, your mother would never approve of you marrying a taxi driver -- and him a foreigner too.'

He didn't eat mealie-meal like most of the other drivers: he preferred meat and potatoes with lots of gravy, and afterwards he usually chose a piece of her mother's home-made mango pie. She always made sure his plate was full, but when she carried it across, she shook so much that she was afraid of spilling the gravy onto his smart blue uniform.

Some of the lorry drivers used to tease him about that uniform, which upset her. They could be a bit more careful with their personal hygiene before criticising her George (for that was how she already thought of him). But she listened-in carefully to their conversations to see what more she could discover about him. She found out that he was single, which was a tremendous relief, and that he lodged in Morogoro Road with a lady who did not provide meals. That was why he came to the restaurant so regularly.

Of course, she was not naive, and soon became aware that the man was also interested in her. They began to have little conversations. He asked her what she was studying at school and she hoped he was not put off when she told him she hoped to study chemistry at the university. She didn't want him to think she was an intellectual.

It was all going very well, but she knew that Miriam was right. Her mother would never approve, even when she discovered that he owned the taxi and had set up his friend in another. Some stratagy must be devised if the affair was to proceed further. She needed more information about him but she could not approach him directly. If only his friend had not stopped coming.

Then she has a stroke of luck. It was on Independence Anniversary day.
 Her parents had gone to the parade ground to see the pageant, leaving her and Miriam in charge of the restaurant. This was a public holiday and few customers were expected, but in walked Wilbert. He was wearing the same uniform as George wore. Miriam was on her way to serve him but Mercy got there first.

'I remember you', she said. You always came in with a friend. We haven't seen you for a long time.' She had to risk appearing to take an interest in Wilbert, to get onto the subject of George.

'I come in all the time,' he replied, 'but in the daytime, while you are still at school. I take the early airport shift and my friend takes the afternoons --- well, he's my boss really. He's called George Bwalya and he has started a taxi business.'

She took Wilbert's order. Good, now at least she knew George's second name.

There was no one else in the restaurant, so when she had served him his stew she hung around, hoping that he would chat. He asked her to sit with him.

81

'I suppose everybody is at the festival ground,' he said.

'Or asleep,' she suggested. 'I expect your friend is asleep.'

'Yes, he's a wonderful sleeper. It comes from the old truck driving days. You had to sleep whenever you got the chance.'

'You are not from Bandari, are you? I heard them saying you were both Zambians.'

'That's right Miss, a couple of foreigners we are. We used to drive for George's uncle; he lives in Lusaka. They are a well-known family where I come from. George and went to school together, up in the East of Zambia near the Tanzania border, not all that far from here really. His Dad is the District Chief in our area.'

Mercy offered a silent prayer. Oh please, dear God, make George the eldest son. Her mother was an awful snob and might accept a future Chief as her son-in-law, even if he was at present only a taxi driver.

She was right. Soon after her nineteenth birthday she walked up the aisle of the Lutheran Church as Mrs George Bwalya. After they became engaged George said he had fallen in love with her the first time he saw her. That was why his taxis were painted that shade of blue.

*

The twins had been making a nuisance of themselves. Mercy let slip that George may bring 'Harry uncle' with him. They were over-excited, asking how long it would be before Daddy came back. They had made some place mats for Harry to take home to his fiancée.

Mercy had always been proud of their bungalow which George had bought with the money he saved from the lorry driving. It was one of three originally built for the managers of the dairy.

82

When Ian Smith declared Rhodesia independent, George had gone back to lorry driving. He returned to Lusaka, taking two of the taxi drivers with him. The closure of the border between Rhodesia and Zambia meant that all the copper was exported through Dar es Salaam, which involved transit through Bandari. This became a bonanza for transport operators, albeit a very dangerous one.

George's uncle found it economic to use Karibune as the site for his depot. George made a lot of money from his three trucks, but he only spent the occasional night at home. Mercy had hated being alone, knowing the dangers he was facing on what they called 'the Hell Run.' After just over a year she persuaded him to give it up.

She liked having her cousin Myra so near. She prayed that George would reconsider moving to Zambia. Of course, they would have to go down there one day. When his father died, George would become Chief. But to go now? George was over-reacting.

It started last Christmas when the girls came home from a party.

'Daddy is not a foreigner is he, Mummy? Tommy Kilewo says we are not real Bandaris and we ought to go home, but this is our home, isn't it?'

She had always wanted George to take citizenship; Festus would arrange it, she was sure. And why on earth had he told the girls about moving? They started boasting they were going to live on a big farm, and that their daddy would be a Chief in Zambia when his daddy died. Her visit to the doctor next week might change things. He never said so, but she knew how much he wanted a son. If only God would let her carry it through this time, she was sure it would be a boy.

She heard the Land Rover engine before it turned the corner and the girls were already there when Harry opened his door. They had their presents with them.

'Look, Harry uncle, these are for your wife.'

'They're lovely, Pipit. Did you really make these yourselves?'

'Mummy helped a bit', said Marika, 'but she helped Poppet more than she helped me'.

It used to amuse Mercy that Harry claimed he could not tell them apart, nor remember their names. He decided to call them Pipit and Poppet. They liked the names, but they teased him by changing which one was which. He really was the nicest European she had met. George would miss him, and she knew that Festus wanted him to come back for another contract.

Perhaps she could arrange something to encourage him to do so. She was good at arranging things, after all she had managed to arrange her marriage by playing on her mother's snobbery. If Harry stayed, so might George.

Something George had told her just might prove to be the solution. When she next saw Festus she would mention it.

She helped load Harry's things into the Land Rover and George persuaded her to allow the girls to go into town with them.

EIGHTEEN

My door key gave me private access to the flat, through the stock room. As I let George and the girls in the light was still on in the shop, so I signalled they should be quiet. I peeped through the bead curtain and saw Wellington drinking tea with Poonam, Mary's secretary. He had heard us.

'Come here young man. This young lady is here to see you; being a most reliable secretary she was not willing to divulge the reason until you came.

George and the twins followed me.

'And welcome to you, Bwana Bwalya. A long time since I saw you at Rotary, and surely these cannot be your little girls? My goodness, what big girls you are now.'

Poonam passed me a silent message indicating the stairs. 'Do excuse us, Wellington,' I said. 'Maybe George and the girls could have a look round your shop?' He looked aggrieved as we left but, nevertheless, started the Bwalyas on a tour of the 'emporium'.

Poonam had kindly stayed on until I got back from Langwa, so she could let me in to use the IALO phone. She told me there had been a call from Richard Butterworth. I was to phone him at home. That could mean only one thing: ever since taking on the Bandari contract I had worried that my grandfather may not last out until I returned. When I left, he was physically well, though his mental condition continued to worsen. Now the decision about staying on in Bandari was being settled for me.

As we left, I asked George to unload my belongings, leaving behind the disappointed twins and an even more disappointed Wellington, who was obviously dying to know what had happened.

We were lucky in getting a clear line. It was good to hear Richard's voice again, though the news I was sure he was about to give me cast gloom over the conversation.

'Hello Harry, glad I caught you before you left East Africa. I tried that number in Malua that you gave me, but the chemist chap said you had packed up and were on your way home, so I rang the Karibune office. Now listen, I know this is an expensive call, so I suggest you just let me talk. We can chat afterwards if you wish.'

'It's about Grandpa, is it?'

'No, don't worry about Mr Paine; he's fine. I saw him last week. It was one of his good spells and he recognised who I was. In fact, we had a nice chat about the old days. It's something totally unexpected that has turned up.'

'Please hold on a minute, Richard,' I intervened. 'I have a friend here who can take this down in shorthand.' I gestured to Poonam to pick up the extension phone. She took a notebook from her desk drawer.

'Ready now?' Poonam nodded.

'Yes, go on.'

Well, Janet --- you remember Janet, my chief clerk? She reads the legal notices in the newspapers as a matter of routine and she came across one yesterday in the *Telegraph* and *The Times.* I have it here, hold on

Would Mary Spencer Paine (née Brown) otherwise known as Polly Brown or Polly Paine, formerly of Levenshulme, Manchester and Eldoret and Kisule, Kenya or any person knowing her whereabouts please contact Justin Farrugia, Advocate at 92b St Publius Street, Valletta, Malta' . . . then he gives the phone number.

Well, I phoned him this morning. It seems genuine because he wouldn't talk, until he had looked me up in the British legal directory. Then he phoned me back.'

'Can you repeat the name?'

'Farrugia. That's two 'r's, one 'g' and an 'i'.' Poonam signalled OK.

'Go ahead, Richard.'

'A man called Hector Brown has died, in Malta. Brown was a Squadron Leader in the Royal Air Force and he'd been stationed there during the war. Apparently, he developed a liking for the island and went back to settle there, after what sounds like a bit of a nomadic career.   He died intestate and Farrugia has been given the job of sorting out the estate. Farrugia sensibly went to RAF records and the surprise is that he found out that this chap Brown had named your mother as next of kin in his demob records. Don't suppose you know what the relationship was, do you? Did you ever hear your mother mention a Cousin Hector?'

'She was an only child, but I can't remember her mentioning cousins.'

'Pity. Anyway, I told Farrugia who you were and what had happened to your parents and Barbara. He circulated the statutory announcements widely but got no replies until mine. However, he needs to wait and see if there is any other response to this latest advert. Assuming you are 'it', if you know what I mean, I don't suppose you are going to get much. It seems Brown got through his capital in his later years. There is a house though, in a place called Santarita. Am I going too fast for your friend?'

Poonam shook her head.

'No, carry on.'

'Brown moved to a rented flat in Sliema towards the end, but he never got round to selling the house. Sounds posh, called Villa Buenvista --- but I suppose they all have fancy names over there. Oh, and there are some books, antiquarian books. Farrugia doesn't want to spend money having them valued until he knows where the intestacy is heading and whether he will get paid. You see, Harry, us lawyers always think about our fees. That's about it. Have you got it?'

Poonam lifted her pen to show that she had it all recorded.

'Yes,' I said, 'but I can't pretend to have taken it all in. I'll have to study what my friend has taken down. Can you carry on dealing with this? I've decided to hang on here for a few more weeks.'

'I have the power of attorney you gave me, but Farrugia will need to see you. I'll send him a certified copy of your birth certificate tomorrow but he won't be happy if he has to wait much longer. I suggest you get yourself to Malta on your way home. Can you still hear me? I'm getting some interference'

'Yes'.

'There is one other thing. I'm still under a lot of pressure from David and Kitty Masters about buying Brough Farm. Can I give them a definite answer?'

'I need more time, especially now this Mr Brown thing has come up.'

'All right, I'll keep stalling. Bye, then. Keep in touch.'

Poonam said, 'What a mysterious man you are, Mr Paine. May I tell Mary about this?'

'I'd rather you didn't --- not yet. Charge the call to my account. I hope you'll also let me pay you for the transcript, and your time of course.'

'Certainly not. I would willingly pay *you*: it all sounds so exciting. I'll type it up at home and drop it in at Wellington Stores. If I were you, I would be on the next plane to Malta.'

This mystery only served to increase the frustration I had felt since the visit to Kisule. All Grandpa had been able to tell me about my maternal grandparents, the Browns, was that they were killed in 1942 when a bomb destroyed their house on the outskirts of Manchester. If Mum did have cousins, there may yet be others contacting this Farrugia chap. Any potential legacy could be widely divided.

When I left the IALO office I decided to walk over to the Kiboko. Mary might be there, despite her health conference duties. I wanted her to fix a meeting with the American computer chap she mentioned. I must get down to some proper work again, even though I would officially be on leave as from Sunday.

Something about Malta rang a bell. I remember Mum was going to Malta in my summer holidays from Castleberg in 1962. It wasn't to see a man, though, it was a Maltese woman friend from her WAAF days.

But let things rest until I hear more from Richard.

I took the elevator to the roof bar. This time the joint was jumping, and the quartet was playing, not usual during the 'happy hour'. I saw no one I knew, they all appeared to be conference delegates. Lucky was having difficulty coping on his own and some of them were getting cross. I got hostile stares when Lucky passed over a Tusker, shouting 'On the slate.'

'Mary?' I shouted back.

'Gone five minutes ago. Said she may be back.'

The atmosphere was jolly so I decided to stay. This was exactly what I needed, to mix with total strangers, to pretend I was already on leave, to forget Bandari for a while, to put Malta out of my mind.

I summoned up courage to ask for a dance. A group were returning to their table after a Latin American medley. I picked out a lady who had seemed reluctant to sit down and asked her to dance. The band began a Burt Bacharach number. Much to my embarrassment we were the only couple on the floor for a while, but she was an excellent dancer and took the lead. The rest of her party eventually got up to join us, and when the music stopped, they invited me to their table. I went to get drinks for them. They spoke excellent English and I asked where they came from.

'We are all from Malta.', my dancing partner said. She looked surprised when I laughed, but I didn't explain.

Mary returned about an hour later, with Potty in tow. By then, I must have been rather drunk.

89

'Wasn't it a good idea of mine to get the band,' Mary said as she and Potty came over to me and the Maltese group. 'I see you've picked up our most eligible bachelor. Don't worry, you can keep him, Mr Potgeiter and I are just passing through. I was hoping you might be here, Harry. Wayne Marshall said you can call at the university any time to talk about using the computer. Here's his card. Don't let this boy get too drunk, darlings. See you all at the conference tomorrow. Come on Potty.'

NINETEEN

A day spent on the university's new computer helped me put the Brown mystery to the back of my mind. Wayne had been seconded from USAID and was glad to input my report, as a training exercise for the team he was assembling. One student was keen to help and I was impressed by the way she set out the technical data. These facilities equalled anything I would have had in Cambridge, plus providing computer expertise beyond mine.

I had decided that my monthly reports could be abridged into a satisfactory final draft, which Haskins and Ede could then dress up for their presentation to WAFCO. I would need to input the commentary myself, to keep that part confidential. My experience of Festus Kasonde raised suspicions as to how far the Ministry's tentacles might reach, and the timely appearance of this clever young woman, eager to get her hands on the report, made me cautious.

As I returned to Wellington Stores and paid off the Banzam taxi, I felt rather pleased with what had been achieved, but I now had to prepare for the ordeal of my daily de-briefing by Wellington. What a confined life it must be for him, stuck in the shop every working day, with only the evening drive, his visits to the mosque and Rotary once a week to break the tedium. I now provided a view into the outside world, and the daily reports I gave him were the least I could do to expand his horizons.

There were two customers in the shop, browsing among the dolls, which meant that Wellington could not corner me on this occasion, but he left them for a moment to hand me a piece of paper.

'Your friend Oscar came over with this.'

It was from Inge, a *While you were out* note from the hotel. Wellington had obviously read it.

'By the way', he said, 'my wife said she hoped the young lady enjoyed her cream cake, but you really must tell her to drive more carefully. She almost scraped my car with her motor bicycle.'

He moved, smiling, towards a customer carrying a large black doll, but came back to say, 'If you would like to join your friend on the road, I have two second-hand machines in the storeroom for you to look at; very cheap, both running perfectly. Some friends who have gone on holiday to Pakistan asked me to dispose of them.'

Inge must have called at the hotel and been given my new address. Her handwriting was calligraphic, which gave no further clue to her personality. I had hoped for something less formal, but the message was stark :
I will not be going to the beach house tomorrow. Can I see you? Phone me on Monday at the mill, 7283, extension 825.

I went into the stock room to have a look at the motorcycles, two 100cc Hondas with hardly any mileage on the clock. Although George had arranged the use of a Banzam cab whenever I needed one, I wanted to be independent, so I chose one. I would surprise Inge on Monday by calling at the textile mill on the way back from the university. I went back into the shop to haggle with Wellington, aware that I was taking on a Grand Master at that game.

*

There was a sparse attendance at the beach house that Sunday. It had rained in the morning and a mist lay over the ocean. People were drifting away. Part of the reason for the exodus may have been Mary's mood; she was always the catalyst. Today she was unusually remote, as if she had a problem on her mind.

Pete Larsen had teased me when I arrived on the little Honda but Mary said, 'How sweet; let's have a ride after lunch.' So about three o'clock we left the others and rode up the coast road to the Lundini Beach Hotel. It was full of German tourists, but the manager saw us arrive and almost fell over himself rushing to greet Mary. He had a table brought out and placed for us in a quiet corner. It was time for me to reveal what Festus had said last Tuesday.

When I had finished reporting his plans for Lexfar, she said, 'I'm not surprised. I knew it would be something like that, but I'm sorry you didn't tell me straight away. You should have known I can be trusted not to say anything.'

'I know but I did promise to keep it to myself.'

'Anyway, you are forgiven, it doesn't matter now. I gather Kenneth has already told Daddy.'

'Thanks Mary. I am glad you know about it because, as usual, I need your help. Do you think your father might be willing to see me before I make up my mind? George and I met him in the hotel in Lassita and he gave me the brush-off. Didn't he once own it?'

'Yes, the Lassita Palace was the first one he bought. It used to be called the Brigmar before it was nationalised.'

'I didn't realise that Brigmar was his company.'

'Yes,' she explained, 'I'm Mar, my sister Brigid is Brig. Brig-Mar, get it?'

'Of course,' I said. 'Anyway, Kasonde's plan hinges on whether they can get aid for the project and I really can't allow this to influence the recommendations I make in my final report. I think Festus knows me well enough to realise that.'

'We all know that sweetie. I agree you ought to talk to Daddy, but he is so difficult these days. He sits up there in Lassita and doesn't want to see anyone, even me. Especially not me I sometimes think. He won't stay at our Karibune house. He hasn't spent one night in the place since Mummy said she was not coming back; it must have too many memories for him. He gave 'Magoulas' to me outright, along with the rest of his Karibune property. It's almost like he took a vow of poverty, except he still has so much coming in that he couldn't give it all away.'

'How does your sister feel about that? Did she get anything?'

'My dear, you must be joking! She and Mummy got all his overseas assets between them. Before he and I took Bandari citizenship he felt he ought to cut his financial links abroad and this was his way of looking after Mummy and Brigid at the same time.'

'So, is there no chance of your parents getting together again?'

'I've always hoped that someday they might, but they are both proud people. He would never leave Africa and she is committed to Ireland. I saw a lot of Mummy when I was at university in Dublin, but I realised just how much we had grown apart; how much . . . what did you once say about yourself? How much I am a child of East Africa.'

'What does he do with his time now? He was obviously such an active person.'

'It's so sad, Harry. I don't think he has any hobbies. He still owns the construction company, but he takes no part in the management, as far as I know. Then there's Lexfar, of course, he still takes an interest in that. Then he has his vegetable garden. But what he does to keep his mind active I really have no idea. He never was a great reader.'

'He must have *some* visitors.'

'Well, yes. Katerina Voyantzis comes down quite often. She returned to Kenya after her divorce. Her brother is Alex Constantinedes.'

'You mean the shipping tycoon?'

'That's him. Their father started out here in the sisal business, like my Grandfather did. The family went back to Greece in the early thirties. I've met her twice and she seems very nice. I suspect they would like to marry if Daddy got divorced, which of course he never can. He and Mum were married in the Catholic Church. Yes, do go and meet him. I'll try to see him too. Isn't that awful, a daughter having to make an appointment to see her own Dad?'

'I'd be most grateful if you could arrange it, but not yet. I may take a short break in Europe.'

Then I told her about Hector Brown.

TWENTY

On Monday I had difficulty getting into the textile mill to see Inge, perhaps the Russian guards became suspicious when they saw me arriving on the little Honda. They took me to an interview room, where I spent about ten minutes persuading an official that I had not come to blow the place up. A guard escorted me to the design studio.

'How did you manage to get in here?' Her eyes showed that she was pleased to see me. 'They always make Mary wait in the entrance hall.'

She introduced me to two of her colleagues Michael and Esther. The tiny Bandarian girl sat on a high stool at a drawing board.

'Explain to Harry what you are doing, Esther.'

'Well', she said, 'our khangas and vitenge used to come from China or India. Some of the designs, 'motifs' we call them, date back to when the cloth used to come from Lancashire in England. Inge is helping us adapt African motifs into designs suitable for printing. The one I am doing here is based on body painting. Some men still do it on special occasions. The trouble is that a lot of our women don't like any changes in the way they dress, so we must adapt a bit at a time if we want them to buy our fabrics. Mike will show you his conch shell design. Michael is our star, though he won't admit it.'

In the next department Inge showed me how the designs were transferred onto rollers or silk screens and then she took me into the factory to see the printing. It was a revelation to see all this happening here in Karibune. She wanted to show me the rest of the factory, but the hooter sounded for change of shift.

On the way back to town she restrained her machine to keep pace with my Honda.

We went in quietly through the stock room to my flat. I had bought a lemon for her tea and had been to the New Bandari to buy some of the cheesecake she liked. She walked round the apartment before she said anything.

'This place is not nice. Why didn't you take one of Mary's flats? Three are empty in the block where I am staying.'

'It suits me fine thank you.'

'Maybe you are tight with your money? That tiny motor bike you bought makes me think so.' She suddenly grinned, as though she had found the answer. 'Oh, I see what you are doing. You want to teach me a lesson. You are telling me that you don't need to have a big machine to show that you are a big boy.'

After I brewed the tea we sat together on the settee. She had surprising news.

'Why I left you that note is because I had a visit from the police on Friday; two policewomen. They asked questions about the hen party last Sunday. I think maybe Mary needs help. They had a complaint from the parents of a young Bandarian girl, I remember her being drunk before I left. Marie-Louise brought her. You know the one I mean, the fat one. She normally comes with that other French girl.'

'Lisette.'

'Yes, her. Lisette is pretty, isn't she? I guess they must have had a quarrel about this girl, because Lisette didn't come on Sunday. Well, by about five o'clock there was no wine left, and everybody was quite drunk, but Mary found some bottles of Martini, the sweet kind. I do not like it, and anyway I'd had enough, and some women were beginning to be silly.'

'Silly?'

'Kissing.'

'I see. But why would the police be interested?'

'Because the local girl is only sixteen. When they took her home she was very drunk and she told her parents about the party. Her father is a *bwana mkubwa*, a big man at one of the marketing boards. By the way, I didn't say to the police anything like I am telling you. I just said it was a swimming party. They asked me why there were not any men there and I said because it is more relaxing that way. Just like Mary told us to say.'

'But did Mary know she was only sixteen. Did she look sixteen?'

'Oh no, much older. She has big bosoms, much bigger than mine.'

'Why did you leave?'

96

'I was angry because Marie-Louise and the African girl started teasing me about being so tall, and Mary did not do anything to stop them. I changed out of my swimsuit and said I was going for a walk on the beach. That is why Mary was angry with me at the Kiboko last Monday, because I did not like dancing with those women and I just, well . . . I just went home.'

'How did the police know you were involved?'

'I have no idea. I don't think the African girl even knew my second name, but one of the policewomen said, 'I understand you are a close friend of Miss Costas, so can you explain why you left the party early?'

She looked a bit unpleasant when she asked me that. I think the police will want to see Mary about it.'

'Maybe they have seen her already.'

'No, if they had she would have told me. I think they are leaving her until they have, you know, more evidence. I am very worried about her and there was only you I could think of to tell about this. If I told Peter he would get cross with me and anyway he talks to Potty, and Potty tells everything to anybody. What do you think I should do, Harry? Should we tell Mary about the police coming? I didn't want to worry her if you think it is not necessary. In Denmark that sort of thing would not matter one little bit. At the art school in Copenhagen there were parties like that all the time, even worse ones.'

'I think we should tell Mary. But first I think we should get advice, and I think I know the right man. Let's go downstairs.'

After I had introduced Inge Wellington went to lock the shop door. He put up the 'closed' sign, then took us through to his room behind the counter and put the kettle on. Neither of us wanted more tea but this was one of his rituals. Wellington listened in silence (a rare achievement for him) while I gave an edited version of the story.

He did not reply immediately and went to brew the tea. Surprisingly, he did not seem shocked by what he had been told.

When he had poured us each a cup of tea he said, 'It is good that you have come to me so quickly. These things can be arranged. There will be no need to tell Miss Costas about the visit of the police ladies, or that you have mentioned anything to me. Better she does not know that I am concerned in the matter.'

George was right. This Mr Chaudhuri was a different character from the one I remembered from our first meeting. Gone were the exaggerated gestures and the hectic barrage of words: this was a clever man of the world. It had been the right thing to approach him. I hesitated to enquire too deeply as to what he proposed to do but curiosity led me to ask, 'So you think you may be able to sort this out, Wellington?'

'In the old days I would have handled the matter personally,' he replied. 'but times have changed. Nowadays, intervention by someone of my colour may not be a good idea. Let me tell you, Harry, such behaviour is not surprising me in the least. Before Independence some of the Europeans were holding very wild parties, and we used to hear stories which were most shocking. I have known Mary since she was a little tot. She is a young lady of East Africa if I may put it so. Such a problem is arising not for first time.

All I will tell you is that John Costas is a friend from the old days. I have his telephone number.'

He went to open a cupboard and brought out two plates. 'I understand Miss Jensen is fond of sweet cake. Please try some of this, made by my dear wife. I am confident you will both find it very tasty. If you will excuse me, I must re-open the shop.'

'He is a very nice man,' Inge said when we returned to my flat. 'Already I feel better. It is so good that I got to know you, Harry.'

'Right then' I said. 'Let me have some information in return for my help. You said, "Some day I shall tell you all about me". So?'

'There is nothing interesting about me, I think.'

'Tell me about your family. Do you have brothers or sisters?'

'No, only me. I will tell you about my mummy and daddy, though. Mary said you always want to know about people's parents and mine are perhaps a bit interesting. Mama is Swedish, which is why I was able to get the SIDA grant for my work here. Papa is an accountant and he works for the Government in Copenhagen. They are divorced. Even while he and Mama were married, he had lady friends, but five years ago he fell in love with this woman he lives with now. She is one who works in a casino, I do not know what you call them in English; we in Denmark use a French word. She gives out the cards or chips, or whatever it is. What do you call them?'

'Croupier.'

'Yes, that's it, the same word we use. She is not much older than me, about twenty-six I think, and he is now forty-seven. I know definitely she sleeps with other men. She calls herself 'Bee-bee', can you imagine that? He believes she is wonderful, but I think she is not even attractive. I still love him, but I am sure that one day she will just go away and leave him unhappy. It is sad.'

'Oh dear. And your mother? Did she re-marry?'

'No, but she has a man. At least she did not do like Papa and choose somebody young. She could have done because she is still nice looking. Erik is fifty. He is a bus driver and he lives with us in Odense. But when he is not working, they drink and when he is drunk he tries to . . . he tries to 'be nice' to me. My mother thinks it is *me* that encourages *him*.'

She seemed unaffected by what she was saying, as if this was a story about a third person.

'And what made you come to Africa?'

99

'Mostly to get away from him. He came into my bedroom once but I threw a glass of water over him.'

'What will you do when your contract is finished?'

'I don't know. I don't have any money, and to get an apartment in Denmark is very expensive. Maybe I will go to my grand-mother, but she lives in the North and there are not any jobs where she is living. By then this woman may have left my father and I could go to look after him, but I do not know how to cook properly. So, like I said, I am not a very interesting per-son.'

'How do I know? You have said nothing about yourself, except that you can't cook. You said you were at an art college. Tell me about that.'

'I am a good painter, that is what I did best at school and when I was seventeen, I got a scholarship to go to the college in Copen-hagen. I studied textile design but what I like best is making portraits. If you were here longer, I would like to paint you. I am doing one of Mary. It's not quite finished but I would like you to see it, just so you can see I am not a useless person. I en-joyed the art college very much, but I always had a problem be-cause I am pretty.'

She never ceased to amaze me. 'And how can that possibly be a problem?'

'Oh, please don't get me wrong, I like being pretty. I'm sure you know what I mean because you are handsome. Women are jeal-ous of me and the ones who *do* like me are usually the wrong sort. Is it not the same for men?'
'Not really.'

'I'm sure it would be easier to make real women friends if I were not pretty --- and men friends too. I mean friends, not boyfriends. You see I don't want to make sex with men before I am married, and the men I meet always want to make sex with me. Except you, of course.'

How did one respond to that? To deny it could end our friendship, so I said nothing.

'Ever since I was at school I seem to attract women. Sometimes I meet one that I like, but a lot of them are too much, well, you know what I mean. So, it is nice to meet a man like you, who doesn't want to fuck me.'

She put a hand over her mouth. 'I'm sorry. I used that naughty word again. Now I must powder my nose. OK, I can see where to go.'

I knew exactly why Mary was drawn to her. Apart from Inge's obvious physical charms, she had a complete lack of guile. It was not quite naiveté yet not an affectation. All I did know was that I very much wanted her in the way she had just ruled out.

Although I was becoming used to her rapid changes of subject, what she said when she returned completely baffled me.

'Do you think Mary should have the new nose? My bewilderment must have been apparent.

'Sorry, did you not know?' she said. 'I thought everybody knew about it. Potty told me that is why she took the job at IALO --- to get enough foreign money for the operation.'

'Don't believe everything Potty tells you.'

'Oh, but I know it is true, Harry. One hen-party day at the beach house she showed us this very funny brochure from a clinic in Los Angeles and we had a competition to choose the best shape for her new nose. I think she would be beautiful with a new nose, because she has such lovely hair and a nice body, and when she is not wearing her eyeglasses she looks really pretty. You know what I think? I think that she is going to buy herself a new nose, then she will come to England to find you, and you will fall in love with her, and she will go down on one knee and ask you to marry her.'

I was relieved to see that Inge was laughing at this.

TWENTY-ONE

I ought to have waited until Richard's letter arrived, but Mary was eager to discover more about this mysterious Hector Brown. I let her book me on the Thursday flight to Rome, with a connection to Malta the next morning.

It appeared the holiday season had not yet started. The plane from Rome was less than half full. After going through Customs, I pushed my squeaky baggage trolley through the concourse of Luqa airport. The echo was like that in an empty cathedral.

I followed the sign to 'Hotel Enquiries', where I was almost pounced upon by the two tourist board staff. They were most helpful and went through almost the whole list of the island's accommodation. I decided to book for just two nights into a hotel in Valletta, hoping the business side of the visit could be conducted quickly. I would then move to one of the coastal re-sorts for the rest of the week's stay.

Once established in the hotel I searched the telephone directory for the home number of Justin Farrugia. Clearly, there were few surnames among the Maltese; 'Farrugias' took up most of one page but only one of the 'Justins' was an attorney. He sounded cross that I had arrived in Malta unannounced.

'Didn't you get the message I sent through Mr Butterworth?'

'No, I'm sorry. I had to leave before his letter arrived. Is there something more I should know?'

'I will explain when we meet. My office is at number ninety-two, St Publius Street, that is . . .'

'Thank you, I have a map.'

Despite Farrugia's brusque tone, he seemed to be taking me seriously.

'Am I to be hopeful?' I asked.

'Suffice it to say that I am now satisfied you are the person I have been seeking. I have also been contacted by a lady who knew your parents when they were here in Malta during the war. I will see you in my office at nine in the morning. Good evening Mr Paine.'

He rang off. Perhaps I had interrupted his dinner.

The hotel dining room was on the top floor and had a splendid outlook over the Grand Harbour. Airline food never satisfies me and I was enjoying the rabbit stew, which the waiter had recommended as a local speciality. At last I felt I was on holiday, though most of the other diners did not seem to be tourists. The majority sat alone, some hiding behind paperback books or newspapers.

One man looked at me as though he wished to enter into conversation. He was probably in his fifties, below medium height and beginning to run to fat. He wore a well-cut linen suit, but the tie was rather loud. He broke the silence and was clearly addressing me. It was a Lancashire accent.

'Like a bloody morgue in here, isn't it,' the man said. 'Mind if I join you?' and did so without waiting for an answer. He brought over his bottle of wine, which he had almost emptied.

'Good stuff is this. Cheap, too; have a slurp.' He poured me what remained.

'You here on business?'

'A little legal matter; family business you might call it.'

'What you want to do,' he continued, taking no notice of what I had just said, 'is to buy yourself some property in Malta. That's what I'm here for. You've heard of Mintoff, have you?'

'Yes, the new Prime Minister.'

'Full marks, lad. Bloody good bloke is Mintoff. Got rid of all them British tax dodgers, 'sixpenny settlers' they were called. That's what the tax used to be, you see, sixpence in the pound. Came out here on their pensions thinking they'd live like millionaires. But he's put them right, has Mintoff. Now they're scuttling off back home like frightened rabbits. You can pick up a house here at the moment for t' price of a packet of tea. It'll all blow over in a bit but by that time I'll have made a killing, mark my words. You look like you've got a bob or two to invest. Get in there quick, that's my advice. Tommy Fothergill, by the way. And you?'

'Harry Paine.'

'Right, Harry. Stick by Tommy and you won't go so far wrong. Sup up, we could do with another of these.'

Tommy looked as though he might be interesting company, but a bottle of wine later I excused myself and went off to bed.

*

Farrugia's office was in a narrow lane leading off Merchants Street, down towards the sea. Four people were already waiting to see him and looked annoyed when he stuck his head round the door and invited me in. The voice on the telephone last night sounded like that of an older man, but he was in his midforties, small and lean, with dark curly hair.

'Before we start,' he said, 'I suggest you read this.'

17 Annunciation Street, Santarita

Dear Sir,

Reference your advertisement in the English 'Daily Telegraph'; I *knew Polly Brown when she was in charge of the billeting office at RAF HQ during the war. I am sorry to say that she was killed in Kenya in tragic circumstances in 1962. She married a man called Henry Paine who was an RAF pilot and they migrated to Kenya when he was demobbed in 1945. She had a son and a daughter, but the girl died along with her parents. The son was also Henry but they called him Harry. He was at school in England when his family died. You may be able to find him through his auntie or his grandfather. She is called Anne and was <u>Miss</u> Paine when I last heard. They were living at Brough Farm, Tor View Lane, Matlock, Derbyshire. I was given this address by Polly   because she should have been coming to see me in August 1962 but I got a message from a Mr Finnigan in the July to tell me of their tragic death. My name was in her address book.*

I am not on the telephone but you can leave a message at Santarita Butchers, Amy Grech is my sister-in-law. I can come to see you if you really want, but the above is all I can tell you. Please acknowledge that you have received this.

Yours faithfully,

Doris Grech (née Mercieca)

'I am sorry you did not let me know you were coming to Malta.' he continued. 'I would have preferred more warning. But now that you *are* here, perhaps we can make some progress towards settling this matter. Quite frankly, it has been taking up a disproportionate amount of my time. I have a full diary today. Are you free tomorrow?'

I tried to counter his rather aggressive tone. 'Since this is the sole reason for my coming all this way to Malta, I am free whenever you need me.'

'Right, the same time tomorrow morning. We will need to go to another attorney to swear an affidavit. I have the title deeds and the keys to the
deceased's property in Santarita. I will give you a note of authority to inspect the books. They are in locked cases in the

morning room of the villa.'

'Does this mean I am accepted as the beneficiary?'

'That will not be my decision, but the only responses I have had were from your solicitor and Mrs Grech. The heir to a first cousin would qualify as beneficiary, but Mr Butterworth said you don't know how Mr Brown was related to your mother. Is that correct?'

'Not yet, but Mrs Grech might know. She was obviously a good friend of my mother and perhaps she knew the Squadron Leader. Doesn't his naming my mother as next of kin count?'

'The phrase 'next of kin' does normally indicate a family connection between the nominator and the nominee. I must point out, however, that our Probate Office may not be satisfied by simply establishing your connection with the person named as next of kin. They may be willing to waive the formality in this case, as there is only a small estate involved, but I feel I should point out the possibility of such a contingency.'

I was becoming tired of this legal-speak. I asked him for a photocopy of Mrs Grech's letter, for which he charged me fifty cents. The meeting had taken less than ten minutes.

I decided that Mr Farrugia was not going to be my closest friend on Malta.

In the ground floor coffee shop, Tommy Fothergill was having a late breakfast. His Hawaiian shirt was only slightly more colourful than his complexion. Tommy's enthusiastic sampling of the Maltese wine on the previous evening had apparently not agreed with him.

'Bloody gut rot, that stuff,' he remarked. 'How did it suit you?'

'Fine. A nice change for me, we don't have local wine where I come from.'

'Happen it were that rabbit then. Something certainly upset me.'

English people abroad seem to follow a set pattern on first meeting.

Information is traded as in the opening moves at chess. I was called upon to reveal a little about myself, to which Tommy would respond with a snippet of his own background but, as the opening pawns in the game were cleared away, he began to open up freely. His natural exuberance won through.

He had built up his father's dress shop in Burnley into a small chain, with branches in several other Northern towns, and had sold out to a larger group in 1972. He was now, to use his own words, 'footloose and fancy free', his wife having run off with a member of the local golf club. If his account was true, he was well on the way to becoming a property magnate. Rightly or wrongly, I decided to tell Tommy the reason I was in Malta.

'You want to watch them lawyers,' he commented. 'I've had my fill of lawyers these last two years. Believe me, Harry, my former wife has a lot to thank them for. Never came across a straightforward one yet, and I'll warrant this one of yours, Farouk or whatever you call him --- he'll have had his spoon in the honey-pot already, mark my words. Has he left much, this Brown?' Tommy's eyes brightened when he heard there was a house involved.

'It's a place I have on my list, is Santarita. Sounds like a good area, out beyond the Three Cities. I'll tell you what, when you get the keys to this Villa what's-its-name, I'll come along with you. Give you the benefit of my expertise. How would that suit you?'

I said I would be pleased if Tommy would accompany me to Villa Buenvista. In fact, it would be good to have a companion.

But not on the first visit to Santarita. I wanted to meet Mrs Grech alone.

Wandering the narrow streets of Malta's capital, one understood why visitors could become so fond of Valletta, especially
the British. There were reminders that, until recently, it had
been a British possession --- red phone boxes, helmeted Bob-
bies.

Catching my reflection in a shop window, I saw that I badly
needed a haircut. Looking down a narrow street leading to the
sea, I noticed a striped pole projecting from above one of the
shops, such as one saw during my schooldays. The interior was
a typical English barber's shop from a 1930's film. The inscription on the washbasin read *Twyfords. By appointment.*

The man enquired, 'Just a trim, sir?' This could have been the
barber's in Matlock that Grandpa used to take me to.

People I spoke to seemed well disposed to the British and interested to know where I hailed from. I always found it easier to
say I was from Derbyshire; the full story was too complicated.
The lady in the shop where I bought a sweater had a relative in
Derby. She bemoaned the departure of so many British, making
it clear that she was not a supporter of the Malta Labour Party.

I took an early lunch outdoors, in a square off Republic Street
beside a statue of Queen Victoria, and marvelled that so many of
the magnificent buildings had survived the bombing. This train
of thought caused me to think of Mum's friend Mrs Grech. I decided I could wait no longer.

*

The journey to Santarita was not encouraging. The bus hesitated and spluttered as it met the few inclines along the way.
There was hardly a gap in the buildings, as we passed through
Floriana to Marsa and Paola. At the dockyards there was a mass
exodus, leaving me and three others on the bus.

Santarita was to be the last stop on the bus route. As we moved into open country my spirits rose. This part of Malta was very different from the conurbation I had travelled through since leaving Valletta. The bus stopped at the gate of a farmhouse, where the three remaining passengers got off and I was left in splendid isolation. They waved me goodbye as the bus set off again.

Five minutes later the driver turned left through a medieval archway and down a narrow road, bringing me to the sea. Brightly painted fishing boats lay at anchor in a small bay, a terrace of fine houses with protruding balconies bordered the road. The bus drew into a parking bay in the main square of the village. As I alighted, I thanked the driver who was already preparing to turn the bus for its return journey.

No one was waiting for the trip back to Valletta. In fact, the square was deserted, except for a street cleaner, who had parked his cart and was sitting on a metal bench in the shade of a row of trees alongside the waterfront. A sign on the shop at the far end of the square read, 'Debono. Family Butcher'. I went to enquire where I might find Annunciation Street. There was no response to my knocking on the shop door.

Of course, I should have realised, this was siesta time. The habits of Mediterranean people die hard. Despite the present mild temperature, the village was asleep, or if not asleep, unavailable for the enquiries of an English visitor. Help must come from the street sweeper and I crossed to ask him the way. As I drew near, I was encouraged to see the cart was decorated with the emblem of Manchester United football club. Everybody I had met so far spoke good English, but here was the exception. When I spoke to him he gave a smart military salute and said, 'Bobby Charlton, Matt Busby. Very nice.'

'Mrs Grech, Annunciation Street. Which way, please?'

'Coming with me,' said the gentleman and set off with his cart. I followed him past the church and into a steep street leading from the harbour, then left into Annunciation Street. I knocked on the door of number 17. There was no reply.

'Goodbye, thank you', said my guide as he turned his cart to return to the seafront. I called him back to thank him and shake his hand. I gave him fifty cents, but the sweeper handed the coin back. He saluted again and said,

'Thank you. Wembley Stadium,' then resumed his journey.

As I too started off down the hill the door of number 15 opened.

'Hello. Did you want Doris?'

'Yes, I was hoping to see Mrs Grech.'

'I'm Mrs Mallia. would you like to come in and wait? Doris should be back soon she has gone to clean a house on the seafront. Or you could go down to see her if you like.'

'Thanks. Can you tell me the way?'

'Turn right at the church, then it's the fifth house along on the seafront, a large white house with marble steps. You can't miss it. It's called Villa Buenvista.'

TWENTY-TWO

As I reached the villa she was just leaving, a well-dressed woman who looked to be in her forties, though a quick mental calculation made me realise that she must be over fifty. She was short, like most Maltese. Her dark hair was closely trimmed, with only the odd fleck of grey. I saw signs of arthritis in both hands as she locked the door, and she came down the six marble steps with some difficulty.

'*Gesu Marija*. You are Polly's boy. It is Harry, isn't it?'
'Yes, I'm Harry Paine.'
'You are the living image of her. Come and give me a kiss.'

On the way back to Annunciation Street she told me she had

110

just emerged from a year's mourning after the death of her husband. She asked if my family still lived at Matlock. I told her my aunt had died and explained that I had just come from Africa for a short visit. We entered the neat terraced house.

'Oh, Harry, it is so good to meet you at last. Let me make coffee.'

'I'd prefer tea if that's possible.'

'Course it is, but let me leave you for a minute while I go next door to borrow some bottled water. I missed the shop this morning. Water in Malta is not good for making tea.' She was out of the door before I could tell her not to bother.

I looked round the comfortable front room. In an alcove by the fireplace was a silver-framed photograph, placed on the top shelf of a little shrine to the Virgin. This was obviously her late husband. He must have been several years older than Doris. Over the mantelpiece was a picture of the Pope and on the wall to the right there was a group photograph, apparently taken during the war. A group of about thirty, most of them in uniform.

At once I recognised Mum. She was dressed in WAAF uniform, standing next to a young civilian woman who was clearly Doris, looking not much different from the person who had just left the room. I searched for my father.

'Can you find them?' she asked as she returned with the water.

'Is Dad on this, then?'

'There, you see, standing in the second row, third from the right. With the moustache.' She pointed to a thin man in RAF officer's uniform, with a bushy moustache. I could hardly recognise this young man as Dad.
'It's strange', I said. 'I always imagined him as being taller. Of course, there aren't many photographs of him. He was almost always behind the camera.'

'Isn't it amazing how children seem to be so much taller than their parents these days? Since the war I mean. I don't know why it is. We find this in Malta, too.'

'I suppose it was the moustache that confused me.'

'He was proud of that moustache, but your mother didn't like it. She made him shave it off before they got married.'

'I wonder if there is an officer called Hector Brown in this photo?'

'Yes, I guessed why you were here. That one is Hector --- at the other end of the second row.'

I studied the likeness of the man I had come so far to trace, hoping he would now be revealed to me in this small front parlour in Malta. In the black and white photograph his uniform appeared darker than my father's. He looked much older than the rest of the group, except the naval officer in the centre of the front row. I remarked on this.

'Yes, he was older than most. Let me see, that was taken in 1942 so he would be forty-two or three then. The *Times of Malta* said he was seventy-three when he died.'

'His uniform looks darker than Dad's.'

'That's right, dark blue, like a naval uniform. Hector was still in the Fleet Air Arm then. I can't remember what they called his rank, but it was like a Flight Lieutenant. You can see, can't you, that he was very good looking?'

'Did he fly with Dad?'

'He was flying a Fairey Fulmar from Hal-Far when that was taken, but when we started losing Hurricane pilots he applied for transfer to the RAF and joined Henry's squadron at Luqa. Come into the kitchen and talk to me while I make the tea. I want to know all about you. Are you married?'

For the moment I was content to be the one questioned. What I had come to find out was so important to me that, suddenly, I felt reticent about questioning Doris. I showed her some of the family photographs I had brought to show Farrugia. We looked through them while we drank tea.

The photographs of my mother at Brough Farm brought tears to her eyes. I told her what I could remember about our life in Kenya, then about Castleberg, Cambridge and Bandari. I was used to the response of 'poor Harry' whenever I told my story, but Doris resisted that cliché of sympathy. Instead she said, 'You have made a good life for yourself, Harry. That's something your parents would have been proud of.'

It was she who changed the subject. I had no need to prompt her.

'So now, about Hector. That is why you came isn't it?' I nodded. 'Have you heard of HMS Illustrious?'

'The aircraft carrier? Yes. I read books about the war. It came into Malta for repairs.'

'That was later. At the time I am telling you about she was still based in Egypt. There was a night raid on the Italian fleet in harbour at Taranto and the planes took off from Illustrious. Hector was flying one of those old biplanes that used to carry torpedoes, what were they called? Gladiators? No, those were the fighters.'

'You mean the Swordfish.'

'That's it. How clever of you to know that.'

'I made a model of one when I was a boy.'

'Well, Hector's Swordfish was hit by the Italian shore defences, destroying the undercarriage. He might have damaged the aircraft carrier if he tried to land on the deck, so he decided to try

113

to reach Malta. If he didn't, he would 'ditch' in the sea, as they used to say. Your mother was on duty in the ops room that night. They saw a single dot approaching on the radar. We had radar then, though it was very secret. Polly and most of the ops team went up from the bunker as dawn was breaking, and they saw a lone bomber coming in, with no undercarriage. There had been a raid on Luqa the day before and the airstrip was still full of bomb craters. If he had hit one it would have been . . . just a minute, what was it they used to say? It would have been 'curtains'.

He overshot the runway and made a belly landing --- it's interesting how these phrases come back. I don't suppose I have said that since the war. Anyway, he completed the landing on grass. That's probably what saved them.'

'He had someone else with him?'

'A gunner. Just the two of them, no navigator that day, which made it more of a triumph, finding their way to Malta. Do you know what he said, Harry, when he clambered from the cockpit?

He said, "Good morning ladies and gentlemen. Sorry to have got you up so early." That just about sums up Hector Brown.'

'Try to imagine those days, Harry. From 1940 to 1942 we were bombed every day. First it was the Italians, then the Germans. I'd just started as an infant schoolteacher when the war began, but the school was closed in the third week of bombing. Our pupils were found places in other schools all over the island. Thank God, they *did* close my school, or we would have lost our children. It was completely destroyed during the high-level bombing by the Italians. You could hardly hear their planes they were so far up. But then the Luftwaffe came along with their Stukas --- they were horrible, those Stukas.'

'So how did you come to meet my mother?'

'After the school was destroyed, I applied to the naval people in

114

Kalkara. I became what they called 'billeting liaison clerk', and that's when we first met. She was just a year older than me. I knew from the start that we would get on. I suppose you know she volunteered in the first week of the war?'

'No, I had no idea'.

Less than three weeks ago I had stood at their graveside, at the end of a fruitless search for information. Now my parents were coming alive to me.

'Polly was the sergeant in charge of billeting. She was my boss really, but we became close friends. She was always tremendous fun and, of course she was very pretty. I have to say, at that time, I was quite good looking.'

'What do you mean? You still are.'

'Sorry, I wasn't fishing for compliments. Anyway, hardly anyone could put up a serviceman. Many would have liked to, but if their house was still standing it would be full of other relatives whose property had been destroyed. Almost everybody in Malta spent the night underground in those days, either in their cellars or in special shelters, even in the catacombs.'

'I've read about it,' I said, 'about why the island was awarded the George Cross. It must have been awful. How anyone could lead a normal life in those conditions, I can't imagine.'

'Of course, life was far from normal, but after a year or so the bombing became routine. Just carrying on with our everyday lives was like . . . how shall I put it? A gesture of defiance, that's it. The worst thing was always being hungry; we Maltese do like our food'

She asked me to carry the tea tray into the sitting room. As we passed the little alcove she said, 'Albert was the best thing that ever happened to me. I do miss him so much, Harry. You have had a loss much greater than mine, so you know what I mean. He never earned much money, poor lamb. They don't pay good wages in the dockyard, even now. After the war I got a job with a firm of estate agents, which enabled us to buy this place. Then he had to give up his job --- lung trouble. Eventually I needed to give up work to look after him. I'm sorry. You didn't come here to listen to my troubles, did you? Let me go back to happier times.'

The phrase puzzled me. 'Happy times, Doris? In wartime Malta?'

'Well, yes. So many people were killed, so many buildings ruined. Each day we woke and were still alive was a new gift from God, so each day must be lived to the full. Yes, Harry, sometimes we *were* happy. Happy to fight back, to see one of those awful bombers fall into the Grand Harbour.

When the billeting office closed, I trained as a cipher clerk. I speak fluent Italian and I learnt German at school. Where we worked was a maze of tunnels, like a little underground city. It was under Fort St Angelo and it was *so* damp: I put down my arthritis to those days. We never knew what our island would look like when we ventured above ground again. But for two young women like us it was heaven to be with such brave, care-free men; not that we allowed them to stray beyond what was proper. At least I certainly didn't, and I'm sure your mother didn't either, not until . . . until she *really* fell in love. I hope you don't mind my going on and on like this. Seeing you brought it all flooding back --- you haven't finished your tea. I hope it's all right.'

'The tea is fine' I said, 'and I want to know everything you can tell me. You've no idea what a thrill it is to hear you talk about Mum. But, as you guessed, just now the person who interests me most is Squadron Leader Brown. Do you know how he was related to my mother? Was he a cousin?'

'Before I answer that you should know more about Hector. As far as I know, he never told anyone the full story, even after he came to live here in retirement. He was a person who would let you know just so much and then a sort of 'veil' would come down. He would be pleasant --- no, more than pleasant, charming. But, when you reached a certain point you knew there would be no more answers.'

It was five o'clock before she finished the story of Hector, approaching time for my bus back to Valletta. I felt I was beginning to know the man. There were surprising parallels with my own life.

Hector Brown was born in a small town on the Scottish borders. He was orphaned early in life and brought up by a maiden aunt. He had inherited enough to allow him to stay on at boarding school and to go to university. Then, like me he lived the life of an expatriate. After St Andrew's University he went out to work for a rubber planter in Johore. Later he moved up to Penang, where he had his own plantation. Immediately war was declared, Hector went down to Singapore to enlist in the Royal Navy. But when they found out he had got a pilot's licence, they put him into the Fleet Air Arm and sent him to Egypt.

That was all he had felt it necessary to reveal about his background, up to the day his Swordfish limped in to Luqa airfield. When he transferred to the RAF there was no place for an extra Squadron Leader so, despite his rank, Hector became a Hurricane pilot, alongside men much junior in rank and in age. Doris described the excitement of watching the Hurricanes battling with advancing masses of German planes, darting and diving, but taking great care to remain outside the area of what was known as the 'box barrage', which shielded the Grand Harbour and the dockyards.

Hector was popular with his male colleagues but, according to Doris, his effect upon women was devastating. Many could not believe that such an attractive man in his early forties was still a bachelor. Doris Mercieca and Polly Brown received most of his attention, and Henry Paine made up the fourth in this group of close companions. Doris thought Polly was in love with both men, but everyone assumed it was Hector she preferred. It was a surprise when, just as the war in Europe was about to end, the engagement was announced between Polly Brown and Henry

Paine. They obtained permission to be married while still serving in Malta. At the wedding in St Paul's Anglican cathedral in Valletta, the chief bridesmaid was Doris and Hector the best man. Within two months Hector was posted back to Britain and Henry and Polly Paine were demobilised, preparing for a new life in Kenya.

'Do you really have to go so soon? I can get Ivan next door to drive you back to your hotel. There's a lot more to tell you.'

'There's a lot more I want to hear, Doris, but I must get back to Valletta. I have to make a phone call to England.'

'All right then, but do come and see me again.'

'May I come tomorrow afternoon, and may I bring a man who knows about property?'

'Please do. I'll find a letter you ought to see.'

TWENTY-THREE

Richard Butterworth was just as surprised to hear me as Mr Farrugia had been but delighted that I had come to Malta. He was intrigued by what I had so far discovered about Hector Brown and surprisingly, since he too was a lawyer, he took more-or-less the same line as Tommy Fothergill about how Farrugia should be handled.

'Go carefully before you sign anything. I've been thinking about Brown leaving that villa empty. If he was short of money, why not sell up before he moving to Sliema? I suggest you carry on your enquiries with Mrs Grech before you put your name to any sort of clearance certificate.

The affidavit you mention seems OK, probably just an acknowledgement that you are who you say you are, but I'd like you to get me involved in any final disposal of assets. I appreciate that Farrugia wants this intestacy wound up as soon as possible, but there ought to be a full search of Brown's effects before we agree a formal release. Is there any chance of you coming over here before you go back to Africa?'

'I hadn't intended to.'

'Do try, Harry. Mr Paine keeps asking about you, though quite frankly I think he sometimes gets you mixed up with your father.   The other week, when Betty and I went to see him, he said, 'I'd like to see my lad before I go. I'd like to bury the hatchet'. We didn't have the heart to put him straight.

Then there's the question of what to do with Brough Farm. Kitty is pressing hard to buy it, and one can always get a good price from a keen buyer. You should give them a decision soon, one way or the other.'

My ticket was open dated, so I agreed to fly to Manchester for three or four days. I very much wanted to see Grandpa again but felt unable to make a firm decision on whether to sell Brough Farm; not until I knew what Malta held in store. Richard kindly agreed to meet me and put me up. The chance of meeting Kitty again was particularly attractive.

*

This was a friendly hotel and I decided to extend for the re-mainder of my stay. After I had done the booking, I went to have a drink before dinner. Tommy was ensconced at the bar, looking pleased with himself.

'Come here lad, what are you having?   Drinks are on me to-night, I'm celebrating.'

I accepted a gin and tonic. Tommy had pulled off a deal to buy a block of four flats on the seafront at St Julians.

'Guess how much I paid for a block of two-bedroomed flats right on the bloody sea-shore? Only built six years ago?'

I named a figure at random, which Tommy almost halved. I began to think that inheriting Villa Buenvista may not be the prize I had hoped it was. We had dinner together. Tommy renewed his friendship with Maltese wine and, during the meal, already fortified by several pre-prandial gins, he revealed a side of his character not apparent in our previous encounters. A man who had built up a successful group of stores could be nobody's fool, but he turned out also to be something of a philosopher.

'Have you ever thought what we're put here for?' he asked.

'Sorry, I don't understand the question.'

'I mean, what is the purpose in you and me being where we are today, and why at this precise moment? You've come from some place in Africa that I've never even heard of, and I don't suppose you've ever been to Burnley. So why are we sitting together in a hotel in Malta, where neither of us has come before? Is that chance or design? What would you say?'

'Are you asking me if I believe in God? Well, yes I suppose I do.'

'You don't have to,' said Tommy. 'I'm not sure as I do or not. What I do know, though, is that there's a reason for us being here --- and being here right now. I've proved it many times. In fact, I've put it to good use in my business career. I've learned to recognise when a particular circumstance matters and when it isn't important. You and me, here, now; I have a feeling as this is one of them occasions when it's important. I've a feeling we ought to see a lot of each other. Since I met you I've pulled off what could be t' best deal of me life, and I have a hunch about you --- that I have a good turn to do you in return. Did you say you're going to look at that house tomorrow? I think I'd better come with you.'

'That's good' I said. 'I was just about to ask you.'

*

Next morning, when I went up to breakfast, Mr Farrugia was sitting at my table in the dining room, drinking mineral water.

'Won't you join me in some coffee?' I asked the lawyer.

'Thank you, but I have to be careful in the mornings. I would love to have coffee, only it is early in the mornings when my ulcer troubles me most.'

That may explain his dyspeptic attitude the day before.

'Since our appointment is in Old Bakery Street it would be a waste of your time to come to my office, so I thought I might as well pick you up here and explain what has to be done. This morning you are going to swear that you are indeed the son of Mary Brown, and this will be attested by the other attorney. I have given Mr Camilleri a copy of your birth certificate, but we have no death certificate for your parents, so he may want to ask you some questions about them. Oh, and bring your passport along.'

It was somewhat disconcerting to have an audience as I ate breakfast, but Farrugia was in a much better mood now than at the previous meeting. I took the opportunity to ask him how much he knew of Hector Brown's story.

'My colleague Emmanuel Camilleri knew him as well as anyone was able to know him; Mr Brown was a very private individual. Manny did the legal work when he bought Villa Buenvista and often tried to persuade him to make a will but, rest his soul, Mr Brown was rather an awkward person in his later years. Emmanuel told me that, right up to the end, he said he was not ready to commit himself. It was thought he was once a man of some substance, but he tended to be secretive about his background. Perhaps Mrs Grech may be able to enlighten you on this when you go to see her.'

I decided not to mention that I had already met her, hoping that

121

Farrugia would continue to talk about Brown.

'The only time I can recall seeing him was at a meeting of the Valletta Literary Circle. It must have been soon after he returned to Malta, 1964 or '65. He gave a most interesting talk on the development of bookbinding in the Renaissance. He was very knowledgeable, but he declined our invitation to become a member. Later, I understand, he became rather a heavy drinker and something of a recluse.

Santarita is a small, quiet place. I'm not surprised he moved to the more anonymous surroundings of Sliema, but for some reason he kept the Villa Buenvista --- against Emmanuel's advice. Perhaps he thought of going back to live there one day. His cheque stubs show that he had been paying ten pounds a month for the past two years, which I assumed was for looking after the house. On the cheque stubs he wrote 'Grech Santarita'. It occurred to me that the lady you are going to see is the person who cleaned for him, but Grech is a common name here. When you see her, try to find out? Assuming she has carried on with the cleaning, she will be owed money.'

Emmanuel Camilleri was in his early forties but already quite bald, a much more affable character than Farrugia. There was no problem with the affidavit, but Camilleri seemed reluctant to conclude our meeting. He wanted me to tell him about East Africa, since he was considering taking his family on a safari holiday. I was enjoying our chat but could see that Justin was keen to be away, so I invited Emmanuel for a drink at the hotel that evening. He readily accepted and promised to bring his wife. We excused ourselves and walked back to Farrugia's office, where he gave me the keys to Villa Buenvista and to the cases containing the books

If I needed more legal work done in Malta I would choose Emmanuel.

*

I was back in the hotel before eleven and found Tommy waiting

122

for me. He had hired a car for the day and wanted to whisk me off to see his block of flats before we went out to Santarita.

'Get yourself out of that suit, lad, and into something comfort-able'.

He was wearing another highly-coloured Hawaiian shirt, so when I went upstairs to change I put on my nearest comparat-ive garment – a Tanzanian kitenge. I am a good six inches taller than Tommy and we must have looked an unlikely pair as we walked to the City Gate, where the hire car was parked.

Once more he managed to surprise me. I had expected some-thing like a Mini or a Morris Minor but what was parked in front of us was a gleaming two-tone Chevrolet, the like of which I had not so far seen on Malta.

'Might as well do the job properly,' said Tommy, showing a de-gree of self-mockery. 'You are now in the presence of a leading property owner. Us tycoons don't arrive in cheap motors --- got to make the right impression, haven't I?'

He drove us through the crowded streets of Floriana towards Sliema and along the coast to St Julians. So far, I had seen noth-ing of 'holiday' Malta and by the time we reached Sliema I was surprised to see so many tourists, soaking up the early spring sunshine.

My legal formalities were now underway and I was looking for-ward to what Tommy called 'a proper day out.'   We drew up at an estate agents' office in the centre of St Julians. Tommy was in there before I had opened my car door and, by the time I entered, he was already in conversation with a lovely dark-haired young woman, sitting alone in the office. She had a slightly dated 'beehive' hairdo and wore a grey business suit.

'Harry, meet Maggie. Maggie, Harry Paine.' She came out from the desk to shake hands.

'Hello, I'm Maggie Mercieca' (She pronounced it 'mer-shaker').

My eyes were drawn downward, for the skirt of her suit was as short as anything I had seen since my first visit to the King's Road in Chelsea, and that was almost ten years ago. It was clear why she kept up this now out-dated fashion; she had the best legs I had seen since I came to Malta.

'Harry is a property owner like myself,' added Tommy.

'I hope I am about to be,' I said. 'Do you know Santarita?'

'Yes, of course I know it, but we don't get out there much. It's not a popular place with foreign buyers and most Maltese make their own arrangements when selling their property. They don't like paying our fees.'

'It's worth any fee, just to meet you, my darling,' said Tommy, making my stomach cringe, but Maggie appeared to accept the laboured compliment in good part.

'And now you'll be wanting to have the keys,' she said. 'Do you mind if I don't come with you this time, Mr Fothergill? I'm manning the office while Charles is out with a client. I suppose manning is the wrong word but I can't say 'girling' can I?' She had a charming laugh.

'We close for lunch at one o'clock until three, so if it's after one when you finish please push the keys into the letter box.'

The phone rang and she smiled a goodbye. Tommy left the car parked outside the office and we walked down to the seafront.

'You could be in there, lad,' he said. 'I could tell by the way she looked at you. In fact, I might have a go myself if you're not interested.'

Although the property was badly in need of redecoration it was quite clear that Tommy was getting a bargain. From each of the balconies there was a fine view over the bay of St Julians. When I considered that this block of four apartments was selling for less than half the current valuation of Brough Farm one could feel sympathy for the 'sixpenny settlers', who were going back to try to resume their life in Britain and faced the cost of buying property there again. Tommy said he planned to keep the top apartment for himself and to let out the others as holiday flats.

'This is just the start, Harry me lad. I've got a budget twice what I've already spent here, so you'll have to help me invest it. That place of yours could be the next . . . hey up, there's someone coming upstairs.'

It was young Maggie.

'Charles came back,' she said, 'so I thought I would come and see how you are getting on,' she said. 'Well Mr Fothergill, are you still pleased with your purchase on second viewing? I have the preliminary agreement in the office ready for you to sign, but I should explain that here in Malta we do things a bit differently from UK. Once you sign and pay the deposit, that money can't be refunded --- we call it an 'encomium'.   So be quite certain before you sign.'

'Any time you like, my dear,' said Tommy, 'and anything similar that you have on your books would suit me and all. I'm going this afternoon to look at this young man's property, despite what you say about it being in an unfashionable part of the island.'

'Oh no, I didn't mean to say that Santarita was unfashionable, it's lovely – my Aunt lives there. It's just that we sell mostly to British or German people and they want to be in Sliema or around here in St Julians.   If you need any advice on property you really ought to see Auntie. It was she who got me this job: she was the star negotiator with our firm for many years. Doris, her name is. I'll give you her address.'

It is, after all, a small island!

Maggie had come to take us out to lunch. We walked a short distance to a restaurant which had been converted from a splendid villa. We sat on a terrace overlooking the harbour. I suggested she choose for us. The hors d'oeuvres could have been a meal in itself but she followed this with some delicious local fish, called lampuka. Then we shared a deep apple pie, with vanilla ice cream. It was all delicious. After his third beer Tommy resumed his clumsy courtship of Maggie, who winked at me when he was not looking. She said it was almost time for her to reopen the office and gave me her aunt's address. As I had expected, it was 17 Annunciation Street.

When we got to the car I suggested I would drive. Tommy had drunk four beers. 'All right lad,' he said. 'You know the way, don't you?'

He continued to enthuse about Maggie. 'If the auntie's owt like t' niece, she'll suit me.'

TWENTY-FOUR

Today Santarita was buzzing with activity. A bread van stood in the main square, with women of the village queueing to buy hard-crusted loaves, as were served in our hotel. In the playground by the seashore, kids ran about and screamed, while old men sat talking, in the shade of tall trees which lined the promenade. I could see my friend the sweeper standing beside his cart, taking part in their discussion.

The arrival of the Chevrolet was greeted with great excitement by the children, who ceased their games to crowd around us, as I parked alongside the bread van. They tugged at our shirts and only laughed when Tommy tried to scare them away. They followed us to Annunciation Street as if we were two Pied Pipers which, in our motley array, we may have resembled. It was only when we reached number 17 and Doris spoke to them that they reluctantly dispersed back to the seafront.

Tommy was sober now and uncharacteristically restrained. I feared that he might repeat the heavy-handed flirtation which failed to impress Maggie, but with Doris he was quietly polite.

126

She showed him the group photograph and he surprised us both, by correctly guessing which was my mother. Tommy seemed to be making a good impression on Doris. When he told her about his purchase of the flats in St Julians, it was not to boast, but to get her opinion. She was business-like and knowledgeable, showing her experience not only of the local property market but of the islands' politics, which, she made clear, was the dominant factor in the present market.

'Unless you plan to stay permanently in Malta, Mr Fothergill, you should get a reliable agent, or else set up your own company. We don't know yet how this new government is going to react to foreign investment. The Libyans are showing a lot of interest, but I'm not sure that British owners will remain so welcome. Had you thought of registering a business here in Malta, with local directors? You keep the controlling interest, of course. But do forgive me, I realise you are a businessman and have probably thought of this already.'

The look on Tommy's face showed him to be very impressed.

'But now I suppose you want to see Villa Buenvista. I have tried to keep it looking presentable, but I suggest you open all the windows as soon as you go in. It can get a bit stuffy, even in this cool season.' She did not offer to come with us.

'Come back to see me before you leave, Harry. I have found that letter to give to you.'

The front door of Villa Buenvista was opened with a large heavy key, which must have been the original. Tommy murmured in appreciation as we entered the hallway, floored with large black and white tiles in a chessboard pattern. Through glass swing-doors was a wide inner hall, with the same flooring but with the walls half-tiled, in a design of different old roses. A marble staircase led off to the left.

The first room on the right was a panelled library with a fine marble fireplace and mahogany shelves, covering two of the walls to roof height. The shelves were now empty, but this had obviously been Brown's library. To the left we entered a large, well-proportioned room with a pair of matching desks and a four-piece suite in antique brocade. The arms of the chairs were almost threadbare. There were ten locked cabin trunks on the floor. This would be what Farrugia had called the morning room.

'Bloody good so far', Tommy said.

Further up the hall there was a dining room, unfurnished save for a big table covered with a dust sheet. The matching room across the passage was completely empty. We had seen beautiful glass chandeliers in every room. At the far end of the hall we opened another pair of glass-doors. To our left was a large kitchen; dating back to the nineteenth century. It had a stone-flagged floor, marble worktops and two Belfast sinks. The cupboards were probably the originals. There was a cooker, operated by bottled gas, but no other equipment.

Leading off the kitchen was a larder with shelves and wine racks almost up to the roof. A side door from the kitchen led into a paved courtyard. There was a well, served by a windlass. Across the courtyard, opposite the kitchen, was another room with a locked door. I had trouble in finding the right key. This proved to be a WC, which had an ancient lavatory, set on a plinth, two steps up from the floor.

Tommy said hardly a word during our tour. His silence spoke volumes.

From the end of the courtyard a flight of stone steps led up to a small walled garden. Before we returned to the house, we sat down on a metal bench. Tommy spoke at last.

'Well, my word, what a house you'll have,' was his response.

'Doris has certainly looked after the place,' I said.

'She's quite a woman, isn't she?' he replied. 'I've decided to ask if she'll be my representative on Malta. Do you think she might agree?'

'It may be a bit soon to ask. I mean, she has only just met us. But you couldn't do better. I'm meeting a lawyer tonight who may be able to help you. Let's go back in and have a look upstairs.'

At the top of the stairs there was a spacious landing with antique ceramic floor tiles. Open double-doors led us into the long drawing room, which was also empty of furniture. On the wall there were some Victorian still-life pictures which looked to be original, though in a style which I could not imagine being appreciated by a man of Brown's apparent discrimination.

Ahead, through beaded glass doors, was an enclosed balcony running the entire width of the room. From the balcony we looked out over Santarita Bay, with a distant view of Valletta across the Grand Harbour. There were four bedrooms, only two containing beds. As Doris had warned us, it was very stuffy upstairs. We threw open all the windows to let the light breeze from the sea clear the atmosphere.

The bathroom was spacious and quite up to date, the only room to have been modernised. The door to the room across the landing from the bathroom was locked and I had to search once more among the bunch of keys.

'Now then, *there's* a surprise,' said Tommy, as we walked into a billiard room equipped with scoreboard and cue racks. Tommy drew back the dust cover to reveal a full-sized table with the baize in good condition. I declined his offer of a game and we carried on up a further flight of stairs onto the flat roof. A room built into one corner proved to be a laundry, with quite a modern twin-tub washing machine.

We closed the windows and went down to the morning room and sat in the only available chairs, to take stock of this surprising house.

'You mustn't think of selling this,' said Tommy. 'It's a bloody gem. I'd buy it off you like a shot but just think what you could make of it if you spent a bit of money doing it up and furnishing it properly. A young lad like you could have years of enjoyment out of a place like this. If I were you, I'd go straight back and ask that young Maggie to marry me and settle down here to raise a family with her.'

When we got back to Annunciation Street Doris had the kettle on, ready to make tea. A big smile spread across her face as soon as she saw us.

'I can see from your expressions what you thought of it. It's a trick I learned when I was selling houses; if you are confident about the property, let the clients explore for themselves and let the house sell itself. I was not so sure of you, Mr Fothergill, because this is the first time I have met you, but I was certain that Harry would fall in love with the place at once. And the look on your faces tells me that Villa Buenvista has won you both over.'

The way Tommy looked at Doris showed that it was not only the house that had captivated him. Amazingly, he seemed lost for words.

I tried to think of a way I could tactfully ask Doris about payment for her cleaning Villa Buenvista but decided this was not the moment. Then I remembered that she had something to give me, and Tommy's presence may be a problem, but she forestalled this.

'Will you come into the kitchen, Harry?' she asked. 'I am never quite sure how you English people like your tea. Do excuse us for a moment, will you, Mr Fothergill? If you need the bathroom, it's to the left at the top of the stairs.'

I followed her into the kitchen. She opened a drawer and handed me a plain envelope. 'In here is the last letter your mother wrote to me. I kept it all these years, hoping that someday I may be able to give it to you. It will explain things better than I could --- but I do ask one thing of you, my dear.

130

Before you open it, find a quiet place where you are at peace with yourself. And try to remember what I told you about the war. Remember how it was for us.'

*

Mr and Mrs Camilleri brought their two children with them to the hotel, a boy and girl in their late teens, old enough to drink wine. Tommy insisted on paying. The family's holiday plans were soon settled. They fixed on the Serengeti, and I persuaded them to add the optional three-day visit to the Lassita Lake resort in Bandari.

We went on to discuss property. Emmanuel was an ardent Labour supporter and believed that the new regime heralded the coming of age for Malta, as an independent force in the Mediterranean area. He sought to dispel any doubts we may have had about investing in the islands. This was just what Tommy wanted to hear.

The Camilleris took us both back for dinner at their home, a recently built house in a place called Swiegi, above St Julians. On the way we passed Tommy's block of flats, which they agreed was a bargain purchase.

By the end of dinner, it had been decided that Emmanuel would form a company for Tommy, just as Doris had recommended, with himself as a director and Tommy as chairman. Emmanuel knew Doris's reputation as a property expert, and it was agreed that he should approach her to be managing director of the new company.

I was fascinated to hear all this going on but could not give it full attention. My mind was on a sealed white envelope in the drawer of the bedside cabinet of my hotel room.

TWENTY-FIVE

I kept the promise I made to Doris Grech. The letter lay un-

131

touched all night, but I slept fitfully and was awake by six in the morning and out into the street, just as the hotel was opening. It was a warm morning with the promise of a hot afternoon, only a few high clouds disturbed the solid blue of the spring sky.

This was Sunday. The early buses unloaded worshippers on their way to church, and a few workers were arriving to start the capital on its new day, walking briskly down each side of Republic Street to restaurant or shop.

In a way, I envied them their sense of purpose. I had no plans, except somehow, I must put myself into a frame of mind which would enable me to fulfil the promise I had made. Intense curiosity was mingled with apprehension. What would the letter reveal? I could not remember receiving a complete letter from Mum, only brief postscripts, designed to lighten the tone of what Dad wrote. Would I even recognise her handwriting?

I walked down to the Grand Harbour and watched traders on the quay outside the fish market, haggling over the remaining crates of last night's catch. Then along towards Fort St Elmo, before I negotiated one of the steep alleys leading back to the city. As I made my way up the steep steps from the harbour, I could hear Mass being sung, and peeped into a beautiful little church. Soon I was in Merchants Street and back at the hotel.

The concierge, who never seemed to be off duty, was already busy at his accounts. 'Do you *ever* take time off?' I asked him. 'What would you be doing on a lovely day like this if you didn't have to be here on duty ?'

'Please don't make me envious, sir. I have just been to Mass and would not wish to sin so early in the day. But, if I had the opportunity, the best thing I can think of on such a beautiful day would be to take the ferry across to Gozo.'

'How do I get there?'

'You don't need to wait for the tourist trips to begin, you can catch a bus to the ferry. Why not go up now and have an early

132

breakfast, then take the number forty-five to Marfa. You will have lots of time to catch the nine-thirty ferry and you will be there before the tourists. You will never find a quieter and more peaceful place. We have a rude joke about Gozitans which I cannot repeat to you so soon after Mass.'

By eight o'clock I had breakfasted, donned my shorts and put on my walking shoes. Wearing a bush hat, I set off to the bus station. In the airline shoulder bag, all I carried was a camera, a ballpoint pen, a bar of chocolate and a sealed white envelope.

As the concierge had forecast, I was at the ferry terminal before the minibuses arrived to disgorge their cargoes of tourists. I purchased a ticket and went into the small shop on the quayside. I came out with a screw-topped bottle of lemonade. I also bought five postcards and stamps, two for England and three for Africa. I would act the part of holidaymaker, on this day at least.

I wrote the postcards during the ferry crossing --- to Mary, Mercy and George and to Inge, although I would probably be back in Karibune before the cards arrived. The other two cards I sent to the Butterworths and Grandpa.

I had no wish to enter into conversation, so after writing the cards I went on deck to enjoy the sea air and watched the tiny isle of Comino glide by to starboard. This was what I had wanted; time to be alone with my thoughts, the day of peace and quiet that Doris had decreed. As the ship approached the small harbour, I could take in the whole of Gozo without a turn of the head. I picked out a high point which would be my destination.

Six or seven minibuses were lined up by the dockside in Mgarr waiting to receive the day trippers, and a service bus stood ready to take others to the capital, Victoria, but I went to post the cards and then into the little terminal building. I bought a map of the island and sat down to decide on my route. The buses had all set off by the time I emerged to begin the walk, up the hill from the ferry landing and onto a path, which led along the coast to a place called Qala.

Since boarding the ferry, I had spoken to nobody but the shop-keeper, and I met not a soul on the way to the little town. Rabbits scampered in and out of the dunes along the coastal path: the only sounds I heard were the cry of gulls and the sea beating at the rocks below. After about forty minutes I had passed through Qala and started to double back, heading inland. My destination was the prehistoric temple of Ggantia. I had five hours to spend before the return ferry. No need to hurry.

After I passed through Nadur, a larger place than I expected, I pulled off the road and into a meadow, to eat half the block of chocolate. Sparrows twittered in the gorse bushes which lined the road, lucky survivors of the marksmen of Malta. Even at this elevation I could look out over the greater part of the island; there was no sound, nor sight of any human activity. I knew that here was the right place.

My first disappointment was when I reached the temples; the minibus parties had beaten me there, but I could wait until later to view the remains. I walked past the crowds and further up the incline, to look down on the scene, far enough away from hearing the tourists, but yet able to draw something from the atmosphere of this ancient place.

I must have sat for about a quarter of an hour before I reached into my bag to open the envelope.

PO Box 27, Kisule, Kenya   27th May, 1962

Dear Dodo,

Well dear, it's all fixed. Barbara has a school friend whose father owns a travel business and they have managed to get me a ticket which allows me to make a side trip from Manchester to Malta for only an extra nine pounds. Even Henry couldn't object to that! We have to fly Alitalia whereas I always like dear old BOAC, but beggars can't be choosers. Believe me sweetie, that's just what we are according to Henry (beggars, I mean).

I'm so much looking forward to seeing you again but you will have to put up with me looking like the poor relation. I have simply <u>nothing</u> to wear. I am assuming that it will be nice and warm in Malta and I shall be able to wear some of my cotton frocks, dreadfully dated though they are. But what to wear in cold old England? That's the problem. However, I think I told you about Alice, who works for us. She is an absolute treasure and the children are devoted to her. Henry says we can't afford her and don't need her now they are away at school, but we pay her a pitiful amount. (It makes me ashamed sometimes.) Anyway, I digress. This Alice is a bit of a dressmaker and I am going to get her to try and make me a suit for UK. I found a lovely piece of some sort of new Japanese material in the store in Kitale. Not quite my colour, a sort of deep blush pink if you know what I mean, but it was in the sales and very cheap, and I was able to buy it from the housekeeping without Henry knowing. So, all being well, I should be able to present myself to the dreaded in-laws without looking too much of a frump.

OK, sweetie, now for THE NEWS! Just guess who turned up in Kisule ten days ago, saying he was just passing through? Ridiculous! Nobody 'passes through' this dump, it is the absolute end of the line, believe me Doris.

Anyway, I didn't say, did I? None other than <u>Hector</u>, that's who. Henry is convinced he came hoping to see Barbara, though he promised he never would, and the atmosphere was very frosty I can tell you. In fact, Henry told him he couldn't stay here and he found a room at the club. But, Dodo, he is still <u>so</u> handsome, my heart turned over!

The real surprise was that for years he was working just down the road in Tanganyika on that ridiculous groundnut scheme, you must have heard of it. Quite the most stupid thing you can imagine, except trying to grow coffee in Kisule. Anyway, he still looks absolutely gorgeous. Do you remember how his hair used to curl behind his ears, even just after he had had it cut? Well, it's completely grey now, not that white kind of grey, if you understand me, but like, what shall I say, battleship -- that sort of colour.

135

Mine is starting to go, and there's no hairdresser in this dump to dye it for me. No secrets from you, darling. You know just how old I am, don't you? But I'm sure you aren't going grey, you have that lovely Maltese hair that never goes grey, lucky old you.

Digression again, sorry.

Right, back to Hector's visit. After the groundnut thing fizzled out he went back to Penang and tried to get a job in the rubber business, but they have their own people now, of course, and Hector had to find any sort of job just to keep himself going. He didn't say exactly what he did but I gather he was some sort of head waiter in a posh hotel out there. Come to think of it I can just picture him doing that, can't you? I can just see the old biddies having palpitations as he showed them to their seats. He's gone very thin though and he's very brown. He has obviously spent too much time in the sun, which means he is lined -- much more than Henry. But still as fanciable as ever.

Well, it all got better after about three days. Henry showed him round the farm and in the evening we all went back to the club and had lots of pink gins and then things got a bit more friendly. Henry never left us alone together, though. Not that I would have 'slipped' or anything. Frankly dear, I think the fire has gone out, if you know what I mean. About time too, I hear you saying! Do you remember the old days, Dodo? After the bombing had finished? Of course you do. Those naughty sailors! But you were always a bit of a 'goody two shoes' if you don't mind my saying so. Sorry, darling, of course you were quite right. Keep it for the right man, that's what a good girl ought to do, and it's paid off, I can see.

Your Albert sounds to be a lovely man and fourteen years difference is nothing. Just imagine if I had married Hector, twenty years it would have been. And thank God I didn't. The poor dear never seems to have made a success of anything.

Oh, but I forgot to tell you, he's suddenly well off. His maiden aunt, who must have been absolutely <u>ancient</u>, well, she died and he inherited this estate in Galloway (that's in Scotland) which he sold and is now rich -- I mean '<u>rolling</u>' darling. That's how he can *afford to roam around the world and come to look up his old cast-off.*

Anyway, he's gone now and life is back to absolutely normal, which I mean is zero, boredom, nothing. Sorry, sweetie, you don't need to hear about that do you? At least I have this lovely holiday to look forward to, and I'm longing to see Harry. Did I tell you how clever he is? He writes such fantastic letters I never know how to reply. But soon I'll be able to hug him and show him just how much his old mother loves him. I do think these boarding schools are an absolute abomination, though I have to admit that the one in Nairobi seems to be doing wonders for Barbara. Thank God she looks like me -- not a trace of Hector about her, praise the Lord (as her new teachers would say). She used to be so like him in the way she behaved, but now she is becoming a real young lady, -- something you could never accuse her wicked mother of being, hey? Those nuns must have beaten the tomboy out of her somehow, though really they are very nice people. When I go to see Barbara I always call in to see the boss-woman and we have a drink together.

What I think <u>will</u> interest you is that Barbara seems to have taken to your brand of religion, which personally I think is a good thing, but Henry is <u>so</u> bigoted. You would think she had decided to turn into a satanist the way he carries on. He keeps threatening to take her away from the convent school, though personally I think it's the fees. He never lets me know anything about money but the way he carries on we can't be making any. I told him that they would waive the fees if he only asked them, but you know him. It's pride, I tell him, and we can't afford to be proud. I've just read over what I've written and I can only apologise. I shouldn't moan. I have a lot to thank Henry for -- not many men would do what he has done. Still at least I can get it off my chest to you, old chum. By the way, on no account let your lovely Albert read this and when you reply don't mention anything of what I have written. It won't be long before I can cry on your shoulder, my dear, darling Dodo. Think of the old days and what fun we had. I do, all the time.

I'm enclosing a copy of the itinerary. As you see, I should be arriv-

137

ing in Malta on 8th August, having dumped dear Harry and Barbara with Auntie Annie, poor things. Let me know you have received this and make sure you have some angosturas in the cupboard for the jolly old 'pinkers'.

See you soon. Lots of love.

Polly

Was it hunger that made me unwilling to accept the obvious message behind what I had just read? I reached into the bag and ate the other half of the bar of chocolate. When I get back to town I must ask the concierge to tell me the joke about Gozitans. Why is it that the people of small islands are always the butt of jokes? In-breeding, that's what the jokes are usually about.   My mind refused to turn to what should have been uppermost. I was back in 1962, a schoolboy revising from his Latin primer on the bank beside the cricket field at Castleberg.

Towns, small islands, 'domus' and 'rus'.

What was it they have in common? I could not remember, and it would never matter. The mnemonics lingered on long after the need to remember their meaning.

A dative put, remember pray, after envy, spare, obey.

Who cares, apart from some long-gone examiner? There was a conjunction between towns, small islands, house and countryside, but what conjoined them I failed to recall. That's pedantic, I said to myself. I remember being told at school not to be pompous.

'Forswear pomposity, my son, else thou shalt end thy days a dry old pedagogue like me'. It was old Hollick who said that. He was my housemaster and fifth-form English teacher; he could have conducted a whole lesson in blank verse. In fact, he wasn't old --- died at the age of fifty-two. Alas poor Hollick.

Why has Hector Brown's legacy suddenly become so tainted?

Just about my age you would be then, wouldn't you Mother? With you there were no 'incestuous sheets'; you were young and single, free as I am now. Come on Harry be reasonable, less of the brooding Hamlet. What was it Doris said? *Remember what I told you about the war. Remember how it was for us.*

Am I like you, Mum? As soon as I saw Maggie Mercieca yesterday, I wanted her in my bed --- a bit of a tumble, that's what they say, isn't it? Come on, admit it Harry, you need a woman. Tell yourself that it's only for companionship but what wouldn't you give for Inge here beside you now? Is that love or is it just the thrill of the chase?

Mary has said she loves me. We have much in common, settlers' children both. Of course, Kitty has always been the one I should have had, dear beautiful Kitty. Did she ever love me? Doesn't matter now does it? Too late. Forget Kitty; forget Mrs Masters. And what about Gaynor? Gaynor, who has been my wife in all but name. Is *she* also lost to me – and why was she the last to come into my mind?
Towns, small islands, 'domus' and 'rus'. The jingle would not leave my mind. I found myself searching for an association.

Town. Matlock, where better?

Island. Would Malta fill the bill?

Domus. Obviously, this now becomes Villa Buenvista.

That leaves *Rus*?

And then an important decision came to me. Only in the countryside am I truly myself --- in the bush forests of Kenya, the green dales of Yorkshire, the Peaks of Derbyshire. I won't sell Brough Farm; that will be my home. That is where I shall end my days.

Looking down to the temple ruins I saw that the site was now empty; the tourists were off to their next scheduled attraction. I went down to wander among the ancient stones, hoping these relics of a once-sacred site might restore calm; the calm I had felt before I read the letter. On the hill above I felt I had shared the atmosphere of a holy place, but down here among the ruins I felt nothing. They were just stones.

It was like that day I had in Rome after the interview with WAFCO. I had walked along the banks of the Tiber, all the way to the Vatican. Excitement mounted when I saw the dome of St Peter's. Then awful disappointment when at last I entered the great square. I was a stranger in an alien crowd, isolated from the believers. By the time I entered the basilica the euphoria had gone. The place I had been drawn to was, for me, a mirage.

I fail to share their faith, but I am always impressed by the devotion of Roman Catholics, nowhere more so than here in Malta. Faith suffuses these small islands. From where I sat now, I could see three great churches towering over their little towns, buildings inspired not only by faith, but by defiance, by grandeur of spirit which defied the material poverty of those who built them. It struck me that, had she lived, Barbara may be a catholic. I might have had a catholic nephew or niece. Hold on, I said, not niece, half-niece. Is there such a thing as a half-niece?

Towns, small islands, domus and rus. That stupid jingle would not go away. Hunger dominated my confused mind. It was time to get down into Victoria and see if I was not too late to find some lunch.

The weather on the return journey was cold and the sky overcast, so most of the passengers were down in the bar. I found a quiet place on my own in the saloon. This would be the end of my fourth day in Malta. So far, I had been driven by events. I must take control of the situation, organise the remainder of the stay and plan for my brief visit to England.

TWENTY-SIX

It was just after nine o'clock the following morning and already

140

there were items ticked off on the list.

I waited on the doorstep of the BOAC office before it opened and made a booking on the Friday flight to Manchester, with on-ward flights from London to Karibune four days later. I had fixed a final appointment with Farrugia for the next afternoon. But my plan to see Emmanuel Camilleri after I left Farrugia had not worked out. When I telephoned him, he said, 'Sorry, old chap, no chance of seeing you at all this week during working hours. However, my wife picks me up every day after work and we wait until the rush hour traffic has sorted itself out before we go home. Usually we have a beer in the Upper Barrakka gardens near your hotel. How about we meet you there this evening?'

One important task remained. I needed to take a look at Squad-ron-Leader Brown's book collection. Ideally, I should make a full list to show to Richard Butterworth when I visited Matlock. There must be a huge number, assuming all the packing cases were full. So, when I got back from Gozo, I had prepared pro-forma sheets on which I would list the titles, dates of publica-tion and the author of each book, with an extra column for notes on the binding or general condition. However, I would need help, even to make a sample list. Tommy was my man for that.

Taking the bus to Santarita was a comedown after our stately progress in the hired Chevrolet. It was the same elderly vehicle as on my first visit and the same driver; maybe he was the only driver on that run. He recognised me from last time and said *bon`gu* as he accepted the ridiculously low fares. As we left Val-letta, Tommy asked, 'Why do they all cross themselves?' There was no attempt to lower his voice.

'Happen they know summat we don't. Just as well to have the Good Lord on our side.' I dug him in the ribs and whispered, 'Do shut up. I hope you realise they all understand what you say. The Maltese are very religious, that's why they do that.'

Tommy was not a bit contrite and grinned to himself at his witticism.

We opened up the villa and prepared to begin work. Tommy sat at one desk and I at the other, with the windows opened wide. A familiar rich scent pervaded the morning room, borne on a pleasant light breeze blowing in from the sea. We were separated from the house next door by a stone wall, over which the neighbour had trained a creeper with trumpet-shaped flowers. It smelled like the Cape honeysuckle which grew round our farmhouse.

We had each pulled one of the cabin trunks to the side of our desk. I was right in thinking there would be no chance of listing the whole library. Even a sample list was going to be quite a task, and we had to finish before five o'clock so that I could be back in Valletta to meet Camilleri.

Brown had arranged the books systematically; obviously, he had packed them in the order they were taken from the shelves. My trunk contained titles with a political or sociological theme; what looked like a complete set of the Disraeli novels, as well as one or two rarer items such as an early edition of Hobbes' 'Leviathan'. There were also some prints, Gillray and Rowlandson cartoons. I was tempted to linger over some of these items but reminded myself that the aim was purely to catalogue. It was already apparent that Brown had been a man of taste.

Tommy, meanwhile, was making rather heavy weather of his batch, a selection of early prints and etchings of scenes from Malaya and Borneo. He did have a problem; some were untitled, and most were not bound. We worked for about ten minutes without speaking. Tommy had a slightly irritating habit of humming to himself.

Then he said, 'I don't suppose she will, do you?'

'Who? Do what?'

'Oh, sorry, my mind was wandering. I mean Doris; she may not want to go back into the property business for me. She seems nicely settled as she is. Do you think I ought to go and ask her myself or should I leave it to the lawyer? I don't always have the right way of putting things to people.' He saw the expression on my face.

'Sorry lad, I'll shut up and let you get on with it.'

My case of books was more straightforward than his, so I asked him to swap places. There was silence again for about ten minutes, before Tommy said, 'I don't know about you, but I could do with a cup of tea. I'll go and ask her to make us one.'

'No Tommy, I'll go. I can ask her about joining your property company. It may be easier for her to tell me rather than you how she feels about it.'

Doris was talking to her neighbour.

'Hello again', said Mrs Mallia. 'We met briefly didn't we? We do hope you will be coming to live here; it will be lovely to have the villa occupied again.
But you will be wanting to talk to Doris, won't you, and I must get my ironing done before Ivan gets back for his lunch, or I shall never hear the last of it.'

'You should have called here before you went to the house', said Doris when her friend had left. 'I could have given you a thermos. And why have you left Mr Fothergill alone? He's such a nice man, isn't he?

Did you say he was a widower?'

'No, divorced.'

'Oh dear, what a pity.'

I followed her to the kitchen. She filled the kettle with bottled water. I had purposely not called on her. There was yet no way I could describe how I felt, after my visit to Gozo. But after she had brewed the tea, she said, 'You read it, did you?'

'Yes. You were right to suggest I find somewhere quiet. I went over to Gozo yesterday. Now I understand.'

'No questions?'

'The letter needs no explanation', I said, 'but is it possible that Mum and Hector could nevertheless have been relatives? The lawyers will want to know.'

'I thought at first that they might be, but Polly explained that Brown is a common name in Britain, like Grech is here. I shall tell the lawyer I'm not sure. I know how important it is to you.'

'I wouldn't want you to lie,' I said, 'but why do you think he made her his next of kin?' Even before I had finished the question, I knew the answer.

'Doesn't the letter tell you why?'

'Yes, of course, I see it now. Because of Barbara, you mean.'

'I'm sure that's why. But I have no intention of telling Mr Farrugia what I just told you. Let the law take its course. Polly was intended to inherit, or at least Barbara was. And now you should. If there is any natural justice, you should be the heir of Hector Brown. Is that the only question?'

'One more. Did you ever meet a man called Finnigan?'

'Arthur? Yes, of course I knew him. A tall fellow from Northern Ireland. He and Henry were good friends before he was posted to Kenya. Wasn't he in partnership with your father to begin with?'

'Yes, but they quarrelled. I wonder if she ever told you why.'

'No, Polly never mentioned it in any of her letters. I hope you won't mind me saying this, Harry, but your father was a very in-dependent man and he did have a bit of a temper. It doesn't sur-

144

prise me he couldn't get on with a partner. Anything else?'

'Yes, there is one other matter. It's really Mr Fothergill who should be asking you this, but he was a bit shy about raising it.'

Not only did Doris appear keen and grateful to take up Tommy's offer, but she was happy to accept payment for cleaning the house, and said she wanted to continue looking after it. 'I wouldn't trust anyone else to do it properly. It's a difficult place and you have to know your way round.'

I returned to the villa armed with a vacuum flask full of tea and two big pieces of home-made ginger cake. Tommy was delighted to hear that his offer had been accepted. He had made good headway with the cataloguing.

'I couldn't make head nor tail of that first lot you gave me, but I think I've done well with yours.'

He had kept out two books, which he had put at the back of his desk. 'I wanted you to see these. I've never come across anybody else who spells your name like you do.'

The first was *The Rights of Man* by Thomas Paine, the man who became such a hero of the American revolutionaries. I had never read *The Age of Reason.* This one was a 1794 first edition, printed in the United States. In it there was a buff envelope on which was written *'Polly'*. I put it into my jacket pocket.

'Don't be so daft lad,' said Tommy. 'Open it up. It's happen a Will.'

*

I was about ten minutes late entering the gardens. Camilleri and his wife were already sitting at a table. As I approached them, I suddenly realised I had no idea how to raise the subject. I could not very well say to Emmanuel, do you think your friend Justin is cheating me and hiding some of Brown's assets with a view to pinching them when I have signed the certificate of satisfaction?

Emmanuel had already bought me a Hop Leaf beer and the three of us made small talk until I had almost finished it. I went to the kiosk to buy refills. Emmanuel was not quite hiding his impatience.

'You wanted to see me about Hector Brown?'

I decided to lay the blame on Richard Butterworth.

'Well, yes. You see, my lawyer is a suspicious old cove, and he told me I should make quite sure that all the assets are 'on the table', so to speak. Since you seem to be the person who knew Mr Brown best, I wondered if you could say how he got through all his money.'

I was now into subterfuge. 'I heard that, some years ago, he came into quite a large inheritance and wondered how it all disappeared.'

Emmanuel took a sip of beer. 'I hope I misunderstand the implication, but you appear to think my colleague may not have been entirely open with you.'

'Oh no,' I interjected, 'It's simply that I have developed a great interest in this mysterious man, who I hope will prove to be my benefactor.'

'I see,' said Emmanuel. 'Yes, I do understand. However, I can't pretend I knew him *well*. I first met him when he bought the Santarita premises. That accounted for around fifteen thousand Maltese pounds at the time --- you could probably more than double that now --- but the rest must have gone on books and drawings. You met him, Marion, what do you think?'

'I used to see him in the Union Club sometimes,' his wife said. 'He always had a story to tell of his forays to London or Edinburgh to buy some old book or other. To be perfectly frank, Harry, he was regarded as a bit of a bore on the subject. He showed no sign of being particularly rich though. I gather he had wandered the world quite a bit. That's where the money must have gone.'

Her husband did not agree. 'No, dear, I believe the books and drawings must have accounted for most of it. Justin has been chary of having them valued, because that's always charged on a percentage basis, but I looked round his library once and would say that it must be worth . . . I don't really know exactly how much. I'm no expert, but shall we say around --- let's say ninety or a hundred thousand pounds. Sterling, I mean, not Maltese. But, as I said, I'm not an expert.   They could be worth more.'

The envelope in my inside pocket assumed a greater import- ance.

It was not quite dark when they left. I decided to take a stroll and called into the hotel to collect my guidebook.

After the shops and offices have closed and daytime visitors have gone back to their hotels, Valletta reverts to its true medi- eval character. This is the best time to savour the splendour of the architecture, many of the buildings constructed by the Knights of Malta. Most miraculously survived the attempts of the Axis powers to bring them low, just as Grand Master de la Valette with a handful of knights and the loyal Maltese protec- ted them from Suleiman the Magnificent four centuries ago. My guidebook led me to the various 'Auberges', each of which was the hostel of one of the nations that made up de la Valette's brave defenders.

As I walked along Merchants Street, I could hear evening mass being sung in St John's Co-Cathedral, but my destination was a church I had passed the previous Sunday before I went to Gozo. It was set at the top of steep steps, in an unpretentious narrow street which led up from the Grand Harbour and was dedicated to the arrival of St Paul on Malta after his shipwreck.

I entered the crowded little church and found a seat at the back, absorbing an atmosphere of quiet devotion, hoping that I might share some of the strength which these believers were deriving from the ceremony. I could not understand much of the Latin, so I let my mind range over the events which had brought me to this island. I thought of my dead sister and of the friends who had become so important to me, and I managed to frame a prayer which brought together all that I wished for them and for myself.

Then I heard the congregation begin to recite words which were at last familiar, and I joined them in the universal prayer. *Pater noster, qui es in caelis . . .*

Emerging into the street, I stood apart, watching the congregation chatting to their friends, until they gradually moved off back to their homes and their families. I waited for quiet to return to the city and I was alone again.

On the way back to the hotel I noticed a small sign on one of the houses, displaying the bill of fare for a restaurant. I was certainly ready to eat. This looked like a private house, but I went in, down worn stone steps, into what probably had once been the cellar of the house of one of the Knights. After the silence of the deserted streets this was a scene of colour and of jollity. Banners displaying coats of arms were suspended from the low rounded ceiling. Noisy groups of diners turned to greet me as I was shown to a table by the kitchen door, and I sat down, relaxed, spiritually refreshed, and hungry.

After taking my order, the waiter placed a bottle of red wine on the table. 'I'm sorry, I didn't order wine. Would you bring me a Cisk lager, please?'

'No sir, it is from the lady over there.'

Looking round, I recognised my dancing partner from Karibune, the doctor I met at the Kiboko roof bar! She waved, and came over to my table, with a man at her side.

'I knew it was you as soon as you came in,' she said. 'What a surprise to see you here. Welcome to Malta. May I introduce my husband? Geoff, this is Harry Paine, the one who flirted with me in Bandari. I told you about him and his friend Mary Costas.'

'Don't believe a word she says Mr . . . I'm sorry. I never got to know your wife's second name.'

'It's Grech'.

*

When I got back to the hotel about nine o'clock Tommy was waiting for me with a proposal.

'I've been on the phone since we got back from Santarita. I spoke to young Maggie about renting an office in Malta and, while we were talking, it struck me, why not Harry's place? It would be handy for Doris. I asked Maggie how much I ought to pay and she suggested six hundred Maltese Liri a year. It doesn't sound much, I know, but she said it were the going rate. You can check with another agent if you want. What do you think?'

'Remember there's no furniture,' I reminded Tommy.

'I'd furnish it for you. Downstairs would be the office and I'd live upstairs, at least until I decide if I want to move over here permanent. Then I can let that top flat in St Julians that I were going to live in. Whenever you come back, you'd have some- where to stay --- if you could put up with me being there too that is. Would you mind if I put a swimming pool in your back garden? At my expense of course. Maggie said that would help if you ever wanted to let it out as a holiday home and I like a dip now and then myself.'

I shook Tommy's hand. 'Done,' I said.

Half an hour later I was in bed and ready to open Hector's en- velope, the second message from the past.

It was not a letter, just a collection of well-thumbed photographs of my mother, several of her wearing a bathing costume.

TWENTY -SEVEN

To be seeing Kitty on my first evening was an unexpected pleasure. Elizabeth Butterworth met me at Manchester Airport:
Richard had an appointment he could not miss. He had arranged that the Masters would come to dinner, so that the issue
of Brough Farm could be settled as soon as possible.

Despite the rush hour we were in Matlock before six, thanks to
Elizabeth's somewhat aggressive driving, in her little Triumph
Spitfire. On the way, she brought me up to date with local news,
most of which was of no interest to me as I did not know, or
could not remember, the people she was talking about. I had to
remind her that my time at Matlock was confined largely to
school holidays. I asked after her children, a girl and a boy, who
were both at boarding school, the boy at Castleberg. I could not
remember their names.

What did interest me was to learn how Kitty and her husband
were getting on, but I had to undergo a 'poor Harry' encounter
before finding that out. Elizabeth put her foot down to pass two
buses, without a break in the conversation.

'Richard told me about Gaynor going to America. We liked her
so much when you came up for the funeral and I said to Dick
she was the one for you. We were hoping to hear wedding bells
when you got back from this job, where is it? Northern
Rhodesia? I can never remember.'

'Bandari.'

'Yes, of course. Sorry. They will keep changing the names of
these places, I get confused. This Gaynor seemed such a nice
sort of girl and so clever too. Poor Harry.'

'So how is Kitty these days?'

'I make no secret of the fact that I always hoped you and Kitty would get together, but she was so desperate to get herself fixed up. A girl like that could have had anybody she wanted. Not that she hasn't done very well for herself, and I'm sure it'll work out all right again. Every marriage has its ups-and-downs, doesn't it?'

I was hungry after the flight. Airline food never satisfies me. Elizabeth knew me well enough to remember this.

'You'll be hungry, won't you?' she said. 'No need to worry, dinner should be ready by the time we get home. Kitty offered to do the meal for us. She said, 'I know *him*; he'll be off that aeroplane ready to eat a horse.' I must admit she does make a lovely steak and kidney pie. We'll be able to sit down as soon as you want, because David was already there when I left, and Richard promised faithfully he would be home by six. Oh Harry, it *is* good to see you again.'

I had never met David Masters before and was prepared to dislike him. They had invited me to their wedding, but I made an excuse. I said I wasn't able to get away from Cambridge during term time, which was not strictly true. The last thing I had wanted was to watch Kitty walking out of church on the arm of some other man.

David was in the sitting room when we arrived. He proved to be affable, charming even. I grudgingly accepted that he was good-looking; about my height, fair hair, slightly receding, which pleased me in a way that was unworthy of me. Richard wanted to have the business talk before dinner, but I asked to delay. He took my case upstairs and I went into the kitchen.

She was listening to the news on the radio, wearing a flower-patterned pinafore over a royal blue velvet dress, stirring a pan of gravy, perspiring, hair somewhat awry. She obviously had not heard us arrive. I kissed the back of her neck and she turned around in surprise. I had never seen anyone look lovelier.

151

'Oh, no,' she said, 'not *you*! How did you get here so quickly? I could see no way you would be here before seven. I must look an awful fright. Keep stirring this while I go and do something to make myself presentable. No, don't look at me.' She rushed out of the kitchen and was on her way upstairs.

Elizabeth came in to relieve her at the Aga. 'Richard has drinks ready, go and join them in the sitting room. You remember where the loo is, don't you? I'll be joining you in a minute after I've brought that foolish lass down again.'

It was not altogether a happy dinner. David monopolised the conversation. He had left Granada to set up his own production company in Manchester and told us in detail about his new game show called 'Pick your Fortune', which had secured a prime-time slot on Wednesday evenings. The programme sounded particularly silly. Kitty was pointedly scathing about it.

Elizabeth tried to be polite. 'We watched it last week, didn't we Richard? The audience certainly enjoyed it and some of the questions were quite difficult, but we missed the end. We had to change over; we needed to see something on the BBC news.'

David was keen to talk about Brough Farm. I could have cut him short by making clear there and then that I had no intention of selling, but I was waiting for an opportunity to explain in private to Kitty why I wanted to keep it. Richard changed the subject, but David soon brought the conversation back to property.

'We are really happy at Brough Farm, aren't we darling, but renting isn't a sensible option in the present financial situation. I feel it's vital to have one's own stake in the housing market, with prices rising every year. As a matter of fact, I've bought myself a little *pied à terre* in Manchester, chiefly as an investment. We record the show on Saturdays, that's when we get the best audience, and one tends to be rather whacked when it's all over. It's handy to be able to stop over rather than drive all this way home.'

'Yes, Richard finds it extremely handy, don't you, darling', Kitty said, in a tone of voice that did not at all match that of her husband. There was a spark of anger.

I had not seen her since my aunt's funeral. She had still been modelling then and had the thin figure that her profession demanded, but it had given a slightly peaky look to her lovely face. Now she had matured into true beauty, or so it seemed to me. She wore the cameo brooch my aunt had given her, a family heirloom that would have gone to Barbara. I was glad Kitty had it. I wondered whether they had chosen not to have children.

David was addressing me, but I had not absorbed what he said.

'I'm sorry?'

'I was saying that it must be difficult living in places where they don't have television. Do you miss it terribly?'

There was nothing to be gained by denigrating the man's raison d'être.

'A bit, sometimes,' I replied.

I offered to help with the washing-up, but Elizabeth said it was no trouble for her to load the dishwasher, so the rest of us went into the study for the business talk. Only twenty minutes later it was over. Kitty took my refusal to sell harder than did David, though I made it clear that they could remain at Brough Farm for at least another five years. Richard would draw up a new lease.

Frustrated that I had not been able to talk to Kitty alone, I said I might call on her parents in the morning, after I had seen my grandfather. I hoped she might take the hint and come with me to the nursing home. To my delight she said, 'Why not let me pick you up from here around nine. We'll go together to see Mr Paine and then we can take a couple of horses to ride over to see Mum and Dad. Poor David is busy all day, aren't you darling?'

'Make sure you wrap up well, dears,' said Elizabeth, 'the weather forecast for tomorrow isn't very good.'

TWENTY-EIGHT

'You are lucky to have caught him on a good day', the matron told me as we walked along the corridor to Grandpa's room.

'By the way, I know all about you. We read him your letters. I hope you don't mind; it's not that I'm being nosey or anything, but his attention span doesn't allow him to read through a whole letter. It sounds like a lovely place, where you are.'

She opened the door of his room. 'Here Mr Paine --- here he is, that young man you are forever telling me about. I'll bring you both some coffee in a minute or two.'

It was an emotional embrace. There seemed to be so little of him; his shoulder blades were sharp beneath my hands. What had been a strong broad-shouldered man was now a doll in striped pyjamas.

'You're looking well Grandpa.'

'Don't come that with me, lad. I'm a daft old man and don't start trying to soft-soap me.'

He was far from 'daft' today. This may be just 'one of his better days', but he listened carefully as I related some of the adventures George and I had had. His eyes were bright and he showed interest in the crops that were grown in a tropical climate. Of course, he was born into farming, but it came as a surprise that he still took such an interest. In return, he gave me some quite hilarious insights into life in this nursing home. The whole house must have heard our laughter.

'Have you done out there?' he asked at one stage.

'I have to go back for three weeks or so, but I promise I'll come and see you again as soon as I return to England.'

'I've been thinking about you a lot recently, lad,' he went on. 'What happened to that smart young woman you brought up to Annie's funeral? Are you still seeing her? Don't you think it's about time you were getting yourself married? You'd best get on with it, I'd like to see a grandchild before I go.'

I decided not to point out that I was his grandchild.

'We are still friends,' I replied, 'but she has just gone off to live in America for a bit.'

'She's not so damn much use to you over there is she? You want to have a look around; there's plenty more. There's a lovely lass comes in now and then to take me out in my Bentley. Must work for that taxi firm. She says she knows you. I think I might have got it mixed up, but I'm sure she said she was young Bill Palmer's daughter, but Billy wouldn't be old enough to have a girl that age, would he?'

His mention of taxis reminded me I needed to book a car.

'I need to go down to Cambridge, Grandpa, but I'll try to come again before I go back to Africa.'

'Would you like to use the Bentley? I made sure you were kept on the insurance. I told Dickie Butterworth you might want to use it when you came home.'

I remembered now. I had agreed with Richard that the old car should be kept on the road so that Grandpa could be taken for a drive in it from time to time.

It did not seem long before Matron came to take away the coffee tray.

'Do you realise that you two have been talking for an hour and a half?' she said. 'Come on, Mr Paine, it's time for you to have your massage, and then you must get yourself dressed and take your little walk.'

'Go and take a walk yourself,' he said. 'We've a lot to say to each other yet.'

'Don't you get cheeky with me or you won't get your Mackeson tonight. We have Mrs Masters in the waiting room, ready to take this young man away. I'll tell her she can have five minutes with you and then I'm going to throw the pair of them out. You've done quite enough talking for one day, thank you very much.'

The leave taking was made easier by knowing that we would see each other again within a few weeks. As Kitty and I were leaving, the old man said, 'Think on what I said about getting wed; there's plenty of nice girls around. I want to see that grandchild of mine.'

There was now no doubt in my mind that this was the right place for him.

But I am sad that he never lived to see my daughter.

TWENTY-NINE

The Volvo smelt of riding tack and Kitty's perfume, scents happily reminiscent of my youth. She said she had been shopping at the new supermarket in Matlock while I had been with Grandad.

'But I purposely didn't buy any frozen things, because you are taking me for lunch. That's the least a rich landlord can do for his poor tenant --- and you can't make an excuse, I've just called into the Cromwell and booked us a table.'

Today being Saturday, the hotel dining room was full. Some

tourists were talking loudly about their visit to Matlock Bath, but most of the other diners appeared to be locals. Things that I most wanted to say to her could not be said in these surroundings, for many people in the dining room knew Kitty, and some must have been aware who I was. No doubt there were several keen ears trained onto our conversation.

I had dressed ready for the ride, in a fawn polo-necked sweater, brown corduroys and an old hacking jacket borrowed from Richard. I felt out of place in this smart hotel. Kitty, on the other hand, was the complete country lady. She wore an expensive-looking suit of pastel checks, a sweater of a similar colour to mine and beige woollen stockings. Her brogues looked like Clark's. She must have realised I was embarrassed to be wearing Richard's old jacket.

'I can't understand why they always keep this place like a hothouse,' she said. 'Why don't we take our coats off?' I removed mine and she slipped hers over the back of her chair. I tried to keep my eyes away from her perfect bust. She kept playing with her rings, as nervous as I was.

'I do hope David gets to hear about this,' she said. 'I'm sure he will, with all these people looking on. Let's say something outrageous to make it worth their while. Better still why not give me a great big sloppy kiss?'

'Later,' I said.

I gave her an account of the events of the last month, a slightly abridged and edited version of what I had told Richard the night before. When I had finished, she said, 'My word you certainly are a good catch for someone now, aren't you? And Gaynor? I hear she is off to America. Will you be joining her there?'

'Quite honestly Kitty, just now I have no idea what I'll do. The last three or four weeks have put so many options in front of me that I'm tempted just to toss a coin.'

'Lucky old you, to have choices. Now I know how rich you are

157

I'll have some wine, please.'

She signalled to the waiter.

*

The rain had held off but there was a chill breeze as she parked outside the stables. It would be getting dark in a couple of hours, but Kitty decided that there was time for a hack up towards the Tor and that we should then drive across to see her parents, rather than ride. Although I had come dressed for the ride, I would need an overcoat to face the hill.

'Look in the tack room,' Kitty said, 'the door's open. I'm sure your leather coat is still hanging on a peg on the wall. Then go and have a look at my horses while I'm changing. I'll bring the Bentley keys with me. If you're driving it down to Cambridge it will be a good idea to turn it over. The old dear normally starts first time but it's about three weeks since I took your grandfather out to Dovedale.'

What was now the tack room used to be the farm office. My old coat felt a bit damp but would serve to keep out the weather. I lingered, to enjoy the childhood memories which the place evoked. As I left to go to the stables, she emerged from the house in her jodhpurs and, as she walked towards me, the same old thrill returned. She carried a black riding-coat over her arm, with her helmet in one hand and another for me.

The car started at once. I pulled it into the yard, ready for when we got back. It was 'Hobson's choice' in the stables; her own two hacks were nearest the door and they were eager to be out. To take one of the livery horses on the rough track up the Tor would have been risky. There was a young girl mucking them out. Kitty did not introduce her.

A weak sun was breaking through the western cloud as we set off up the hill. The last time I had been up there was with Gaynor, after the funeral. It had been one of my favourite walks in the old days.

'I'm going to take you to one of my special places,' said Kitty. 'When I was a girl I loved to ride up to the old farm. Perhaps you remember it? Even then one wall had disappeared and it's completely derelict now. I used to pretend it was my house. I had just put the children to bed and was sitting with my lovely husband on our veranda, before the butler called us in to dinner. I always had ideas above my station, you see.'

'And who was this 'lovely husband'?'

'Oh, it varied. Some boy from school I was in love with at the time, or Cary Grant. Yes, come to think of it, it was usually Cary Grant.'

The horses needed no guidance, they knew the way as well as either of us. As we got further up the hill, the sky became clearer and by the time we reached the ruins of Corbett's Farm we were in full sun, albeit a weak, watery one. We went into the roofless building and sat together on a large fallen transom, that had once supported the main window. We looked down onto Matlock Road and the homes of our childhood, with their damp slate roofs reflecting the wintry sunshine. The two horses grazed contentedly in the long-neglected meadow.

'You know', she said, 'I don't think I could live anywhere but around here. I hate towns but Matlock is just about right, don't you agree? If I left here then I would go to somewhere like that little island you were telling us about. What did you call it?'

'Gozo.'

'Yes, that sounds nice but here suits me. If I can't stay on at Brough Farm I may try to buy a little house in Matlock and rent a field for my horses. Of course, I would have to give up the livery side of the business.'

'But why? I agreed that you and David can keep it on for five years maybe longer. It's just that I feel exactly as you do about Matlock, and I love Brough. It may be years before I can come back to live there but I'm absolutely certain that this is where I want to settle down.'

'What I didn't want to have to tell you,' she said, 'is that I am planning to divorce David. It's all too sordid to explain, but that's why I was so keen for us to own Brough Farm. The stables and the riding lessons I give could just about support me. David put most of our money into this new production company, but we could just about manage to buy Brough Farm. I couldn't be thrown out if we owned it, so the house would sort of be my alimony. I'm not begging you Harry, but I want you to understand why I was so keen to buy.'

'You could go back to modelling'

'I'm too fat now.'

'Nonsense!'

'Have you seen the kids these days? Like beanpoles. I suppose at a pinch I could transfer my own horses to Dad and Mum's place, but they don't really have room for my loose boxes and your meadow is ideal for my jumping classes.'

I should have known better but, without thinking, I said, 'Poor Kitty'.

'Yes, poor me.'

There was a wry smile on her face. She said what had been in my mind ever since I saw her in the kitchen the previous evening.

'I should have waited for you to grow up'.

'You know I loved you,' I said. 'Always have.'

'Did we know what love was in those days? I don't think I did. Of course, it was quite apparent that you fancied me. Your feelings for me were rather obvious if I may say so. In the turnip field? Remember? I was very flattered at the time.'

'Oh dear, so you did notice. I just couldn't help it.'

The horses had stopped grazing and curiosity had driven them into the old house. They stepped over the stones and stood in what had been the kitchen, staring at us.

'What can I do, Harry? I'm so mixed up I need someone sensible to guide me.'

A thought came to my mind. 'Perhaps Richard could arrange some sort of sale and re-purchase agreement, so I could buy Brough back from you once I settle down in Britain again. Does he know how things are between you and David?'

'Elizabeth has probably told him. She knows about Karen --- that's her name, by the way. She's what they call a 'hostess' on that stupid show of his, and he has this flat in Fallowfield where they go after the show. They will be there tonight. Round about eight o' clock he'll ring up and say something like, "It's been an absolutely shattering show, darling and I really couldn't face the drive back." Our life is a complete sham.'

Kitty had been holding my hand while she was telling her story and, without realising what was happening, we were kissing. I now knew that Kitty's feelings for me were all that I had ever hoped. My dreams were at last becoming reality. But it ended all too soon, one of the horses tried to put its face between us and we both burst out laughing.

'Come on,' she said, 'time to go. It seems I have brought a chaperone with me. Let's go down and take the Bentley across to my parents' place.'

Kitty's parents appeared unaware of her marital problems. They enthused over their son-in-law and his success in the world of television. I could see that this was hard for Kitty to bear. It was good to be once more in the company of these friends, but Kitty said she could not stay long because she needed to feed the horses, so after tea we excused ourselves. I told the Palmers I would be back within a month.

As I started the car, Kitty asked me to stop the engine.

'I have something to say to you before we set off. I've been rehearsing it all the time you were talking to Mum and Dad. Let me get through it before you speak.'

I covered my lips to show obedience.

'What I want most of all right now is that you should take me back to Brough Farm and that we should go up to your old room and make love. I know you have wanted that all day and it's what I have been trying to resist, ever since you kissed me at the old farm. Dear sweet Harry, I want you so much, deep inside me . . . but if I let that happen it would make me just the same as David.'

'It's no more than he deserves. We could start again --- together.'

'No, darling, I'm not right for you. Much as I love you, I can't take you away from Gaynor. From what she told me at the funeral I know she loves you deeply. That would always be an obstacle in my mind. You must marry Gaynor, bring her back to Matlock, and I'll be your best friend. We have to forget what might have been.'

'No. Why can't we . . .' She would not let me go on.

'Please don't say anything more or I shall begin to cry. You deserve the happiness I could never bring you. Take me back home now.'

As I switched on the engine again she placed her hand on mine.

'But, on the way, do you think we could pull into the lay-by where the bus stops. I would like to finish that kiss the horse

162

interrupted.'

THIRTY

Nothing had changed in the porter's lodge of Erasmus College except names on the post racks. There was the pervading smell of lavender furniture polish from the gleaming counter. A coal fire burned cosily in the hearth at the back of the lodge.

'Very nice to have you with us again, sir,' said Mr Barnett, the head porter.
His bowler hat still hung on the coat rack behind the counter. 'You've been in foreign parts I see. Paine, H. A., 66 to '69. Agriculture, if I'm not mistaken.' He lifted the flap and came out to shake my hand.

'Thank you, Barnett,' I said, 'I'm glad to find you still here, but now I am pleased to call you *Mr* Barnett.'

He gave me a key to one of the guest rooms. There was no room number on the tag. 'I've put you in T staircase, the set right at the top. I'm sure you remember the way, though as I recall we never had you in college, did we? You lodged with Gladys Miller.'

College servants have remarkable memories. Even in a small one like Erasmus there were over a hundred men passing through in each annual intake, yet Barnett could remember my name, initials, years of residence, the subject I studied and where I had lived.

'That young lady of yours come in the other week with a suitcase and a tennis racquet. Professor Beeson asked me to put them in the guest room for you. A lovely person she is, I must say. She told me she was going abroad but I didn't put two and two together. It'll be nice to have her with you again, I'm sure. Seven pounds for the room, I'm afraid.'

I paid him and he went back behind the counter to make out a receipt.

'Oh, dear me, I almost forgot. Professor Beeson said he'd be pleased if you would join him for dinner in Hall, second sitting. I put you an MA gown on the bed; you won't need a hood. And could you join him for a glass of sherry in the Senior Common Room before dinner. Half past six, he said.'

I thanked him and prepared to leave, but he obviously wanted a chat.

'You know, Mr Paine, they're not like they were when you was up, the undergraduates I mean. Heads forever stuck in their books these days. The job's not the same, I'm sorry to say. We don't have the trouble with them like we had in your day. My word, that play you were in was a right to-do, wasn't it? What was it called?'

'Private Lives.'

'That's it. Me and the wife saw it. You and your lady friend were very good, and do you know what? That post-graduate chap who called himself an anarchist is standing for Parliament --- you know what as? A Tory, that's what. Amazing how when they get out into the real world they learn a bit of sense. Well, mustn't keep you.'

As I was opening the lodge door, he said, 'You can leave the key in the door when you've finished tomorrow but do call in again. Jarvis will be on duty in the morning and he'll be glad to see you, if he can recognise you under all that tan. I put a fire in your room. You'll be glad of that, coming from where you've been. Like Siberia up there it is in this sort of weather.'

I went up to dump my overnight bag, poked the fire, put on more coal and then set off for Sidney Street.

The building that was now the offices of Haskins and Ede had formerly been student lodgings. Its proximity to several university faculties and the old Cavendish Laboratory impressed upon

164

visitors that they were in the heart of academia, but the domestic atmosphere had been deliberately maintained. The only concession to 'trade' was a discreet brass plate, set beneath the bell-push. Clients mounting the stairs would feel assured that their fees were not supporting extravagant overheads.

For me this was just a courtesy visit. I had nothing to say that was not already in the monthly reports, but Cambridge is a close-knit community. They may well hear that I had been in town and be offended if I did not call.

Today, Sylvester Ede could have been mistaken for a minor poet. He was wearing a plum-coloured corduroy jacket, pale green slacks and, despite the winter weather, open-toed sandals, revealing a pair of yellow socks. His long hair had now started to thin on top, and he had adopted pince-nez spectacles, which only added to his studied eccentricity. In fact, he was not only a brilliant scientist but possessed a business brain that had helped him and Brian Haskins build up one of the most respected technical consultancies in Britain. Neither had yet reached forty.

He had adopted a languid air while at the university.

'My dear Harry, come shake the hand. So kind of you to call, and congratulations on a job well done; or perhaps I should say, on the point of completion. Of course, you are quite right to take a little breather, why not? Are you to be here for long?'

'No, only a few days. I had to pop back for some family business.'

'Why not, indeed. As you said in that most succinct telex message you sent us, everything is under control. I'm sure you will have it all buttoned up by the deadline. Just to remind you, though, we do need to have everything here by the end of this month. Brian and I will need a day or two to jolly it up into the sort of thing that WAFCO like to see. So, enjoy yourself.'

'It's not exactly a holiday.'

165

'Business, holiday --- entirely your own affair, dear boy. By the way, you seem to have made a hit out there. I had a letter from that Deputy Perm Sec chappie, saying that we must definitely put in a bid for the implementation phase, and insisting that you should lead the team. I do hope all this adulation hasn't made you too expensive for us. We are a struggling little firm, as you know.'

As I was preparing to leave, Sylvester said, 'Just a thought, but if the Bandari submission falls through, would you consider Nepal? No need for a decision now, but read up on rice, my dear --- just in case.'

I declined the offer of sherry and walked over to Arlington Passage.

There I was greeted like a long-lost son.

'Oh, you do look well, Harry. My Harry will be sorry to have missed you. Can you stay to supper? It seems such a long time since I had my two Harrys together.' Mrs Miller was always amused that her husband and her lodger shared the same name. There had often been confusions in the past, as either she or Gaynor called out for their man.

'But we was so worried when Gaynor said she was going America. I said to Harry, 'What he wants to do is get straight back and stop her, that's what I said. I would have wrote you only I knew you was on your way soon. It seems that Yankee man has a wife and two young children. I asked Gaynor outright and she said there was nothing like that going on, but I says to my Harry that nobody looks that way at a young woman if there's nothing going on. I can't remember what he called himself.'

'Professor Morgenthau, Hans Morgenthau.'

'There you are, you see? German. I might have known. Anyway, he was round here two or three times trying to --- what is it? Ingratulate himself? That's not right, is it?'

'Ingratiate?'

'That's the word I wanted. I'm sorry, but I've been on this earth long enough to understand these things. And her such a friendly, trusting person. Maybe she didn't realise what he was after.'

The idea being planted in my mind was repugnant. I tried to allow for Mrs Miller's ingrained suspicions, the result of reading hundreds of cheap romantic novels, but she was opening a wound that had appeared when first I read Gaynor's letter. What was it she had said? *Don't think I'm a husband stealer.* Was I being cast as Othello to Mrs Miller's Iago? I wanted to be out of that house as soon as I decently could. Happy memories were being tarnished. I wanted to get back to college and the warm monastic room that had been prepared for me. I looked forward to getting drunk with Jack Beeson.

THIRTY-ONE

How much should I tell Mary? That was the problem uppermost in my mind on the long boring flight from Heathrow to Karibune. Most of the passengers in the non-smoking section of economy class were elderly tourists, on their way to a safari holiday with SAGA; a jolly bunch, but now all fast asleep since the service of after-dinner liqueurs. The two seats next to me were empty and I was able to stretch out, to relax if not to sleep.

But I must have slept, for I was awakened by the cabin lights being raised and saw the food trolley a few rows ahead. I prepared myself for the miniscule offering that was a BOAC economy-class breakfast. The tray was swept away as soon as the last mouthful was finished and the stewardess, wheeling duty-free temptations was right behind the breakfast trolley. I forced my sleepy brain into action. Only twenty minutes before we are due in; we are being hustled; they must have been late waking us.

Think, quickly. Bottle of whisky for George, scent for Mercy.

167

'And for you, sir?'

'Yes. Johnnie Walker please, and some perfume.'

The stewardess looks as though she knows her smellies.

'Which of these do you think would be nice for a young Bandarian lady?

'Ma Griffe? The local passengers often choose it.'

Despite the gathering dusk, the heat that met me was reminiscent of that arrival two years ago. I was still only half awake while going through immigration and customs. Into the Arrivals hall, and a surprise --- it was not George meeting me, but Mary. She must have left work specially. Of course, silly me, I didn't change my watch. It's six-thirty in the evening, local time. That's why it's getting dark.

'Paine darling, you look awful,' she said. 'You look as though you *need* a holiday not just back from one.'

'No hold on', she told the porter, in Swahili. She jogged out of the door to catch up with him. I had not yet had as much as a welcoming peck on the cheek. By the time I caught them up, the porter was preparing to stuff my cases into the rear engine compartment of Mary's Volkswagen. She showed the man where to find the luggage trunk.

'Sorry I'm not picking you up in style,' she said, as we settled into the little car . 'I never like leaving the Merc in the airport car park. Now, come here you gorgeous man.'

I got my kiss as she switched on the engine. Rather a nice kiss.

'OK, sweetie pie,' she said. 'I want to hear every single thing that happened. First though, you must listen to what I have to tell you. You are spending tonight with me at the beach house. Wellington's gone.'

'Gone? What do you mean, gone?'

'Scarpered, decamped'.

'But why? He can't have left permanently. I knew he was planning to go to New Zealand but he can't just leave like that. What about the shop? What about their house, his car?'

'Left everything.'

'Has Mrs C gone with him?'

'Yes. They both drove up to Nairobi. One of Daddy's Kenya friends rang to tell me. You know that Wellington sold his Mercedes months ago and has been driving around in that old Ford Escort? He just abandoned it in the car park at Nairobi airport and bought a couple of tickets to Bombay. He left the car door unlocked, with the keys in and a note on the dashboard to say it should be sold in aid of the Red Cross.'

'Why on earth would he want to leave so quickly?'

'It appears he was going to be accused of sending money out of the country through the black market.'

'He wouldn't be so stupid as to get caught.'

'Well, no. Personally, I don't think he would get up to that sort of thing. People are always approaching me to get money out, but it's not worth the risk. But he must have got a tip-off that they were after him and didn't want to stay and fight. The police have taken over Wellington Stores.'

'But all my stuff is there.'

'Don't worry, I've had a word with them and they agree you can go in and remove your belongings. George is coming round in the morning to drive you there --- and don't forget it's their wedding anniversary party on Friday evening. You'd better get yourself in trim for that.'

'What about my motor bike?'

'We have that. Inge drove it round to her place. By the way, did you pay him in dollars?'

'For the bike? No. But I did pay the rent in dollars. I suppose that was illegal, was it?'

'Yes, but don't worry. It's not small fry like you they are after. Just don't volunteer the information. The police seem to be very reasonable these days. I had a bit of a problem myself just before you left --- something that they were told happened at the beach house. Nothing serious, just some silly girl inventing stories. They dropped it after a week.'

'I'd better move back to the hotel,' I said,

'You can stay on at the beach house if you like, but it will be busy at weekends, of course. Why not move into one of my apartments?'

'It's most kind of you but I'm sure I'll be able to find somewhere else.'

'Don't be so bloody independent. There's one empty in the block where Inge lives. I'll phone her and she'll get it ready for you to move in tomorrow. I have a couple of Swedes arriving, but not for six weeks.'

'OK, thanks. That sounds perfect, provided you let me pay you.'

'If it makes you feel better you can pay me what you paid Wellington, but not in dollars, please. I would have offered you that apartment originally, rather than send you to see Wellington, but I didn't trust you and Inge together under the same roof.'

'No need to worry on that score,' I said, 'she's keeping herself for 'Mr Right' --- and I'm not him, it seems.'

'Bollocks. She would have your knickers off in a couple of seconds if it suited her. But maybe you're right, maybe she isn't interested. I have my reasons for thinking that she's a bit like me --- you know.'

I did not know and said so.

'Do I really have to spell it out for you? Not sure --- about men. Oh Harry, don't be so thick.'

'Perhaps it's because I'm a bit tired,' I replied.

All the lights were on at the beach house, for security reasons. I carried my cases upstairs and she showed me into the end bedroom, which had a view of the ocean, through the narrow slit of a window. I had never been upstairs before.

'Hope this be OK?' she asked.

It was a single room and fairly basic, but there was a shower cubicle and washbasin. Mary showed me the bathroom cabinet. It was stocked with everything a guest of either sex would need. Shower gel and shampoo, toothbrushes and paste. For the ladies there was night cream and cleanser. For men, razors and shaving cream, expensive aftershave. Some packets of condoms on the top shelf set me thinking. On the bed was a pair of pyjamas still in their plastic wrapping.

She turned back as she was leaving. 'I left your mail over there on the dressing table. There's one from *her*, from America. Oh, and there's a print-out from Wayne Marshall. I know it's private but I did take a peep. Looks very professional. All you do now, I suppose, is add your own bits of secret formula --- like they do in the soap ads. Do make a good job of it darling. We all want you back here.'

'Do I need a net?' I asked.

'Not down near the sea. Just spray the room before you go to bye-byes'.

Mary's cook had left us a lovely supper; prawn cocktail, beef bourguignon and a gateau of her own concoction. We had already disposed of a bottle of champagne by the pool, as I began to report the events of the past two weeks, but I hesitated over whether she should hear the whole story. Should I tell her about Brown and my mother? Brown's visit to Kisule raised possibilities with which I had not yet come to terms. The Costas family connections might provide information on Hector's work on the ground nut scheme, but there was much that I was not yet prepared to discuss with Mary. One step at a time.

Mary said she did not want claret with the beef, so we stuck to champagne. She poured us each another glass.

'By the way', she said. 'I took your advice about vodka. Haven't touched a drop of spirits since you gave me the gypsy's warning, but I've made it up with bubbly. Daddy invested in crates of the stuff, most of which he gave to me when he moved to Lassita. Until now I hadn't bothered with it, but I'm beginning to realise what I've been missing.'

I was always conscious of Mary's generosity and I had tried to repay her kindness from time to time. There was a heavy duty on wine, from which I had diplomatic immunity, but she made it clear when I first brought a bottle to one of her parties that she always provided the booze. Otherwise, she said, some people would be straining to return her hospitality, when they could not afford it. "And I bloody well can," she had said.

'Here's a bit of good news,' she continued. 'You know how George had this crazy idea of going back to Zambia? Well it's all off. Festus has persuaded him that he's indispensable --- indispensable to you, that is. So, you see, there is a lot riding on you making a good job of that report and coming back to us.'

The second bottle of Pol Roger was well down as we finished the stew and she went to the fridge for the dessert. I was getting 'second wind' and she was eager for me to carry on with

172

the story. The Malta characters were already familiar to her.

'Tell me more about this Tommy, he seems like my kind of person. Do you think he will marry Doris?' This had not occurred to me.

'And the niece, Maggie, I assume she fell for you?'

It was easy to keep her entertained with the minor players in the story. I had not told her about meeting Kitty; I would do a little discreet editing of that part of the narrative. More importantly, I still hesitated over my mother's relationship with Hector. And then it struck me. Let her find out the truth as I did. Let her read the letter in bed tonight, here, in the peaceful atmosphere of this beach house by the shore of the Indian Ocean, as I had read it on my quiet small island. Although I don't understand her sexuality, she will appreciate, even better than I do, the feelings of a young woman in time of war, bereft of parents, unsure of her future and needing to be loved.

I still had not reset my watch so asked her the time. Midnight in Bandari meant that I had been awake for over twenty-four hours, apart from the nap on the aeroplane. My mind told me that my body needed sleep.

'Let's have a swim in the morning,' she said. It was more a command than a suggestion.

'Sorry. I didn't pack swim trunks.'

'You won't need them, there's just the two of us. I'm sure you've nothing down below to be ashamed of.'

We left the supper dishes in the sink, kissed each other goodnight and went up the stairs.

'Wait here,' I said, and brought the letter from my bedroom.

'I would like you to read this. It will explain something very important that I discovered in Malta, which I am finding it find it

173

difficult to tell you'.

She took the letter, kissed me again and said, 'Sweet dreams.'

I waited until I was in bed before opening Gaynor's letter. It was chatty, affectionate, amusing --- just as if we were still partners. But the words of Mrs Miller came to mind, as I read, '*And it's so kind of Hans Morgenthau and his wife. They have offered to let me stay at their lovely home, as a paying guest; I'm treated as one of the family.*'

THIRTY-TWO

As I came downstairs next morning, I smelt frying bacon and could hear Mary talking to George in the kitchen. The early swim was now out of the question.

'About time too,' Mary said, as I entered the kitchen. 'Your friend has already eaten most of the bacon and sausage I was cooking for you. You looked so peaceful when I came to waken you that I had a swim on my own.'

George came over and shook my hand, a formality which always struck me as strange, since we were such close friends. And he always preferred to speak English, the language in which he had been educated. Of course, he spoke fluent Kiswahili, but his native language was Chibemba which no one up here spoke.

'Just give me a minute George,' I said, and ran back upstairs. I pulled his whisky out of my case and the perfume for Mercy. I also found the two dresses I bought for the twins. Elizabeth Butterworth chose them with me at Marks and Spencer in Derby.

George was delighted with the presents, but said, 'Half an hour, Harry, and then we must be off to Wellington Stores. I promised Inspector Mac we would be there at ten.'

There could only be one Inspector Mac in the Bandari police

174

force, my former squash partner. 'Not Mac from Malua?'

'Yes, he told us he knows you,' said Mary. 'He's with the currency squad now but don't think your friendship will pull any strings, he's a tough cookie. What's his real name, George?'

'Fulgence Mackeja --- his uncle was our first president. Come on, hurry up bwana, eat your breakfast then go pack your suitcase. I've got the taxi waiting outside and I don't take credit cards.'

*

The stock room door would not open with my key. The locks had been changed, so George and I had to go round to the shop door. Mac was sitting at the counter and two policewomen were making lists of the stock. There were two small boys up stepladders, checking the top shelves. One was Wellington's assistant, the boy with the Gladstone bag.

'Good morning, Mac,' I said. 'It's a surprise meeting you like this.' The other boy came down the ladder when he heard my voice. He ran over to grin at me.

'Oscar, what are *you* doing here?'

Mac answered the question for him. 'Oscar's doing a spot of Saturday overtime, aren't you? He helps us from time to time.'

So, Oscar was their informer in the New Bandari.

Mac took a ruler from a drawer in the counter.

'Put your hand down on here and make a fist.'

I did as I was told. Mac gave me quite a hard smack with the ruler. The two boys danced round the floor in amusement and the policewomen doubled up with laughter.

'There, my Superintendent told me to rap you on the knuckles. You have been a naughty boy.'

175

Wellington's assistant must have reported to them about my paying the rent in dollars. 'I really didn't know I was breaking your rules.'

'Of course, Harry, we realise that. People may think our currency controls are unreasonable, but you must understand how important it is for us to conserve all the foreign exchange we get. We don't have the opportunity to earn much of it.'

'I really am sorry, Mac.'

'OK, you've had your punishment. Instant justice, I think it is called. I checked that you did the right thing when you obtained the dollars, paying for them with your sterling credit card, but when you came back from Kenya you should have changed what was left into Bandari shillings.'

'Understood. It won't happen again.'

Mac grinned, to show that all was forgiven. 'Now I'll come upstairs with you and we'll sort out what is yours. We are taking a full inventory, though a lot of this stock looks unsaleable. Mr Chaudhuri can have his property back if he ever returns and explains himself. Come on Oscar, help Harry and Bwana Bwalya.'

While I packed two suitcases, Oscar and George put the rest of my stuff into cardboard boxes.

When all my stuff was packed, George drove to the block of apartments where I was to stay. I could tell him where to go, having taken Inge there the evening we first met. Once we were on the way, he asked, 'Did Mary tell you our news?'

'Yes, that's great. She said you've changed your mind about going up to Zambia. If my proposals are accepted we can carry on with the implementation together.'

'No, not that. I wondered why you hadn't congratulated me. I thought Mary would have told you. OK, listen my friend, do you have a diary?'

'In my suitcase.'

'When we get into the apartment then, draw a line through the last two weeks in September. Make sure you are back with us by then and leave room for the christening of Master George Harry Bwalya at the Lutheran Church. You see, I have the names ready --- you are going to be his godfather.'

'That's wonderful news. Do congratulate Mercy for me.'

'You seem certain it will be a boy', I said.

What I did not add was, you seem certain that Mercy will complete her pregnancy this time. After two miscarriages.

'No problem, bwana,' George replied. 'My cousin assures me we are going to have a nine-pound boy, in the middle of September.'

'Your cousin? He's a doctor?'

'Sort of. He is fully qualified in traditional medicine, the leading guy in Chinsali District.'

'Really George? I don't believe it! You're relying on a witch doctor? '

'Well, I'm not being entirely truthful. He is not fully qualified.'

We had reached the apartments. As I pressed the entry-phone button for Inge's apartment, a shiver of excitement ran through my body. I now had a key to the front door, but the askari wanted to know who I was and why I was there. I was still explaining myself when Inge opened the door. She wore a dressing gown and had a towel wrapped around her head.

'I saw the cab drive off. I have been washing my hair,' she added superfluously. 'Come up and tell me all about your holiday.

I have made us a smorgasbord. Smorgasbord is all I can do, so you had better get used to it.'

The apartments were as luxurious as I had guessed they might be. Mine had only two bedrooms, but each had an en-suite bathroom with a sunken bath, a feature which must have been ahead of its time when the place was built in the early fifties. There were eight apartments in the block. Mine was on the second floor and Inge's at the top. We both had the same view overlooking the car park, but beyond that lay the creek. If I leaned out of the window, I would catch a glimpse of the Indian Ocean. She told me my motor bike was in the garage assigned to my flat.

She left me at the door of my apartment and went up to dry her hair. It occurred to me that I ought to have bought her a present, and I decided to give her the piece of Maltese glass-ware I had bought for myself.

After I had taken a shower and changed, I went upstairs. 'It is absolutely beautiful,' she said when I gave her the paper-weight. 'You are my very favourite man. I never imagined you would think of me while you were on that beautiful island. And thank you for the postcard, it came yesterday. I was surprised when you said you were going to England. Did you see your grandfather?'

As far as Inge was concerned, this had been purely a vacation, so I was not required to go into the details of my experiences in Malta, but I did tell her about Tommy, and about meeting someone who had been a friend of my mother. The smorgasbord was laid out on her dining table but I told her I was not yet ready to eat.

'That's good.' She smiled a teasing, provocative smile. 'So, we will have time, maybe. When you have finished your beer, I want you to come to my bedroom. I hope you won't be disappointed.'

I could not suppress excitement when she said, 'Excuse me for a moment while I go in and get ready.' She gave another smile as she closed the bedroom door.

I resisted the temptation to gulp down the beer. After a few minutes she pushed the bedroom door slightly ajar. 'I'm ready now. Close your eyes. I felt her taking my hand. Come with me, but keep your eyes tight shut until I tell you'.

I waited in great excitement.

'Now,' she said, 'you may open them.'

It was her portrait of Mary. She was depicted seated on a rock with the Ocean as a backdrop. I recognised the beach house in the middle distance. Her white gown was embroidered in the Greek fashion. Although this was a perfect likeness and beautifully executed, it was not the person I knew. Here was a gentle, vulnerable young woman. There was tenderness I had not seen in Mary, or perhaps never recognised. There was no doubt that this was a woman gazing at her lover.

'This really is a work of art,' I said with complete sincerity. 'You show me a Mary I never saw before. You are a true artist.'

'Oh, Harry, thank you; I was so worried. All day I have wondered whether I dare show it to you. But you are wrong about Mary, that is how she really is. We quarrel, as you know, but truly she is the best friend I will ever have. She could be the same to you, if only you would let her know that you love her a little bit.'

She opened the door again. 'I am sorry for teasing your cock, as Mary would say. I know exactly what you were hoping for and I am sorry I disappointed you. Now I am hungry; let's eat my smorgasbord.'

THIRTY-THREE

179

Dusk was gathering as we drove out of the city to George and Mercy's party. It was a relief to find her in a quiet mood, obviously happy, singing to herself the words of a tune playing on the car tape deck, *High Hopes.*

She had handed my mother's letter back to me without comment when George was there, at breakfast time. I had not been able to speak to her alone since then, but I decided that now was not the time to talk about it. I did not want to disturb this pleasant calm. Until we reached the coast road hardly a word passed between us.

It was one of those marvellous Indian Ocean sunsets. The moon was already there, a huge silver ball resting just above the surface of the sea and giving a cool cast to the gently rippling waves. She took a hand from the wheel to squeeze mine but did not say anything. There was no need for conversation.

I had dressed for the occasion in a new black safari suit; formal, yet not out of place with what the locals might be wearing. Mary had on a long dress with a tight waist, made from kitenge material, with a dark print. I congratulated her.

'Thank you, Inge designed it. You don't look so bad yourself, by the way.'

The neckline of the dress seemed dangerously low. She must have sensed my stare.

'I know what you're thinking, but don't worry. I'm not going to pop out of it, and there's a little coat to cover me up when we arrive. On the back seat.'

'I like the perfume, too.' I said. '*Je Reviens.* Am I correct?'

'Paine, you never cease to surprise me. How could you possibly know that?' Then she realised. 'Oh, I see. Is it Gaynor's too? I'm so sorry. If I'd known that I would have put carbolic behind my ears.'

180

'No, don't be silly. I love it.'

When she drove off the highway, onto the dirt road which led to
George's house, we could already hear the beat of the music. I
recognised it as a Zairean tune that was the current hit. The
twins must have chosen it; George and Mercy's taste was more
old-fashioned.

The Mercedes stood out among the other vehicles parked on the
spare ground in front of the bungalow, some old private taxis, a
few Banzam cabs and a selection of battered pick-up trucks. It
seemed there were no other European guests.

The party was already in full swing. George had certainly gone
to a lot of trouble. The lawn area was covered with a wooden
dance floor, probably borrowed from Mercy's church. Coloured
jam jars, each with a candle burning in it, hung like fairy lights
in the jacaranda trees which lined the garden. A couple of spotlights had been placed high on the veranda and were trained
onto the dance floor.

George rushed across to escort us in. Tonight, he wore a white
safari suit. As we reached the veranda, he turned to display me
to the assembled party.

'Look folks,' he shouted, 'it's the black and white minstrel show.'

This caused great amusement among the more sophisticated
guests, because there had been a campaign in one of the local
newspapers objecting to a television series then popular in Britain.

Mercy was majestic in gold lurex, with an elaborately tied head-
scarf of the same material as her dress. Mary kissed her on the
cheek and, after a momentary hesitation, so did I.

'Watch it bwana,' said George. 'That's my wife you're kissing.
Now you'll have to dance with her.'

George took Mary's hand and the four of us went to the dance

181

floor.

I studied what the other men were doing and tried to copy their movements. It appeared that the male contribution to this type of dancing was secondary. I kept a pivotal role, bending and swaying to the infectious rhythm, as Mercy performed a series of complicated manoeuvres in front of and around me. There was obviously no such formality as an 'excuse me'. Mercy was replaced by one lady and then by another, while I kept up the easy steps, which seemed to suffice. Across the floor I could see Mary, obviously more used to this type of dance. She was matching the African ladies in inventiveness, moving skilfully among a constantly changing group of partners. One of them was Festus Kasonde.

After a while I caught her eye and signalled that we should move off for a drink, but she indicated that she was enjoying herself and did not want to give up, so I went back to the veranda to see Pipit and Poppet, who were in charge of the tape machine.

'You were very good Uncle,' said one of them, Poppet probably; I was never sure. 'Will you dance with us?'

'We have been taking lessons,' said the other twin. 'We can do all sorts of dances.'

'I promise you both a dance later, but could I have a drink first?'

'Daddy told us you like Tusker. I will get you one if you like,' said Pipit, 'but Mummy says we have to make you try her pombe. She and cousin Myra Kasonde made it specially.'

'I'm sure it's lovely dear, but that sort of drink isn't good for my tummy.'

'It is horrible stuff,' said Poppet. 'It makes people get drunk and then they fall down. I'll go get you a beer.'

Pipit ran after her.

Mary came onto the veranda with Festus.

'What can I get you to drink, Harry?' he asked. 'I know Mary likes vodka and tonic.'

'Not tonight,' she said. 'Coca Cola please.'

'And the twins are looking after me,' I said.

Poppet returned with my beer. He whispered in the child's ear and she disappeared to join her sister. Mary followed her.

'I'm glad I caught you, Harry', Festus said. 'I wonder if we could have another chat sometime --- off the record. It's only loosely connected with the other matter, but someone has put an interesting idea into my mind.'

'I'm free on Monday morning. Will you be in the office?'

'Here would be better, he said. 'Some evening preferably. I gather you will be around for a little while longer, so if you could let George know when it might be convenient, I can pop over. We live next door but one.'

'Why not fix it now? Next Tuesday evening? '

'I'll check with Mercy if that's OK. By the way, could we make this one completely private?'

Mary and the twins had returned to the veranda, so I just nodded.

The tape was playing a Nelson Riddle selection. Mary grabbed my hand and took me to dance.

Festus went onto the dance floor to speak to Mercy. Then he left, without having drunk his beer.

Mary kissed my cheek. 'What do you think, Paine? Isn't this the best party ever? Pity it has to end at eleven.'

'Does it?'

'Most people have to work tomorrow,' she said, 'though what those pombe drinkers will feel like in the morning I shudder to think. Come on, don't be so British . . . let's smooch. Then take me over there and feed me.'

We carried our food to one of the tables under the jacaranda trees. As we sat down we heard George call for silence and announce that there was now to be a cabaret. He stood on a chair so that he could operate the two spotlights. Mercy stopped the tape machine and put on some Latin-American music.

Onto the dance floor stepped the twins. One wore a white tuxedo and black bow tie, the other a pink ball gown, liberally scattered with sequins. Their dancing lessons had obviously paid off. They started to the tune of "Blue Tango" making expert swoops and flourishes to rapturous applause. Then came an immaculate rumba, followed by a cha-cha. When the music changed to a foxtrot their parents joined them on the floor, to the acclamation of the whole party. It seemed incredible that George had considered leaving Bandari; he seemed universally popular.

After the foxtrot, Mrs Kasonde put on local music again and I went to give the girls their promised dance. To my dismay, the other guests appeared to think this was an extension of the cabaret, and no one got up to join us. The children were even better at it than their mother, so that I felt the complete amateur of the trio. Rashly, I began to attempt ever more ambitious variations on the theme I had been taught.

Applause followed each move. I began to invent steps, which earned me further applause from the crowd, and the twins responded with new improvisations to match mine. It was a tremendous relief when the music finally ended. The girls gave a curtsey and I bowed. We left the floor hand in hand.

It was a quarter to eleven, almost time for the party to end. I saw Mary sitting under a tree with a group of Mercy's women friends, and took her for a last dance. As the music changed to the Anniversary Waltz, we guests quit the floor, to leave George and Mercy dancing alone. There were tears in Mercy's eyes.

I looked down at Mary as we stood watching them, beneath one of the jacarandas. Her eyes were also wet with tears, though she had the sweetest smile on her face. I took her in my arms and kissed her.

'Yes, you were right. It was. The best party ever.'
On the way back she said, 'I don't think you've ever been to my house, have you? How about coming in for a nightcap?'

'That would be nice,' I said.

THIRTY-FOUR

I had never heard of any of us 'economic mercenaries' being invited to her home. The beach house, of course, was open to all her friends but her home, 'Magoulas' it was called, was her private territory. I had driven past it many times, an odd place when viewed from the main road. Set high on a bluff overlooking the Kinoni residential district, it could be mistaken for a castellated water storage tower. The facade seemed forbidding when viewed from the road. There were no normal windows, just narrow slits, maintaining the 'desert-fort' image of the beach house.

She turned up Kinoni Road, then off onto a dirt track, rising quite steeply. At a pair of wrought-iron gates, she stopped and sounded the horn. A guard emerged from a hut to open the gates. He secured them when she had driven through, then he marched off to the left and opened a large garage. I got out and chatted to him while Mary put the car away. The askari waited with his torch to escort us up to the house, but the terraced garden was illuminated by moonlight. She wished him goodnight.

'Come on,' she said, 'I'll race you up to the house.'

There must have been more than twenty steps up to the front door. She pulled up her skirts and ran ahead. I pretended I was trying to catch her, but took care to remain a step or two behind. Halfway up, she stopped, and I had no choice but to run past her. At the door I turned back to look, and caught her tucking her bust back into her dress.

'All right you won, but I couldn't let you in with my tits hanging out, could I? Now, take a look at the view to your right. You can see why Daddy built the house up here.'

It was magnificent. The whole of Karibune was set out below us like a carpet, with the ocean beyond, shining in the moonlight. We stood at the entrance, panting, while she searched for her keys.

Through the mahogany front door was a broad hall with a terrazzo floor. Furniture was set out like the lobby of a hotel. Marble stairs with art deco metal banisters led up each side, onto a minstrels' gallery overlooking the hall. Carved mahogany double doors underneath the stairs presumably led into the ground floor rooms.

'Come on,' she said, 'more stairs yet; this place was built by a crazy Greek architect friend of Daddy's. Everything is the wrong way round, bedrooms on the ground floor and living rooms upstairs. I'll not race you you've probably had a good look at them already.' Before we reached the lounge all the lights went out.

'Damn, another power cut,' she said. 'Half a mo, I'll switch onto standby.'
She took a small torch from her purse and went downstairs again.

Moonlight flooded in through sliding glass doors, as I made my way into the sitting room. I moved across to admire the view;

the same wonderful vista as at the front door, but now I could see the whole panorama. Lights came on again and the air conditioning started up with a gentle hum. Mary returned and pulled open one of the sliding doors. We went out onto the balcony.

'OK, Paine darling. There's something I want to ask you. You see, I'd like some champagne now and I want to know if I have to drive you home. Will you stay the night? After such a lovely evening I don't want to be alone in the house. No strings, no commitment, your own choice of bedroom --- and I shan't be hurt if you say no.'

'I don't want the evening to end either,' I said.

She put on a record, one of my favourite Mozart piano concertos, and went into the kitchen.

Within a few minutes she was back, carrying a tray, on which was a bottle of champagne, two plates of cold lobster and some brown bread, obviously prepared in advance. She took it to a table at the far end of the balcony. Mozart provided the perfect accompaniment to our meal. The lights of ships twinkled in the harbour below and Mary looked happier than I had ever seen her. The champagne was soon finished, and she suggested opening another, but I pointed out that it was half an hour past midnight and time for bed.

'A goodnight kiss then?' she suggested. 'Or two, perhaps?'

She stood and partly unzipped her dress, then cupped a breast in her hands for me to kiss, first the left and then the right. The fragrance of 'Je Reviens' brought back memories I would rather have avoided.

After the excitement of the kisses I willed myself to leave the balcony and slid open the glass door. 'You offered a bedroom?'

'Come and choose.' Mary led the way downstairs, through the double doors and down a corridor. She indicated the first door

187

on the right.

'That's mine.'

She opened the door of the room opposite. It had white carpet, a double bed with pink counterpane and a dressing table unit which took up the whole of one wall. The bathroom, through an arch, was also in the same shade of pink.

'Not quite you, perhaps,' she said. 'Come on.'

She went past the next door without opening it. 'Not you either. This will be more your sort of room.'

It was as masculine as the first had been feminine. With its four-poster bed and Wilton carpets, it could have been the bedroom of an English country house hotel, were it not for the mosquito net round the bed.

'Am I right?'

'Perfect Mary thanks.'

'Tea or coffee in the morning?'

'Tea please.'

'I'll leave a note for Phyllis. Nine o'clock do?'

'That's fine. You've made this a lovely evening for me,' I said. 'So, here's a thank you kiss.' I took her in my arms.

Neither of us wanted it to end, but it was she who broke off, with a joke to lighten the atmosphere.

'If that was thank you I wonder what 'please' would be like? Goodnight, Paine darling; it's been a lovely evening. Pyjamas in the top drawer and everything you need is in the bathroom cabinet. There's a robe behind the door. Sleep tight.'

She hesitated by the door but said nothing, turned, and went out.

There were two sets of pyjamas, still in their wrappers. The bathroom cabinet was stocked with everything I had found in the beach house bedroom. Instinctively, I placed one of the condoms into the pocket of the white bathrobe. After I had washed, I decided it was a waste to unwrap the pyjamas just for one night, so got into bed.

Despite the late hour I could not sleep. Only the steady low hum of the air conditioning disturbed the quiet. I always find complete silence disorienting, needing to know that I am in a world where life goes on, even though I am taking temporary leave of it. I need reassurance that I am not sinking into a void, alone. It may be the high-pitched hum of mosquitoes flying outside the net, chirping cicadas in the flamboyant trees outside my bedroom in Kisule, creaking beds in the school dormitory, the neighing of shire horses or the low hoot of a barn owl at Brough Farm, the soft breathing of the woman I loved.

I drifted from the memory into a dream.

Mary came to my bed while I was in that half-world between sleep and awareness, a state when the senses respond, though one is not fully awake. Her kisses were a complement to the dream, her perfume was that which I knew so well and, when she slipped astride me, the dream was not broken, for that had been Gaynor's way. She was moving gently above me whispering words I did not understand, some mantra from her Greek heritage. They were words of love, of that I was sure, but part of a private fantasy which I could not share. I closed my eyes and let my own fantasy return. The frustrations of abstinence began to drift away; the long months of loneliness were being erased.

Her slow movements prolonged the pleasure. In my fantasy, I was with Gaynor but as my excitement increased the image changed, to become the tall, lithe figure of Inge. A tempting creature, walking naked ahead of me along a beach, splashing her feet in the warm spray. I quickened pace but could not

189

catch her; the most desirable prize of all remained out of reach. But then she turned and smiled her arch little smile, opening her arms to draw me close to her, to draw me deep inside her. The surging ocean washed over us as I reached my climax. So long delayed, so completely fulfilling.

Suddenly I was awake, overwhelmed by the power and urgency of Mary's response --- a scream!

Then I heard words which deepened the mystery of the woman above me.

'Now. Oh, Barbara darling --- *NOW*.'

THIRTY-FIVE

I was still asleep when the maid brought in tea, and alone. Was Mary just part of my dream? The lingering fragrance of Worth gave the answer.
Beams of sunlight pierced the room through the narrow windows.

Phyllis drew back the netting from around the bed. She was a plump Chagga lady, probably old enough to have been Mary's nursemaid. She spoke good English.

'Morning bwana, here is some tea for you. It's a lovely day outside. Mary has gone for one of her jogs, though why she needs to jog I just do not know. She says I should give you a track suit to wear. I had to leave it outside, let me go get it.' She took away my safari suit and returned almost immediately with a plum-coloured tracksuit, which she placed on the Lloyd Loom chair.

'Breakfast is ready, and I'll be going when I've pressed your nice black outfit.'

'Please don't bother,' I said.

'I like to iron for gentlemen. Thank you for coming here bwana. Mary is too much on her own since Miss Paterson left.'

I was about to ask who Miss Paterson was, but decided that this may lead to a story I would rather not hear. I felt silly, with a sheet pulled up high to cover my nakedness.

'Was it you who made our meal last night?' I asked. 'It was delicious.'

'Lobster is easy but I'm glad you enjoy.'

More mysteries. Who was Miss Paterson? Whose was the track suit?

I took a shower. The tracksuit looked as though it would fit, but I put on the bath robe and set off to find the kitchen. I remembered it was upstairs. On my way through the hall, Mary came, with hair straggled all over her face and perspiration streaming from her.

'You *are* a sod' she said. 'Why is it you catch me like this, either with my breasts hanging out or looking like a scarecrow. Go and put that nice track suit on while I have a quick shower. If you go into the kitchen looking like that we shall have Phyllis raping you.'

I had not shaved. Opening the bathroom cabinet, I considered whether to put the condom back, realising that it had not been used last night. I slipped it into the pocket of the track suit. By the time I had shaved and dressed, Mary was already in the kitchen, eating muesli. Her hair was still wet, the red curls were now an amber cap, framing her glowing, healthy and, yes, beautiful face. She had inherited her mother's Irish complexion.

'I see it's all right for *you* to wear a bath robe, then?' I said.

'You would have been quite safe anyway. Phyllis has gone. There's your safari suit, by the way, hanging on the door.'

191

She made me porridge, followed by poached eggs and bacon. She was her normal self, as though last night had not happened, but I needed to have the mystery resolved. After breakfast I suggested we go onto the veranda. I sat on the swing sofa, while she took a cushion and sat on the floor. The ocean was now a deep blue, true aquamarine. There was no need to question her, for she said at once,

'Yes, I realise what I said last night. I knew your sister. She is the only person I ever truly loved; until you came along.

But let me tell you the story of my family. It may take some time.'

*

JOHN COSTAS

John was proud of his Greek ancestry, but he regarded Africa as home. When he was among Greeks he would stress that he was Cretan. His father, Petros, came to German East Africa in 1912 as manager of a sisal estate owned by an aristocratic Bavarian family, having obtained the position by a letter of application which exaggerated the size and prosperity of his family's olive groves, outside the town of Magoulas on Crete.

When Petros arrived at the estate, near Langwa, he realised that his lack of knowledge of sisal was unlikely to be exposed, since the Baron himself appeared to know little about the business, having only recently inherited the estate. His main interest was in hunting big game and most of his time was spent on expeditions with friends to the lion country along the Kenya border.

Fortunately for Petros there was a foreman, who originally came from Sierra Leone and who could have managed the estate himself, had he had the right skin colour. The Baron insisted on having a European in charge. Petros struck up a friendship with this foreman and gradually learned how the sisal crop should be handled. From the start he began making improvements in the way the estate was organised. It had been a long time since it had received the attention it required.

Petros decided to keep his wife and five-year old son in Crete until he felt established in German East Africa. The manager's bungalow, built for him before his arrival, was superior to the home he and Maria had in Magoulas, but the Baron had an un-predictable nature. Petros wanted to ensure that he was safe in his job before calling his family to join him.

By the end of 1913 he felt secure enough to send for them, but schooling was a problem, and he wrote to tell Maria that young John should stay at home with her brother and go to school in Iraklion: Maria objected. By the time several letters had been exchanged it was too late. A war had broken out in Europe, which was to mean the separation of the family for another five years.

For reasons which no one locally could understand, this European war spread to East Africa, and the British, Belgian and German communities, who had previously co-existed amicably, now found themselves fighting battles over a land to which none had a strong allegiance, taking with them African con-scripts for whom King George and Kaiser Wilhelm were un-known beings from an unknown continent. The Baron sent his family home to Bavaria and raised a company of bewildered es-tate workers, who were marched many miles to engage the en-emy on the border with British East Africa, if any British could be found in that deserted area.

Compared with the horrors of Passchendaele and the Somme, this East African war was a mere sideshow, but it engendered hatreds among the participants which long outlasted the con-flict. Petros was unwittingly cast in the German camp. He struggled to keep the estate alive, with an untrained labour force and with no means of exporting the sisal crop. To bring in some income, as well as to feed himself and the workers, he cleared a large area of sisal and turned it over to the production of vegetables. He converted one of the storage yards to a pig farm and sold the progeny to the German army, and to the mar-kets of Tanga and Dar es Salaam, which were not far south of

Langwa.

His main regret was that he was unable to bring his family to join him, and the question of John's education resolved itself by default. These were five long, lonely years.

By 1919 the Baron had returned to the estate but did not bring his family back from Germany. He showed even less enthusiasm for the place than he had before the war.

When it was decided that Tanganyika Territory was to be a British protectorate he lost all interest, and after spending six months vainly trying to sell the business to his neighbours, most of whom were equally disillusioned, he visited Petros in the estate office, a place he rarely entered these days. He made an offer which combined desperation with generosity. Costas could take over the estate without any down-payment, but a partnership agreement would be drawn up which would be dissolved once the Baron had been paid the specified amount at which he had originally put the business on the market.

Together they visited the Baron's lawyer in the capital, but Petros took the precaution of being accompanied by his own lawyer from Tanga, a fellow Greek. The final deed negotiated, specified that the Baron should be paid half the annual profits until the debt was cleared, with two per cent interest on the balance. The estate house was to go to Petros.

Six weeks later the Baron and his belongings left on one of the first passenger ships to sail from the port of Langwa. Petros moved into what had hitherto been known as 'the schloss' but which he now renamed 'Knossos.'

The foreman took over the manager's house. Now, at last, Petros sent for Maria.

She was both amazed and depressed when she saw the house they were to live in. She envied the smart bungalow now occupied by the Sierra Leonian manager, but she set about making a home of the large and rather forbidding building, long neglected

194

both by the Baron and by her husband. She had agreed that
John should remain in Crete; at the age of thirteen he was showing great promise at school and he would be able to come to see
them in the long summer holidays.

Those early years of the 1920's saw an expanding demand for
sisal, as the carpet manufacturers of Europe and the United
States gradually built up production to meet the pent-up demand following the Great War. Shipyards turned from making
warships to passenger liners and freighters, all needing ropes
and cargo nets. Petros was able to re-employ many of the
former estate workers returning from the war, without laying
off those who had replaced them.

*

When John first visited them in 1921 it was a schoolboy's
dream home. He tramped the long cool corridors, imagining he
was a nobleman in the eighteenth century. By day he would go
with his father through the sisal fields and around the farm,
which still grew vegetables and raised pigs. They now had an
abattoir, a factory for curing bacon and an ice-making plant,
which meant that frozen meat and bacon could be packed for
shipment to Dar es Salaam and up the coast to Mombasa. John
spent a lot to time with the manager and learned how the sisal
crop was grown and processed. It was a wrench for him when
the time came to leave for Piraeus and, as he boarded the ship,
he vowed that Tanganyika would be his home.

Petros Costas was not the only Greek estate owner. Albert Constantinides was already established when Petros first arrived.
He owned a small sisal estate, west of Langwa, and bought up
more estates from departing German owners. More Greeks followed, as managers of other plantations. There was a Greek
club in Langwa of which Petros became president, and Maria
was able to visit neighbours in the Ford car they bought.
Gradually they developed a social life, which made her home-
sickness bearable, but she could never learn to love their house
and longed for the comfort of the little farm in Magoulas. She
also longed for a daughter, but that was too late. John was their

195

future.

John returned for the summer of 1922 to find that Alex and Katerina Constantinides had been invited as guests for the holidays. They were at a boarding school in Nairobi and spoke English fluently. John had schoolboy English, which he spoke with some embarrassment, but English was their first language. It did not take him long to realise that the parents had planned this visit as a language school; the guests were to improve John's English and teach him Kiswahili, and he was to encourage them to speak Greek.

Alex was a fat, lazy boy who had no interest in Greek, but Katerina was keen to help John with his English. Swahili had come to him naturally on his tours around the estate. The main result of the visit was that John was able to persuade his father to let him go to the boarding school in Nairobi. His mother needed no persuading. Little Katerina was ecstatic, for John was a good-looking boy.

By 1928 there was a marked reduction in demand for sisal, as Western countries entered the Depression, but the loan to the Baron had been paid off in 1924, so was no longer a drain on the estate income. Petros expanded the farm but looked for a diversification which would cushion the effects of lower sisal sales.

Being a Greek, he naturally turned to the sea.

Langwa had become a busy port during the sisal boom and had begun to rival Tanga and Dar es Salaam as an outlet, not only for sisal but for coffee and cotton exports from the Central regions.

Thus came about the Costas Shipping Agency. Petros himself took charge, but he planned that John should take over.

It was in his new office at the agency that Petros had his heart attack. John did not complete his economics degree at Athens University. He came back for the funeral and never returned to

Greece.

*

We had been on the balcony for over an hour and the sun was striking across it. Mary had taken her cushion from the floor and sat beside me on the swing sofa.

'So, what happened to your sister?'

'What happened to Brigid was a husband and four children, all boys by the way. She met Patrick at University College; he's a doctor now and they live in Cork. They're blissfully happy of course. For Brigid the story has to have a happy ending.'

'And your mother? You never talk about her, do you? I assumed she was dead until you mentioned her the other day at the Lundini Beach.
Sorry, I didn't mean to be so blunt. I suppose it's because I don't have a family, that I always ask about everybody else's.'

'Mummy lives in Cork too, in a flat quite near Pat and Brigid. I'd better carry on with the story.

*

DERVLA SCULLY

For most of Dervla's young life there had been little doubt that she would become a nun. Her eldest brother, Conal, entered a seminary at the age of sixteen and was ordained six years later. Her elder sister Brigid was regarded as 'far too wild', but young Dervla was the pride and joy of her parents. She joined the Children of Mary at fourteen and regularly cleaned the church.

The prospect of having both a priest and a nun in the family filled the Scullys with understandable satisfaction. When Dervla decided to train as a nurse, her parents thought this an excellent preparation for the Order --- and was she not at mass every single day of the year, twice on Sundays?

So, the whole of Loughbarra was shocked when it became known that Dervla was not to take the veil after all, but was to join a missionary order in Africa as a lay sister. No, not the whole of Loughbarra. There were some who said that, with that flaming red hair, she would never be a nun.

In 1935 her parents went with her across to Liverpool, to see her onto the British India steamer to Mombasa. They hid their disappointment behind tears of farewell.

Just short of three years later the news broke in Loughbarra.

'Did I not tell you that red hair would be the ruination of her?' said Mrs
Reilly to Mrs Roberts outside Flaherty's butchers.

'But isn't it romantic?' replied Mrs Roberts, who was a Protest-ant and could not be expected to appreciate the gravity of the case. 'Nursed him from death's door with the malaria she did, and when he wakes up from the very edge of it he thinks she's an angel, herself standing there above him with her red hair shining like the setting sun. There and then he proposes, did you know that? And now here they are on their way to be mar-ried. It's lovely, Molly, so don't you go spoiling it with your stor-ies. She's a good girl and she always has been.'

'Then why is Patrick Scully having the banns called before ever they set foot on Irish soil? Tell me that. If you didn't forever have your head in them romance novels you'd know the fact of the matter. Mary cleaning the house from top to bottom, and him Greek and wouldn't know a decent Irish farmhouse from a hovel.' With that, she went into the butchers to make sure that Mrs Flaherty had heard the news.

*

For Dervla everything had been marvellous so far. In Kisumu they boarded a flying boat, which had taken them all the way to

Alexandria. She had never been on an aeroplane before but was not frightened: being on this was just like being aboard a ship, except for the noise. John got concessionary fares from Imperial Airways because of his agency. Now, here she was in her own room in the Piccadilly Hotel in London, only the second hotel she had ever stayed in. This one was so much better than the one in Liverpool. A single room, of course. John had behaved like the true gentleman he was, and had not been in even to say goodnight, though she wished he had.

Tomorrow they would be in Dublin and her father would meet them in the motor car. It was not yet three years since she had left them crying at the dockside, wondering whether she would ever see them again, and now she was bringing a husband home with her. No, she reminded herself, *almost* a husband.   John had insisted that her father should give his permission for the marriage. She had already written to tell them about him even before he proposed, so when John telephoned them, her Dad had said, 'Why surely, son, if that's what you both want, but her mother would never rest easy if you were not married here by her brother.'

She looked, for the hundredth time, at the lovely engagement ring John had bought in Asprey's that morning. He had kept the wedding rings himself, which was only right and proper.

*

The wagging tongues of the ladies of Loughbarra wagged in vain, because it was more than two years later that Brigid Costas was born.   John's mother never saw her: Maria died from cancer in 1939, after being nursed through a painful illness by her daughter-in-law. When their second daughter was born they named her Maria, though everybody called her Mary, her Irish grandmother's name.

In Europe a second war had come, and gone.

THIRTY-SIX

199

Dervla had never taken to life on the sisal estate and the house was not at all to her liking. She had servants to do the work, the neighbours were far away, and all of them Greek. John spent most of his time now at the agency in Langwa and no longer came home for his lunch. However, she did enjoy going down to Karibune with him. He was investing money in real estate there and he respected her opinions on design of the houses and apartments that his property company was building. But this was not her proper work; nursing was what gave her satisfaction.

Brigid was at school in Dublin and aiming to get into University College, so she no longer had any interest in East Africa. Mary said quite definitely that she did not want to go to school in Ireland and the mission sisters suggested that she be sent to the convent school in Nairobi. Meanwhile, the girl was quite content to be looked after by Phyllis, her young nanny. So Dervla started nursing at the mission again. It was less than an hour away in the car and the sisters welcomed her back.

When John announced that he was building a house for them in Karibune Dervla had mixed feelings; disappointment that this would bring an end to her work at the mission, but immense relief that she would be getting away from the estate. From the start, however, the new house caused a rift between them. While John had been happy to consult her over the apartments he built for renting and sale, he took no notice of her views when it came to what was to be their home, putting his whole trust in a man who had never been to Africa and who planned the whole thing on a drawing board in Athens. So, during term time when Mary was away at school, she decided that rather than sit alone in the estate house she would go to live at the mission, and she took a room there with the sisters.

John became interested in local politics and got mixed up with people who called themselves 'African nationalists'. She could not understand why a man of his background should want to mix with a group of hotheads, who were planning to rid themselves of people who had been so good to them.

God knows, as an Irishwoman, she had little time for the British, but surely John was crazy to think that these new friends of his would ever give credit to a Greek, even if they did get what they were aiming for. He kept taking her to look at this house in Karibune that was taking an eternity to build. Every time she saw it she liked it less.

Mary had started to talk like her English friends and said it was 'absolutely super', but what would a girl of fifteen know about it? Dervla began to feel her daughter was drifting away from her, preferring to stay with her fancy Kenya pals rather than come home to mother.

John said it might be better for Dervla to go back for a holiday in Loughbarra and he would let her know when the new place was finished; he was sure she would change her mind then.

But she never saw 'Magoulas' finished, and never returned to Africa.

THIRTY-SEVEN

'It's getting hot in here. Let me show you the roof. It's always cooler up there.   Phyllis made some fresh lemonade yesterday; it's in the fridge.'

She returned from the kitchen carrying a jug and two glasses on a tray. I took the tray and followed her through the upper hall and along a dark passage. Mary opened a door at the end of the passage. We went up a flight of circular stairs which took us through an attic area used for storage. At the top of the stairs she opened a metal door and we emerged onto the flat roof. A badminton court was laid out at the sea end and Mary asked me to carry the tray to a type of pavilion which was laid out with tables and chairs, like the patio at the beach house. There were sun beds and mattresses piled on the floor. Mary took two out and we sat under the canopy, with a mild breeze blowing in from the sea.

'So you see, Harry. Having a family doesn't guarantee happiness.

I was fascinated by what Mary just told me about her family. Now I could understand why John Costas chose his solitary life up in Lassita, and Mary herself was less of a mystery. But she was yet to mention the name I most wanted to hear.

'And Barbara?' I prompted.

'Help yourself,' she said. I poured two glasses of lemonade.

'Thanks. Well, Barbara was my salvation while all that was going on. She was a year older than me. She would have been thirty last September, wouldn't she? I wonder if you can imagine what it was like at that school for someone like me. I was a little fat dump at that age --- would be now if I didn't exercise. Fat and Greek Irish. An attractive mixture, eh? What do you think of Phyllis's lemonade?'

'Delicious. Go on.'

'Well, the black Kenyan girls were easy to get on with, but the whites were mostly Happy Valley types. You will know what I mean. I came from what they considered to be the absolute 'sticks', and it didn't help that Daddy was richer than almost all their snooty parents. But, of course, Barbara wasn't like that'

'How did you become friends?'

'We were both good at tennis. In fact, she was brilliant, but I was a good doubles partner. After we won the school championship, we were entered for the Nairobi District Juniors tournament. We came second and after the final she kissed me. It was while we were showering in the changing rooms. It was nothing to her, just what you would call a thank-you kiss but for me it was absolute bliss, the best moment of my life. Every night in the dormitory I had dreamed that one day she might kiss me. Then I suppose I must have started crying and I told her about my parents quarrelling.

She said, "Why not ask your mum if you can come up to us for the hols. You could have my brother's room."

'Are you telling me that you knew my parents?'

'Well, yes. I went up to Kisule just that once. I'd seen them together at Speech days twice I think. But your mother came down to the school quite often.'

'What did you think of Mum?'

'Oh, she was really beautiful, but a bit . . . oh dear, I don't mean to be rude and upset you.'

'For heaven's sake, tell me? Don't wrap it up, please. They've been dead for twelve years and you are the only the second person I've ever met who knew her.'

'Well, all I can say is what the nuns would have said in those days; flighty. I'm sorry, Harry, I realise it's your mother I'm talking about, but 'flighty' is all I can think of to say. She used to bring the dishiest men with her. The other boarders always used to look forward to seeing who Mrs Paine would bring with her. She would tell Barbara they were 'Good friends from Nairobi, who had kindly driven her out', but we all imagined they were more than that. Sorry, but we schoolgirls probably put the worst possible construction on it. You've got to remember we were all obsessed by sex at that age.'

'What about when you went up to Kisule? What was that like?'

'Oh, that was lovely. Barbara and I rode all day. My Dad said we couldn't keep horses down in Langwa because of the tsetse fly, and I do so love riding.'

'Go on about my parents. Tell me anything you can remember about them.'

203

'Well, your father didn't look much like you. It's obvious both you and Barbara took after your mother. He was very polite, but quiet, and a bit . . . what shall I say? A bit English, I mean *old-fashioned* English. Reserved, that's the word I wanted. He was reserved. But he did have a temper, not with Barbara, though; despite what we have just found out I could tell that he loved *her*.'

'And Mother? Were there any 'good friends' in Kisule, do you think?'

'I doubt that. It was a dull little place, wasn't it? We certainly didn't find any interesting boys, not that I minded that of course. I was blissfully happy just being with Barbara all day.'

'What did you think of the farm?'

'Not much, I suppose. I only had our own place to compare it with and, to me, yours was a bit poky. Your parents seemed to be struggling to make a living, just like your mother says in that letter. We were all convinced that was why they came to take her away from school.'

The Headmaster's study at Castleberg flashed into my mind.

'But now I'm going to have to disappoint you,' Mary continued. 'You see, I've never discovered *why* they took her away. All those stuck-up bitches who hated her for being so pretty --- they all said that your father should never have sent her if he couldn't afford the fees. "A bush farmer with no background. Should never have come to Kenya in the first place."

'You were there when it happened, Mary. Try to think back.'

'I do remember Barbara being taken out of class to see Mother Superior. At break time I didn't go for milk with the rest. Instead, I sat in the cloister, so that I could see Mother's door. It seemed a long time before Barbara came out and I could see she was crying. Two nuns were with her and I could see they were on the way to the accommodation block, so I rushed to the

204

study we shared. Barbara said they were taking her away and she didn't know why. Her father had been so rude to Mother Joseph and she wanted to die.'

Mary herself was crying now. 'I'm sorry. You'll have to excuse me.'

She broke off and ran into the pavilion, sobbing. I followed and held her tightly in my arms until the tears gradually subsided. Here was someone who loved my dead sister just as I did. No, not in the same way --- in a way I could not understand. But someone who was bound to me by a tie of love for the person who still seemed almost part of me.

'Oh, Harry darling, it was the unhappiest time of my life. I waited and waited for a letter or a telephone call from her, but there was nothing. It was over a week before we were all sent into the assembly hall and told they had been killed in a car crash.'

I led her back outside and we walked around the roof, holding hands and looking at the view. Before we had completed the circuit I had made a decision. For both our sakes I had to find out what happened on that day in June twelve years ago.

'Now,' she continued, 'can you imagine how I felt when I read your CV and saw it was you coming out for the WAFCO project. In my office that first day, I could scarcely look you in the eye. You have no idea how like her you are, the way your eyes twinkle when you smile. You're doing it now.
That smile, it's exactly like hers; the way she used to smile at me and make my knees turn to jelly.'

'I thought at first that you were terribly proper,' I said. 'I wondered if we would ever get on. Only when I went to the beach house did I realised what a lot of fun you are.'

'Yes, that's Mary Costas, isn't it? The comic turn, life and soul of the party. Half past ten every Sunday morning it's down to the beach house and on with the motley, chatting up the new talent.

Searching for another Barbara. Of course, when you first met Inge at the Kiboko I knew at once that you saw the resemblance. I was drunk, but even in that condition it was obvious as soon as you looked at her.'

'No, I still don't know what you mean.'

'Inge and Barbara? I know their colouring is different, but you looked at Inge as though you recognised her. Don't you see that she is the reincarnation of Barbara?'

I thought back to that first meeting in the hotel bar and now knew who it was that I had recognised in Inge. The implication repelled me. Is that why I have fallen in love with her? Is it my dead sister with whom I am in love?

'Then *you* came along,' Mary said. 'The embodiment of Barbara but, what can I say? Attainable, not to put too fine a point on it – male. But there was sodding Gaynor in the way. Sorry about the language, but that's how I thought of her; an obstacle to what I most wanted. And yes, I *am* in love with Inge too. So, that's it, isn't it? The end of the affair?'

'What do you mean? I don't understand.'

'I'm not stupid and I realise what a fool I've made of myself. A man can't respect a woman who throws herself at his feet, especially one who's half queer. But I hope we can still be friends I'm sorry I'm crying again.'

Mary moved to sit on the pile of mattresses and quietly sobbed. I went to sit beside her and placed my arm around her shoulder, but she dragged me down and pulled me hard against her. I kissed the salty tears from her cheeks, I kissed her lips. She opened her bath robe, put her hands onto my shoulders and gently guided me further down her body.

THIRTY-EIGHT

As Mary drove me back to Umoja my mind was on the complexity of this woman, sitting beside me, but distant. She had been so full of passion little more than an hour ago but was now outwardly composed. My body still glowed with excitement, but behind the excitement was guilt, that I had been unfaithful to Gaynor. We exchanged few words and those merely to confirm the arrangements she had made.

Because of her love for Barbara, the mystery surrounding the death of the my family had become equally her concern. She took a decision I had been loath to take. My visit to Kisule had reopened a wound, now made more painful by what I had just learned about my mother. Mary, however, was determined to complete the picture left unfinished since the day Barbara was taken away from their school.

She was going to take a week off. We would drive to Kenya, where the former Mother Superior of her convent school lived in retirement. On the way back we would divert to Lassita to see her father. The latter visit had already been arranged by telephone, but Mary had yet to find out exactly where the Reverend Mother was living. She would ring some of her former school friends who may know.

She dropped me at the apartment block with a casual, 'See you next week.' No kiss.

Inge must have been watching at her window, because by the time I had climbed the stairs she was waiting on the landing outside my door. I still wore the track-suit and carried my safari suit in a plastic bag.

'I'm glad that track-suit fits you. We bought it just before Wellington ran away. Mary measured it against me; I told her you were about ten centimetres taller.'

She smiled knowingly, as though familiar with the whole story of my visit to Mary's house. 'You will need to rest now, I think --- to recover your energy.' She giggled.

The two of them must have planned my seduction in advance. I changed the subject.

'Mary and I have been making plans. We have decided to take a trip up to Nairobi.'

'Oh, how exciting: you are eloping! I will come with you and be her bridesmaid?' She ran upstairs.

For the rest of the afternoon I intended to edit the draft of my report, but my mind would not turn to it. I spent more than an hour pottering round the apartment, admiring ornaments I had hardly noticed before, opening and closing books without any intention of reading them.

My body still glowed from finding the *real* Mary. After two years working so closely with her it was only now that I saw her as desirable. To find such passion in her was a revelation. Yet I did not fully understand how she felt about me. Was I anything more to her than a surrogate for my dead sister? After so many months deprived of the companionship of women, I now found myself totally confused. Out of my depth in this tide of emotion. In order to discipline myself into some useful activity, and knowing there was no hope of being able to concentrate on the report, I took a writing pad to the dining room table and set about the equally daunting task of penning a reply to Gaynor.

Hardly had I sat down when the doorbell rang and there stood Inge, looking delectable in a knee-length cotton shift dress, the colour of ripe apricots. She seldom wore skirts and I had never seen her in anything so short. To complicate the issue further, a vision of Maggie Mercieca appeared in my mind. My surprise at seeing Inge must have been evident. She gave me one of her teasing pouts.

'I have come for tea but I see you do not want me. Goodbye then. I shall go back to my room and cry, then I shall make my own tea and I shall write in my diary that my English gentleman does not like me any more.'

'Come in and don't be so silly,' I said.

She sat on the chair near the window and I went to put the kettle on. I was thoroughly enjoying the luxury of this apartment, after the Spartan existence that George and I had undergone for most of the past two years.

'Tell me about the other residents here,' I said from the kitchen. I had not yet got to know anyone else in the block, although I recognised the couple opposite as people who occasionally came to the beach house.

Inge came to join me. Her synopsis was far from complete but gave an insight as to where her interests lay.

'Right, are you ready? OK, the man in number one sometimes hits his wife. Number two is empty now but a consultant from Sweden is coming to live there next month. Opposite you are the Hewitts from the British Council. You have probably met them at Mary's beach house. Number five and six are both from Germany. Then there is a very nice-looking Belgian boy called Albert Foch. He works as an adviser with the harbour authority and drives a Suzuki like mine. Opposite him are a couple from Mannheim called Beckmann or Bechtiger, something like that and the wife is very bored because her husband works at night at the airport, so when he is at work she goes across to Albert and I think he fucks her. Oh, sorry, I think he makes love with her. That's it, because the other one on my floor is empty. Mary would not give you that one because it is too near my place and she is jealous about you and me. So now you know about everybody and I would like my tea, please.'

During the days that followed, Inge and I established a routine of meeting for coffee or tea whenever we both happened to be in, and on the first Thursday evening she came down for supper. It was nothing ambitious, avocados with prawns, followed by some talapia from Lake Victoria, which I served with Sauce Bercy; a recipe I found in a paperback Larousse that the previous tenant left behind. What she enjoyed most of all was traditional English rice pudding with sultanas and nutmeg, something Auntie Annie taught me how to make.

Inge proved to be more-or-less correct in what she said about her own culinary skills. When she returned my invitation, she made mutton stew which she said was her only alternative to smorgasbord. There was still no indication that she thought of me otherwise than being her 'English gentleman' friend. Nevertheless, the time we spent together was a welcome break for me. I was in a fruitful period of work on the university computer, inputting the final recommendations of my report. An evening with Inge became the focus of my day. I began to imagine what life with her might be like; unpredictable and difficult in many ways, but glorious fun.

As we got to know each other better our conversation blossomed. She was not a lover of modern painting (she made an exception of Picasso) and showed no enthusiasm for the current icon, Andy Warhol. Her passion was for Dutch interiors. One evening she brought a book of reproductions down and we sat side by side on the sofa. She liked to invent a story around the characters in the domestic scenes. Her commentary brought them to life.

'You see that door, half open? The children are hiding behind it listening to the artist talking to their parents. They have been told not to come in until he has finished but they are wanting to interrupt, so they can take a look at the picture. And here, across the page? That little dog has been ordered to wait there until the sitting is over, but she is wanting to powder her nose.' When I pointed out that dogs don't powder their noses, she said, 'This one is an English dog.'

As Inge went through the rest of the illustrations relating her inventions, I sat intrigued by the life she was breathing into these mundane scenes, but at the same time hoping that she might feel the effect of our proximity as I did, and want me to kiss her.

'You know such a lot about art,' I said. 'Don't you find textile design a bit limiting?'

'That is what I do for a living, like you dig up lumps of soil.'

'Is that what you *want* to do though? Just imagine you were able to do exactly what you wanted. What would that be?'

'Oh, that one is easy to answer --- to have my own couture house. One day you will see my name on the most beautiful clothes in the whole world. The Inge Jensen Collection.'

She appeared to be serious.

We would often dine out, usually at the nearby Palm Court Hotel. Potty was there on a couple of occasions with his current girlfriend, Euphemia from the New Bandari. The first time he saw us arrive together he gave me a warning glance, though Mary seldom came to the Palm Court. One evening Pete Larsen came in but when he saw us he quickly left.

Much to my disappointment, the sexual aspect of our relation-ship did not develop as did our conversation. I could not risk breaking what was already so fragile, by pressing it beyond what she wanted. But I was forever looking for some sign that the friendship might be moving to something more intimate. Our farewells were limited to a goodnight kiss, and even this was always on the landing. When we came home, I would es-cort her up to her flat, each time hoping to be invited in, but she would first take out her key and *then* kiss me, sometimes as though this was a duty. I would try to read a message into her response, but it seemed as if she was thinking --- here is a man who has been good to me and he expects to be kissed, so I will make it as nice as possible for him.

Nevertheless, these kisses were the high point of my day. I wandered downstairs in a happy daze, letting my imagination drift to what might be much more than just a kiss.

*

I skipped the beach house parties on the next two Sundays, to concentrate on my report. There was now every chance that I would have it ready to send to Haskins and Ede before Mary and I went up to Kenya. I had still not managed to complete a letter to Gaynor. Several attempts lay in the paper basket. I asked Musa, the cleaner, not to empty it. I might still make a satisfactory reply from the discarded efforts.

On Monday evening Mary came to give me the international driving licence and to confirm the arrangements she had made. We were to spend the first night in Arusha. Separate rooms, she made clear. She did not stay long. The conversation was as formal as if it had been conducted in her office. After she left, I heard her go upstairs to Inge's apartment.

When I looked through the window next morning the Mercedes was still parked outside. Half an hour later she and Inge emerged, laughing, and drove off together.

THIRTY-NINE

Festus Kasonde was already at the Bwalya's bungalow when I arrived. Mercy seemed rather tense, as she ushered me onto the back stoep. George was out at work in one of his taxis. There was no sign of the twins and Mercy disappeared as soon as she had delivered me to Festus, who was dressed in a tee shirt and lungi, not the Nehru style suit he wore at work. It was a humid evening and I was pleased to find a crate of cold beer under the table.

Kasonde moved the crate to give me more leg room. 'I wonder whether we are expected to dispose of all this?' he asked, in Swahili.

I joined him in the same language. 'Let us at least make a start.'

Festus opened two bottles and passed me a glass. 'I am pleased to hear that Mr Marshall was able to help you with entering your data. We are trying to persuade him to stay here on a permanent basis --- just the sort of man we need. And I do agree

212

that it would be a good idea for you to get the opinion of John Costas, now that he knows of our little plan. If he finds someone like you involved he may be better disposed towards it.'

'Is there anything that goes on in this country that you don't get to hear about?'

Kasonde laughed and changed to English.

'Sorry, Harry. Don't think me a Machiavelli; people just tend to tell me things, that's all. Karibune is really like a small village, isn't it? At least the part you and I inhabit is, don't you agree?'

'I disagree. For me it seems more like an expatriate ghetto.'

Festus took a slow sip of beer. 'I think I know what you mean. What a pity that more of the foreigners who come out to help us cannot be like you, and really get out and meet our people.'

'I'm sure they would like to,' I said.

'Yes, I am not blaming them; we need them here in the capital. But I wonder how many of your friends understand as you do what happens once you get away from this town? Even I sometimes need to remind myself that out there is a big country, a country with problems that we are only just starting to tackle. That is why I try to spend as much time as I can back in my home village.'

'Sorry if I sounded rude Festus, but it is disconcerting to see how efficient your information network is.'

I opened two more bottles, while Festus embarked on the topic for which I had been summoned. He reverted to Swahili, probably without realising it.

'I wonder whether you consider that the East African Community is irretrievably lost?'

'Surely your political friends know more about this sort of thing than I do.'

'Of course they do, but it is not often that I get the chance to speak to an outsider who is not grinding his axe . . . that's doesn't quite fit in Swahili, does it?' He changed back into English. 'Who does not have an axe to grind . . . correct? Sometimes it's difficult to translate colloquialisms into our language. President Nyerere must have had an incredibly difficult task with his Shakespeare translations. Have you read them? Absolutely perfect in the purple passages but the language of the ground-lings doesn't seem to work in Swahili.'

My face must have betrayed frustration at Kasonde's failure to come to the point.

'Sorry for the digression --- it's a failing of mine. The reason I asked you to come for this chat is that you know the Kenya situation, and have travelled around Bandari as much as any foreigner I know. I would greatly welcome your opinion.'

I thought back to that driver, Goodwill, and his attitude to the Kikuyu, to the way the twins were regarded as foreigners by their classmates. I phrased my reply with care, lest I offend this man, whom I had come to respect.

'I believe there are still strong arguments in favour of a Community, but I suspect that the nations have been drifting further apart since the original experiment ran into trouble. I had always assumed that your people had some misgivings about the idea, and now don't we also have to consider the problem of Uganda? Surely there can't be a Community without Uganda, and with Amin in control there you surely can't . . .'

'No, of course not; but discount Amin. Frankly, I think we shall need to take some action against Idi. I gather that Julius has some plans --- but keep that to yourself. I mean, do you think the will is there to get together again?'

I pondered this for a moment. 'I have always thought that the countries are potentially a viable entity, but their political and tribal differences make anything but a loose trading bloc difficult to envisage.'

Kasonde seemed pleased by what he heard, but I remained convinced that this preamble was leading to something closer to home.

I concluded by saying, 'To sum up: given a new regime in Uganda there might be a possibility of a 'drawing together', especially if some outside emergency arose to unify the nations. Not necessarily war, I sincerely hope that is out of the question, but some other crisis, possibly economic.'

Festus almost beamed with pleasure and exclaimed, 'Yes, I knew you were our man --- I told them so. Well done Harry!'

I was not quite sure what I had done, apart from having reached the conclusion that Kasonde wanted.

'And don't we have that crisis now?' he asked.

'Do we?'

'Fuel, my dear chap . . . petroleum . . . inflation. Here we are in Bandari, trying to make something of our independence, when the carpet is pulled right out from under us by OPEC.'

'Yes, I see what you mean.'

'It's all right for Nigeria and Libya, even Gabon. Do you know that Gabon's population is far smaller than ours, but now they are one of the richest countries on the continent, purely because of an accident of geology? Who else in the OAU, apart from those I have mentioned, benefits from what's going on? The Arabs are certainly thumbing their noses at the old colonialists, but what about us, their oppressed brothers? What can *we* do to withstand that sort of pressure?'

'Forgive me Festus but I'm way out of my depth here. I'm an agronomist not an economist. Ask me where to plant coffee or how to grow avocados, and I'm your man, but let me pass on this one, please.'

'Sorry, I do tend to get carried away, I'm always being told that. Let me come down to earth then. Ethanol, does that mean anything to you?'

'Yes. You mean ethanol as an additive to petroleum. I gather it's being done in Brazil, but to ship ethanol here would make it as expensive as petrol, and then to convert vehicles . . .'

'Stop. Hold on, Harry. Not *ship* ethanol, *produce* ethanol. Why not make it here?'

'Well, I suppose that with petroleum at present prices you might make it pay, given the right technology.'

'Which I happen to know is already available,' Kasonde interrupted.

'Let me carry on, please. You'll find that there is something to interest you at the end of all this. You see, our National Economic Council has a science sub-committee of which I am what might be termed a lay member. I grant you we don't have the world's leading scientists, but we do have people who can interpret the latest publications. The scientific journal *Nature* recently featured a most interesting treatise on this subject. It was written by someone you know --- know very well, in fact.'

'Now I'm convinced you *are* Machiavelli incarnate. No doubt George told you about Gaynor's article?'

'Well, not directly. George told Mercy about it and it was she who told me. Mercy is a clever lady. She has good Cambridge 'A' levels in chemistry and biology and could have gone on to university. She understood what you told George about using bacteria to produce ethanol, even though he didn't. It was Mercy who suggested that your fiancée might join us.'

216

'I'm sorry Festus, there are problems. First of all Gaynor is only a post-doc researcher. She is certainly interested in the industrial use of biotechnology but right now she's on a two-year assignment in California. Secondly, we have no intention to marry at present. Finally, on a practical point, I believe that marketing a sufficient amount of ethanol wouldn't be feasible. What about raw material for the process? I'm sorry, I don't want to be rude, but don't you think this may be a little beyond the reach of a country like yours?'

Perhaps I had overstepped the mark. Kasonde looked downcast at my response. I had not meant to belittle the East African nations, particularly Bandari. I admired much of what the government was trying to do, but this certainly seemed a grandiose plan.

'Just think about it,' Festus said. 'That's all I ask at this stage.'

'I will indeed. But I asked you about raw material. Bandari needs all its productive land for food supply.'

'Millet?'

Kasonde looked as though he had produced a rabbit from the hat. 'You haven't revealed much to me about your WAFCO proposals but you did say early on that millet was 'a waste of space', if I can recall you said that almost any starch produce could be the input for the process. Why not millet? It's a low value food crop but it will grow on even the poorest land. Does that appear 'pie in the sky'?'

A grandiose project it certainly would be. And yet? If it could be brought to fruition and Gaynor could be working beside me here? Once again, a tempting bait had been laid --- and Festus knew it.

'Here is something you must keep to yourself,' he went on. 'The brewery owners want to cease production in Langwa and centralise down here in Karibune. That would give us our fermentation plant.'

217

'There's still the problem of what to do with so much ethanol,' I said.

'That's why I wanted your views on the East African Community. We could have a market throughout the community and the front-line states down south. There's also a distinct possibility of a free South Africa joining us soon. Is that a big enough market for you?'

'I see. You mean Bandari would be first in the field and there would be no justification for any other African country setting up in competition. A bit of vision and a lot of optimism are needed but I suppose it could happen.'

'Right, that's exactly my view. Think it over.' Now, let me go and find Mercy. We need help in disposing of this beer.'

While Kasonde was away I considered the possibilities. Is Gaynor committed to two years in America? Suppose this project could be made feasible and we work together on it; that would be the best possible outcome. Forget the WAFCO implementation contract, forget Kasonde's hare-brained plans for Lexfar. But does Gaynor still love me, or is what Mrs Miller told me about her and Hans really true? And how do I feel about Inge? It certainly feels like love. Then there is Mary. We were close for that brief amount of time, but what do I truly feel for her or does she feel for me?

I needed to stand back and review the situation in fresh surroundings.

Kasonde had returned. 'Mercy will be joining us soon. She has gone to pick up the twins from my place. Myra has been looking after them while we had our little chat.'

'OK, Festus,' I said. 'You have given me a lot to think about, but I do promise to write and get Gaynor's opinion.'

'That is all I want at this stage,' he replied. 'Now we have several bottles of beer to attend to. Mercy will ask my wife to join us. Myra told me she hardly had a chance to speak to you at the party. The twins were very cross this evening when they were sent away. Since your exhibition dance with them you have become their hero.'

George returned to join the impromptu party around ten o'clock. Fortunately, I met no police on my slow, unsteady, drive back home on the little Honda. By the time I reached Umoja my lungs were full of the fresh sea air and I was sober again.

Now I *was* ready to write to Gaynor.

FORTY

My idea of a convent would have been a cloistered retreat, deep in the countryside, with soberly habited nuns quietly drifting around the grounds, deep in contemplation. The reality was a four-storey building which looked more like an office block than a place of religious devotion, down a busy side street leading off from one of Nairobi's main thoroughfares. Mary rang the doorbell and we were let in by a young African nun dressed in what looked like nurse's uniform, but with a fetching grey wimple instead of a hospital cap.

'Hello Maria,' she said. 'Remember me? I used to be Charity when we were at school.'

'Of course I do,' Mary replied. 'Charity Ndebe. Yes, I remember you well. You did take the veil after all. What do we call you now?'

'Now I am Sister Benedict. She shook hands with me. 'And you must be Barbara's brother. We all loved Barbara, didn't we, Maria? Mother Joseph said you were coming, and you look just like her. Poor Harry.'

I hoped she did not see me wince.

219

'We'll wait,' Mary said. 'We are a few minutes early.'

'No. Mother is ready for you in the refectory. Come with me.'

Sister Benedict led the way up upstairs. 'You have become beautiful Maria.'

The refectory resembled a cafeteria. Mother Joseph sat at a blue formica topped table in the middle of the otherwise empty room. She put down the book she was reading and rose to greet us. I had expected a very old woman, but this lady was probably just nearing seventy. Mary kissed a ring on her finger. I shook her hand.

'Well now Maria Costas. Little Mary. God bless you, you've made a fine young woman, as I knew you would. And you don't have to tell me who this young man is, for is he not the very living image of his poor dead sister?'

She began to walk towards the swing doors at the end of the refectory.
'Come along with me, my dears. This place is not suitable at all, not for the talking we have to do.'

The room she took us to resembled Doris Grech's sitting room, the little shrine to the Madonna, the same picture of the Pope on the wall and comfortable, rather worn furniture. Mary and I had rehearsed the questions we would ask, and it was I who should take the lead.

'It's good of you to see us, Reverend Mother, and we don't expect you to tell us anything which you feel is private to you and my sister. I happened to take a job in Bandari and, by the strangest of coincidences, I came across Mary who was a close friend of Barbara's at your school.'

Mother Joseph smiled. 'Of course, you must realise that is what I would call the will of God.'

'I am beginning to feel you may be right about that. Anyway, as you may recall, I was a boy of fourteen when I learned that my family had been killed, but even at that age I knew that my parents wouldn't take Barbara away before the end of term without a good reason. Mary has told me about the heated discussion before they left. I can't help feeling there may be more that you can tell us?'

As I finished the little speech I had prepared the night before in the Livingstone Hotel in Arusha, I remembered something that Tommy Fothergill had said in that other hotel, in Valletta; something about being in a certain place at a certain time. Was it just coincidence that had brought the three of us together in this convent in the centre of Nairobi, with the Saturday afternoon traffic hooting outside the window of Mother Joseph's comfortable little room?

She put down her rosary beads and did not reply to me. Instead she addressed Mary. 'Tell me Maria, what is this young man to you? I ask you this because what I have to tell him is not for the ears of anyone who does not love him, as I know well you loved his sister.' This remark appeared to disturb Mary. 'Don't be surprised dear', Mother Joseph continued. 'I suppose you thought we were all dried-up spinsters who knew nothing of the emotions of other mortals. But we all of us have eyes, and we all still have the human feelings we were born with. It would make me happy if you told me that Harry is more to you than just Barbara's brother but, if that is all he is, would you leave us for a wee while, before I answer the questions he has come so far to ask. Then he will decide how much to tell you.'

I looked across to Mary. We had not prepared for such a contingency, but she needed no prompting. She picked up her handbag from the side table and went to the door.

'I think I will go and have a word with Sister Benedict,' she said. 'We have a lot to catch up on since I last saw her.'

When the door had closed, Mother Joseph went to a cupboard and brought out a book which looked like a ledger. She spent a few minutes searching and, when she found the page she wanted, she read carefully through it. Then she studied a few more pages. It seemed a long time before she spoke again.

'I told Maria that you would be asking me questions, but I know well what they will be; so sit quietly and listen, while I try to think back to when it all happened. What I have here is my diary for 1962, but what I wrote in there is not good enough for you, I am sure of that. I've been trying to put myself in mind of what took place that day. By the way, will you close that upper window please? I can't reach without a chair.'

I closed the window and she got up to switch on the ceiling fan.

'Thank you. Better to be a little warm than to have that traffic disturbing what I will be telling you. Now, did you know that your sister wanted to turn to the faith?'

'Yes. I have found that out only recently, from a letter my mother wrote to a friend just a few weeks before she died. She made it clear that Barbara wanted to become a Catholic.'

'We never put any pressure on the girl. To tell you the truth, Harry, we were always a bit troubled when a non-Catholic pupil wanted to turn to the faith, because parents would always suspect we were after influencing them. But with Barbara it was never in doubt from the first term. There was a great change in her, but you were never to see what she had become before she left us, God rest her soul.'

'I gather my mother used to visit you.'

'Yes, she would call in to see me whenever she came to visit Barbara. Now there was a fine woman, your mother. I don't just mean beautiful for she was surely that, but a good generous-hearted being that deserved better than the lonely scrimping life she had. In some ways she was a bit like I was before I joined the Order --- spirited.'

'Spirited?' The word surprised me. I had always imagined her

222

to have been subservient to my father. 'In what way, spirited?' I
asked.

'You would meet those that said she was flighty, but in truth she
was a creature who needed the affection of all she came across
-- and, the way this world is created, some of them would have
to be men, wouldn't they? It was nearly always Polly who came
to see Barbara. You don't mind if I call her Polly do you? As I
told you, whenever she came, she would drop in to have a word
with me. In those days I used to take a glass of Guinness, for my
health, you understand. Polly would have a sherry. She would
tell me of the life they led in that small town where you used to
live. What was the name of it, now?'

'Kisule.'

'Ah yes, Kisule. Well, I told her that Barbara had been to see me
about joining the Church and that we had done what we could
to point out all the difficulties. Your mother said she was all in
favour, but that your father would be dead set against it. She
said she would not dare tell him, not him in the state he was.
Bear in mind that it was a difficult time for all of us then. We
knew that there was to be independence and the settlers were
mortally terrified what would become of them when Jomo
Kenyatta got into power, for was he not then the bogey man to
put the fear of the devil into them? As you know, it didn't happen like that at all, but at the time there was a great fear in all of
them.'

She picked up the diary she had been consulting. 'Speech Day
that year was on the twenty-third of May, so it was a surprise to
see them here early in June, especially your father. I could tell
at once that he was a troubled man, but he had that air about
him of someone who contained his troubles. Your mother said
not a word. She seemed scared of him because it was clear he
was in a high temper.

'He started off very quietly. Said how difficult things were on
the farm and that he didn't think he could continue with the
fees for the next term. I said he needn't worry on that score, for

we had arrangements with a lot of the parents to see their daughters through to their certificates. But I could see that this wasn't what was really troubling him. Then he said something like, "Can you not see what you are doing, turning my daughter away from us?" I knew exactly what he meant.'

'So, he knew about Barbara's decision?' I asked.

'It seems that your sister had written to tell him what was in her mind, even though your mother told her not to. Then Polly spoke up, to remind him that I had warned Barbara; that I needed her to be sure she knew what she was taking on. But that only increased his temper. He said I should send Barbara in --- the poor child was waiting in the hall and she could not have missed hearing what he was saying, for he had raised his voice loud.

'When I went out to fetch her, I asked Sister Brendan to come in as well. She was a strong woman, and in the mood your father was in I wondered whether I might need some protection, but when we came back he had somehow gained control of himself. He said to Barbara, very quietly, that they were all going home, and he asked Sister to be so kind as to get somebody to help her pack. Barbara looked terrified. She was fighting back the tears and your poor mother was already weeping. Then he calmly takes out his cheque book and asks me politely how much was needed to settle up to the end of term. He said he must apologise for the angry words. I'll never forget the look of him. He was struggling to keep himself under control, and the unhappiness was there like a dark curtain behind his eyes.'

This was just as I had imagined it --- but was that all she had to tell? Mary's account took over from there. What happened after they left? I imagined my mother and sister getting into the Zephyr, frightened and weeping, my father loading her trunk into the boot and driving off through the school gates. Then the scene dissolved, like the fadeout in a movie. Where was the next location? The car joining the branch road to the Rift valley highway, the tense silence, the reactions of the three of them as they neared Kisule in the darkness? But there was to be no more; the film was over.

'So that's about the size of it,' said Mother Joseph. 'That's all I can tell you. A friend of your father came down next day to say they had not reached home. No, I think I am wrong there; I think it may have been a few days later because, according to my diary, we had the Bishop here for first communions on the day after they took Barbara away.

Then there was an announcement in *The East African Standard* to say they were missing. We tried to make sure the girls didn't see it. My diary tells me it was on the twenty-sixth of June that I got the telephone message telling us the awful news. That's a full nine days after they took her away. I arranged a requiem for her as soon as we heard.'

'Where exactly did the accident happen?' I asked her. 'Who was it that phoned?'

'I'm sorry, Harry, I know no more than I have told you, and I can't recall the name of the man who telephoned, though I do know it was the same person that came to tell me they were missing, a tall fellow with a red face. Wait a minute, I do seem to remember that he was from my part of the world. Yes, I re-call that he had the traces of an Ulster accent.'

'Would his name have been Finnigan?'

'Yes, you are right, that's it, Finnigan.'

*

I was glad to be able to repay some of Mary's generosity. She could use her Bandari shillings in Tanzania but in Kenya we needed foreign exchange, so she had no option but to let me pay. I decided to do things properly and insisted we stay at the best hotel, the New Stanley. I remember that my parents had longed to stay there but were never able to afford.

When we got to the hotel, I managed to change the two single

225

rooms we had booked for a top floor suite. There was a luxurious lounge between the two bedrooms. We sat in there after the short walk from the convent. There was a sense of anti-climax, as I related my conversation with Mother Joseph, because Mary could have written the script for most of what I had just been told. Although our scenario of the events of that day twelve years ago was now confirmed, both of us felt a sense of frustration. The story was still incomplete.

Mary was determined not to let it rest.

'Surely *somebody* in Kisule could tell us what happened. I'm sure you were not firm enough with them. I'll get the information from them. We must go back and try again. I'll ring Daddy and say we'll be arriving three days later. I can call Poonam to tell her to hold the fort a bit longer.'

'No, Mary,' I said. 'You must believe me when I tell you that there is nothing more to be learned up there. Nothing can bring them back. I'm willing to accept things the way they are, and I think you should. Perhaps the end of the story should remain a mystery. Let's take a walk around Nairobi before it gets dark and I'll take you out to dinner tonight. I found an excellent place in Koinange Street when I stayed here last time. I'll phone for a table now, it's a small place and they will be busy on a Saturday night.'

Since my night's stay at Magoulas she had remained somewhat distant with me. I suspected that my burgeoning friendship with Inge might be the cause of this change in her attitude. I saw her visibly relax after we left Bandari, as though she had left her problems at the border. These days alone with her might restore our relationship, at least to where it stood before the night of George's party.

On our stroll through the city we passed a toyshop which had a window full of cuddly animals. I went inside and bought her a little lion and when I presented it to her she kissed me, right there in the street. After that she held my hand as we walked. There was the prospect of an intimate evening.

I was the first to finish changing for dinner and called through to her room to tell her I was pouring drinks. 'Just a tonic water, please,' she shouted.

'Are you sure?'

'Yes, I'm sure, and you don't have to be frightened. Being on the wagon doesn't mean I am going to rape you again.'

FORTY-ONE

Lassita is just about my favourite place in East Africa. It is situated in that strip of the continent where the annexations by Germany and Britain abutted on King Leopold's Congo. In the carve-up of Africa between the European nations, this slice fell to Germany. It is doubtful whether any representative of the three contestants had ever taken the trouble to investigate what was at the top of the range where Lassita now lies.

The plateau on which the town stands had no permanent inhabitants until Dr Heinz Lassiter, an Anglo-German, established a hotel there in the late 1890's. The area had been grazed by the cattle of nomadic pastoral peoples, Nandi and Maasai, each disputing the rights of the other to the land. They faught skirmishes which resolved the supremacy of neither tribe, but which drove wildlife from the plateau. These nomads had no tradition of establishing settlements, so Lassiter was able to say that he had 'discovered' the place. He claimed it as his own.

Heinz was the son of a British-born missionary doctor and his German wife. Although the father was English by birth, he studied medicine at Heidelberg, stayed on there when he married and took German citizenship, before joining a Moravian mission in German East Africa in the 1880's.

Young Heinz trained as a geologist and joined the German colonial service as a surveyor, rising to be Director of Survey to the provincial administration. It was as part of his survey duties that he stumbled upon the place that was to bear his name, though 'stumbled' is perhaps not the word to describe what must, in those days, have been a major expedition. The plateau on which Lassita now nestles is only about two thousand feet high, but rises steeply from the plain. Before the road was built it must have been a two day climb to reach the summit, with all the equipment needed by a survey team.

It seems that Lassiter, then in his late thirties, was so taken with what he found that he immediately resigned from the colonial service, bought the land rights to the area, and set about developing it into a hill station for the recreation of his former colleagues. He used his government connections to have a road built up to his little kingdom and, using his own resources, he built a hotel and several bungalows around the natural lake which lies near the entrance to the plateau.

The small price he paid for the land rights ensured that he became a rich man, for in the early years of the twentieth century many others followed his example and bought plots from him, on which they built retreats where they could escape the oppressive heat of the East African coast. By 1912 it had developed to a point where plans were afoot to make Lassita the summer capital.

But the First World War ensured that this was never to be.

George and I arrived there as part of the WAFCO survey, in the rainy season of 1973. Mary told us that a Canadian water supply project took guests and she wrote to book us rooms for the three weeks we expected to be in the area. We didn't know what to expect, as we drove up the narrow road to the plateau, but what we found proved unforgettable.

The three weeks became almost two months, for it became clear to me that this was the most promising area for agricultural development that we had come upon.

On the day of our arrival we had set off far too late from Malua and it was already dark as the Land Rover climbed the long

228

steep hill. As we reached the pass leading down to the Canadians' camp a heavy mist lay over the small settlement. Our destination was at the far outskirts of the town, just as the tarmac ended. Entering what had clearly been a road builders' camp, we followed a sign which still showed *Brigmar Construction Ltd. -- Site Office*.

A light was on in the wooden office building. George went to knock on the door while I searched for the letter confirming our booking. When the door opened I saw George shake hands with a tall, thin man in a check shirt and corduroys, with a tartan-checked cap on his head. He was smoking a pipe.

'Hi there,' he said as I approached, 'I'm Ted Mackenzie. Welcome to Southern Alberta. Hope you weren't expecting the Hilton.'

He led us down a gravel path to a single-storey terraced block and opened the doors of two adjoining units. The rooms were basic, but spotlessly clean. Compared with some of the accommodation George and I had encountered on visits to more accessible areas of Bandari this was indeed 'the Hilton'.

'There's a shared shower room in between you, but you both look clean enough to join us now for supper. My wife has made a beef stew in your honour. You're a bit later than we expected, so wash up and we'll see you in twenty minutes. The mess room is along past the contemplation block. See you soon.'

Waiting along with Ted in the dining hall were his wife Margaret, their two teenage girls and five men, four of them almost indistinguishable behind full beards. They came and introduced themselves in turn, all Canadians. It was Saturday night, which Ted explained was the only evening when the whole group was together. All the men, apart from him, spent the working week in the villages, but everyone came to base camp on Saturdays so they could hold a service on Sunday mornings.

The aid project provided deep wells to the kiwanja villages on the plateau and was funded by a charity set up by several

229

churches in Canada. Ted and Margaret had been missionaries in Uganda and came out to administer this project after being evicted from their school at the start of Amin's rule.

After dinner, we all listened on the radio to the BBC World Service news. Then there was hymn singing, to a harmonium played by Tammy, the elder of the Mackenzie daughters. George gave a solo performance of 'The Old Rugged Cross' in his fine bass voice, and Margaret joined him in 'Amazing Grace'. It was a pleasant evening in an old-fashioned sort of way, but we excused ourselves at around nine-thirty, claiming tiredness.

As we walked back to our quarters George summed up the group precisely; 'God's engineers' he called them, and that is how they were known to us from then on.

Lassita has a micro-climate all its own. It seldom has the heavy downpours which plague the lower regions, though the annual rainfall is almost identical to that on the plains below. There is steady drizzle for a large part of the year. For the first few days, George and I found it depressing to be in this perpetual mist, but soon began to appreciate the fact that we were missing the deluges afflicting the rest of the country.

On the morning after we arrived, the mist was thick and there was quite a chill in the air. We walked into the small town, before setting off on an exploratory drive round the district. Ted had told us that many of the houses were used only as seasonal retreats by government officials. There was a permanent population of hotel staff and many retired people, including several Europeans, former planters and civil servants.

Until the kiwanja villages were established, development was restricted to the area within two or three miles of town, where plots were able to draw on piped lake water for irrigation.

Lassiter had set up a dairy herd when he first arrived, in order to supply his hotel. When John Costas bought it he developed the herd, through artificial insemination, now available in East Africa. I was pleased to find that the cattle were my favourite breed, Friesians. The Canadian group had established their own dairy, in what had been the tractor shed when road builders had the camp.

Local people were employed to produce butter and yogurt. Two of them delivered milk and cream around the settlement. Petrol being expensive and in unreliable supply, they carried the milk churns in a lumbering ox cart which they led through the town at a stately one mile an hour. I discovered that their main customer was the Costas estate. Before the end of my first week in Lassita I asked Ted how I might arrange an interview with Mr Costas.

'No hope, brother,' Ted replied. 'I've not seen him since we got here. He owns this camp of course. He's very generous --- the project pays no rent. We leave his milk and cream at the gatehouse. I never got to cross the border to the house.'

'Surely you met him when you were negotiating to take over the road camp.'

'No. He has what he calls a bailiff, a guy called Matiba; anything you want concerning the estate, that's the guy you see. You can go to the hotel if you want. None of us has been there but I'm told it's quite splendid. You have to dress up, though. They wouldn't welcome the likes of us in our lumberjack outfits.'

I decided it would be wise to follow the protocol of colonial times. I went to the gatehouse of the Costas fortress to leave my business card, with a note to say that I would greatly welcome a chance to meet Mr Costas, to discuss the WAFCO project. Mr Matiba came down and assured me that the message would be passed to Mr Costas but that he seldom received visitors.

One evening, George and I put on our best suits and went to the hotel for dinner. It was indeed a splendid place, a well-preserved relic of nineteenth century Europe, such as might be found in a German spa town. As we walked into the dining room, we saw the man I recognised as John Costas, seated at the head of a table of foreign guests. Though he was now a recluse, his picture was often in the newspapers. The photo they used was that of a younger man.

As dinner progressed and the party with John Costas became noisier, it became clear that they were travel writers and airline officials. Since the resort had been taken over by the national tourist organisation a visit to Lassita was included in many brochures as an 'add-on' to safari holidays.
Visitors were transported by helicopter from Arusha airport. Lassita Lake was free of bilharzia and three days spent sailing, swimming, and water-skiing on top of an African plateau could well prove to be the highlight of the holiday.

When Mr Costas's party was leaving, I got up and spoke to him.

'Excuse me. My name is Harry Paine. I left you a card.'

Costas shook hands and smiled but said nothing.

'I'd like to thank you for allowing me to stay at Lexfar.'

'That was not my decision,' he replied ungraciously. 'And I know your daughter, of course --- Mary.'

'Oh yes?'

'Will it be possible for us to have a talk?' 'Better not,' he replied. 'Good evening.'

George had heard this conversation. He did not often swear but, as they watched Costas leave the dining room, he said, 'Rude bugger.'

'Perhaps he doesn't like English people,' I speculated.

But I would soon be welcomed into his fortress.

FORTY-TWO

We had finished breakfast in the New Stanley by eight o'clock. Mary ordered packed lunches. Road travel in East Africa is sometimes an adventure and one can seldom find a place to eat. To reach Lassita from Kenya we had to re-enter Tanzania, pass through Arusha and cross the border into Bandari a few a miles beyond Moshi. Once we got to Bandari our route would take us through Malua, where I used to be based. I persuaded Mary that we should set off early, in order to reach Malua by lunch-time. I was hoping to call at the pub where I was once a regular.

Mary looked happy, as we entered the Bandari immigration post to have our passports stamped. After all, this was her country. The welcome the immigration officer gave her was like what royalty must experience.

'Welcome back home, madam,' he said. 'If you are going to Las-sita please use our telephone to let Mr Costas know at what time he may expect you. Go through to my office and dial '9' for an outside line. Do pass on my compliments to your father --- the name is John Mbeya. It seems a long time since we saw him through here; I hope he is keeping well.'

As I waited in front of the counter while Mary telephoned her father, I felt very much like the hired hand.

'Most kind of you John,' she said when she returned. 'He re-membered you.' Mr Mbeya glowed with pleasure. 'Another guest will be passing through later this afternoon and Daddy would be most grateful if you would also let him ring Lassita when he reaches here.'

I had not realised quite how much of a celebrity Mary was in Bandari. The Mlima Inn was my 'local' while I lived in Malua and I used to walk in without anyone even turning a head, but today was different. As I took Mary to my usual place by the dartboard, the landlord came to say he had a special table ready in the lounge bar. The Mayor would be round to meet her in a couple of minutes.

'Why all the fuss, Isaac?' I said. 'Can't we just have a couple of beers and one of your specials? A couple of steaks, medium rare, between two thick slices of bread, oozing butter.'

'OK Harry,' the landlord replied. 'If that is the way you both want it. But I must phone Mr Temba or I will be in trouble, that is for sure.'

We were there almost two hours. My former landlord, Mr Temba, came with his wife and children. The Mayor did turn up, followed by a reporter for the *Bandari Independent*, several members of the farmers' cooperative, plus a lot of people who claimed to be my bosom friends. I could not remember having met some of them in my life. Everyone wanted to buy a drink for Mary, and she agreed that I would drive the rest of the way. Quite a little party we had.

On our way towards Lassita, Mary said, 'You see, Harry? You've got to come back. Where else could you make that impression in such a short stay? Bandarians must be the friendliest people you can find anywhere in the world, so don't let us down.'

'You were the big attraction,' I replied, 'but I take your point.'

Less than a hundred miles remained. Despite our long lunch break, we could easily be there by teatime. It was frustrating that, about twelve miles out of Malua, we passed the range behind which our destination lay, but it was still another thirty miles before we reached the road up the mountain. Heinz Lassiter had the road built to receive visitors from the coast, and this remained the only vehicle access to the plateau. He had it started more than forty miles from the town, and it was cut diagonally into the hill, to make a long gentle approach rather than a sudden steep climb.

When eventually we reached the junction, I topped up with petrol at the filling station and took the precaution of filling the two jerricans, aware that the gas station at Lassita Hotel often ran out of fuel. Two Maasai boys were there, resting before they began to walk their cattle on the same long climb. Mary called them over and handed them our two packed lunches,

234

which they accepted without any display of gratitude, part of their tribal tradition of proud independence, but annoying to the donor.

Like many roads in Africa this had a central track of tarmac, with compacted earth forming the rest of the camber. There was mostly a gentle gradient, but there were parts which needed hairpin bends to negotiate rocky outcrops and passing places had been constructed. The rule of the road was that traffic coming up the hill had priority.

It was most annoying when, just as I was past the first of these bends, I saw two motor cyclists coming down the hill with head-lights blazing, showing no intention of leaving the road to let our car through. They came right up without leaving the central strip and signalled that we should stop. As the motorcyclists drew near Mary said, 'Oh, no. That must be Jonas coming down. Back down to the passing place, darling.'

Jonas Wabandari was now President of the Republic. Until In-dependence he had been a successful barrister in London, and it was regarded as a selfless and patriotic act when he gave all that up to return home to join the new government. He had been born Jonas Jonasson, (it was rumoured that there was Ger-man blood in the family during the nineteenth century) but he had adopted his present name after taking Silk, as a gesture of loyalty to the land of his birth. Some pointed out that it also helped to bring in racial discrimination briefs. He became Justice Minister in the first government and was a surprise choice to replace President Mackeja, who died only three years later. He did an adequate job, but he had certain *follies de grandeur*, one of which was that he demanded the whole road to himself wherever he travelled. However, on this occasion he did not assert the right. When the outriders had reached our Mercedes, we were alerted by a blast on the horn of Jonas's car. We saw him standing in the passing place above, waving to sig-nal us to continue up the hill. When we reached him, we got out to say thank you.

'I am sorry, Mary dear,' said Jonas, in English. 'I realised it must be you. My boys are a little over-zealous I'm afraid. The rule of the road applies equally to presidents, I do realise that.'

Despite the reasonable words he nevertheless gave the impression that he had done us an enormous favour.

'That's most kind of you,' said Mary diplomatically. 'Have you seen Daddy while you were in Lassita?'

'That was the whole point of my visit. I have Simon with me, as you see.' He indicated the Minister of Natural Resources, Kasonde's boss, who was sitting in the back seat but had not troubled to get out.

'Your father said he was expecting you. And this must be Mr Paine. We ought to have met before, young man. Festus has told me what a splendid job you have been doing with WAFCO; be sure you persuade them to implement your proposals. But do excuse me, I have a dinner appointment in Karibune tonight. Come and see my wife again sometime soon Mary. You always make her laugh.'

He shook hands with us both and the entourage was on its way.

A few miles further on, Mary said, 'I suppose you've noticed I haven't been seeing so much of Inge in the last couple of weeks.'

'Well, yes. I assumed you were busy.'

'Not exactly. I thought I should leave the field clear for you --- for her sake mainly.'

'Sorry Mary, you'll have to help me with that. I don't understand. What do you mean by 'leave the field clear for me'?'

'Oh dear, I forget I'm talking to a man. How can I expect someone of your gender to understand such things? OK let me explain.'

We were ahead of time, so I pulled in to one of the passing

places, where there was a deep parking area.

'Let's get out and stretch our legs,' she said. 'There's a good view from here.' She walked to the observation platform and we leaned over the safety barrier, as she continued. 'I did enjoy the sex last night and, of course, that first time when you came to Magoulas. To tell you the truth I'd never done it before, with a man I mean.'

What she said appeared to upset her. We stood looking down from the viewing platform over the plains of Northern Tanzania. It was not so stark a landscape as that from Molson's Peak, where I had stood only a few short eventful weeks ago.

'You see, I used to have a friend staying with me, that was her bedroom you saw at Magoulas, the pink one. She was the matron at the Karibune maternity hospital and we planned to stay together, permanently I mean, but then she got a job in Nigeria. That's where she is now.'

'I'm sorry,' I said. That seemed inadequate, so I asked, 'Do you keep in touch?'

'Not any longer. It was for the best, really. We were too much alike; both of us unreliable. I do love you, Harry. I mean *you,* not Barbara's brother. But I'm deeply in love with Inge. The greatest joy I can imagine is to spend the rest of my life with her. I'm sure we are right for each other, but I want her to find that out for herself. This may sound crazy, but I wanted to see if she would fall in love with you. I wanted her to decide how she feels about you, so that she might discover how she feels about me. Now can you see how mixed-up I am? That doesn't stop me from feeling jealous though, both of her being with you and you being with her.'

I feared she was about to cry again and moved to embrace her. But she had not finished. 'When you come back for your second contract, we will know the answer. At present I think she is just revelling in the idea of having you around, and I know you well enough to realise that you won't press her into a relationship

237

she doesn't want.'

She had recovered her composure now.

'That's all. Let's go and face the music.'

At the gatehouse we both had to sign the visitors' book. I had
never had a proper view of the house. It was screened from the
hotel by a line of conifers. Like 'Knossos', the Costas family
home, it was built in the style of an old European hunting-lodge,
but this place was larger. It lay at the end of an avenue of
cypress trees, the first I could remember seeing in Africa, but
from what I had discovered about Lassita nothing surprised me.
There was a fountain in the centre of the forecourt, playing over
Teutonic water nymphs.

I parked on the gravel beside an identical Mercedes sports car,
which had Kenya plates. While I got out the luggage Mary went
to ring the door bell, an old-fashioned pull-chain. I could hear
the bell and Mr Costas must also have heard it inside the house,
but it was a servant who opened the door and then came out to
relieve me of the luggage.

'The master asked me to say sorry, but he is on the telephone in
the study. You know the way, of course, Miss Mary. I will take
the suitcases up to your rooms.'

'Right, here goes,' Mary drew a deep breath before she led the
way through the panelled hall, down a passage lined with hunting trophies, into a book-filled room, where John Costas sat at a
large desk, still talking on the phone. He smiled and signalled
us to sit.

'OK', he said, into the phone. 'My other guests have just arrived.
We can continue when I see you. Say two hours? I'll have a
drink waiting for you.'

He put down the phone and came to shake hands with me, then
gave his daughter a perfunctory peck on the cheek.

238

The brief encounter in Lassita Hotel had left me with no firm re-collection of his physical appearance. On closer inspection, John Costas did not look much like Mary, except that they shared a Greek profile. He was shorter than her, but he had a trim figure with hardly an ounce of fat on him. He was almost completely bald, though the ring of hair that remained was still dark. His eyes were piercing while he looked at me but then moved quickly on to give his daughter the same brief appraisal, all the while maintaining a charming smile.

'Glad you got through so quickly,' he said. 'Let's go through to the garden. Mrs Voyantzis is picking some asparagus for our dinner. By the way, Harry, I am very proud of my vegetable garden. I shall be pumping you for free advice while you are here.'

He led the way, through French doors, into a formal parterre. Mary went to join him, as we followed the brick path which led around the beds. I kept behind so as not to disturb them. I could hear them in whispered conversation though there was no need for them to whisper; they were speaking Greek. Be-fore they reached a gate in the stone wall which surrounded the garden they stopped, and Mr Costas raised his voice in anger, to which Mary responded with a louder burst of her own.

Then he turned to me with the artificial smile once more on his face.

'Do forgive us Harry. Mary and I can continue our conversation later.'
He gestured for me to join him, as he opened the gate into his vegetable garden, and Mary dropped behind us. By one of the plots at the far end of the garden I could see a lady dressed in cream smock and light blue trousers, talking to two gardeners who carried baskets. On her head was a battered straw hat which I guessed must belong to Mr Costas. He called out to her.

'Our guests have arrived, Katerina.'

FORTY-THREE

We drank afternoon tea in a conservatory which led off from the dining room. When we had finished, the women went back into the house and Mr Costas took me outside again to look at his compost heaps. He rummaged with a trowel, deep under the base of one of the heaps, and brought out a handful of dark brown loamy soil which he ran through his fingers with a look of great satisfaction on his face.

'I consider this compost to be one of my better achievements.'

It seemed odd that this man, who had built a business empire over a large swathe of Africa, should take such great pride in a compost heap.

'There are a few hyrax in the rocks over there, which help keep the snakes away. They will not venture out in full sun, so I have mongoose too.' Four or five of the little animals were play-fighting beside the compost heaps. 'Don't try to pet them, Harry, they bite. One of them caught a puff-adder last week. Come over into the summer house, I have quite a lot to tell you.'

He led the way to what would be better described as a gazebo, an open fronted building in the style of the main house and constructed in the same stone. There was a stone bench around the three walls but it was covered with seed trays. Mr Costas was using it as a potting shed, so we sat on two canvas chairs at an ancient card table. Katerina had already sent out two bottles of beer.

'First of all, let me thank you for alerting me to Mary's problem,' Costas said. 'I had a phone call from Kamal Chaudhuri after you had spoken to him and I was in time to sort things out, but I am very cross with her. I apologise for our little outburst in the rose garden. Also, I owe you an apology for not seeing you while you were staying down there at the road camp. I imagine you thought me extremely rude.'

I was no doubt expected to demur, but the memory still

rankled. 'I was somewhat aggrieved,' I said. 'You also upset my friend.'

'All I can say in my defence is that I must be careful not to appear to exert influence on projects such as yours. I am regarded as something of an *eminence grise* by opponents of our government. No, to tell you the truth, that is not all. In the past I have met several of my daughter's friends, and none of them has been the sort of person I would wish to cultivate. Would you believe me if I said that you are the exception?'

This sounded sincere, but who could tell if what such a man said was genuine? I asked him what he thought of Kasonde's plans for Lexfar.

He poured the beer, 'I'm glad you raised that, Harry; my last visitors have changed what I was going to say. No doubt you passed His Excellency on the way. Jonas agreed to let me pass on at least part of what he just told me, because you seem to have acquired quite a reputation for keeping your own counsel. He says they have had the devil's own job to prise any information from you about your WAFCO study. We will be talking about major developments in the country's affairs, so I must insist that what I tell you goes no further, at least until the news is announced formally. That could mean several months. Finally, we can't burden Mary with this knowledge'.

It had to be a snap decision; John Costas's keen eye was upon me. This was how a poker player must feel on the final hand. I had felt no compunction in reporting village gossip to Terry Canham at the embassy, but this sounded like something more serious. I decided that on this occasion my loyalty would be to Bandari.

'You can rely on my discretion.'

Costas hesitated only slightly. 'Right then --- where to start? I must admit I have hardly taken it all in myself yet. First, concerning Festus Kasonde. There is to be a reshuffle of the cabinet and Festus is going to be offered a ministry, probably Eco-

241

nomic Planning. This means he would be in an even stronger position to push through his plans to develop Lexfar.'

'Suppose Festus does go ahead with his plan?' I asked. 'Do you think the place can operate without Ken Pereira?'

'Ah, so you know about Ken's plans to leave, do you? Wait until I get on to the main point of Jonas's visit before we develop that one. This is the part where sealed lips are called for. OK?'

Costas waited for me once more to signify confirmation before he continued. I nodded.

'It's common knowledge that the West is concerned about our close relations with the Soviet Union. To be frank, Harry, so am I, but I admit the Russians have been most generous --- the textile mill, the Ban-Zam highway, you know what I mean. Anyway, this close interest has brought our friends from the United States into the picture. You will be aware of their Apollo space programme?'

'And they want me to be an astronaut?' I regretted the joke as soon as I made it.

He continued as though I had not spoken. 'They want a site for another satellite tracking station somewhere along the Indian Ocean. An approach has been made to our ambassador in Washington to see if we would be interested in providing one.'

'Knossos?' I suggested.

'Clever fellow. Exactly so. When I became a Bandari citizen, I thought it right to abandon all my overseas holdings. For my own sake I don't in the least regret this, because I can't envisage ever leaving, but I am concerned that the situation here may change. I would like to think that Mary would be provided for, if ever she needed to leave. I must admit I have hoped that one day she might marry and leave this country with a husband, but I know in my heart that this will not happen. So, I want to help her in the best way I can. The President has outlined a proposal that makes it very attractive to accept the offer to make 'Knossos' available to the Americans. I can't go into details, but it would mean that Mary and I would once again have foreign exchange.'

'I hope they wouldn't alter the old house,' I said. 'It's an historic building. There can't be many such places in East Africa still in that state of preservation.'

'You feel that do you? I am pleased that someone else regards the place as I do. It is so much a part of my life and my family history that I made it a condition that Knossos should not be destroyed. Jonas thinks they will be happy, not only to maintain it, but to continue with the renovations, which I know it needs.'

In the distance I heard a ring of the front door-bell. So had Mr Costas.

'That will be my other guest --- he has made good time. I kept this as a surprise for you. Katerina mentioned to her neighbour in Malindi that she was coming down to meet you, and he said he knew you and your family.

I wonder if you remember Arthur Finnigan?

FORTY-FOUR

Mary warned me that dinner here would be formal. I wore my dinner jacket for only the second time since I came to Bandari. She had on the same suit I had helped her remove the previous evening, after our first goodnight kiss.

We sat at a large round table, Katerina to the right of John Costas, Arthur on his left. I was between Katerina and Mary. I had so far exchanged only a few words with Katerina, but already liked her. She was short and rather plump. Her dark hair was probably assisted in its colour.

From the snatch of John's telephone conversation that we heard on arrival, I assumed he and Arthur Finnigan were old friends, but it became clear this was the first time they had met. I had no recollection of how Finnigan looked when I saw him briefly all those years ago. That was at the Nairobi show where he had been on a stand run by the Rift Valley Farmers Association. Barbara had rushed up to embrace him but Dad pulled her away without a word being exchanged.

He had aged badly. I knew he was older than Dad, but he looked to be well into his seventies, whereas he could be no more than sixty-two or three. He was about my height and obviously had been a handsome man, but he was now overweight, with the rubicund complexion of a heavy drinker. I was thinking about how Dad might look now, had he lived, and was not immediately aware that Katerina was addressing me.

'I'm sorry, what were you saying?'

'Day dreaming, weren't you? Mary tells me you are coming back to Bandari after your leave, and I insist that you both come up to stay with me in Malindi. I have tried to persuade her in the past, but she always claims that her office can't run without her. Here she is now, so I know that is not true. We have so much looked forward to meeting her friend.
I must not say 'boyfriend', must I?'

I did not want to disappoint Katerina. 'Thank you for the invitation. It's far from certain that I shall be coming back for another contract, but if I do, I will try to persuade her to come up to Kenya with me.'

Arthur and John were engaged in a discussion of Kenya politics. Katerina lowered her voice, so that only the two of us should hear.

'I hope you don't mind my asking Arthur to join us, Harry. It was pure chance that I happened to mention this visit to him. John had told me you were born in Eldoret and I asked Arthur if he knew you. It was a shock to learn that he and your father were once partners. You know, Harry, I have always been a great believer in the significance of what others may regard as coincidence.'

Tommy Fothergill had said much the same, albeit not so succinctly.

After asparagus came a fish course, talapia meunière. As Arthur's wine glass was refilled yet again, it was clear why he showed his age more than he ought. During pre-prandial cocktails he had suggested that the two of us have a chat after dinner, over a game of snooker. I was now worried whether Arthur would be in a fit state to answer the questions I so much wanted to ask. However, it appeared the drinks were having no effect on him; he was obviously inured to over-indulgence.

As the fish plates were being taken away Katerina announced, 'Tomorrow I shall make you one of my moussakas, but John suggested that on your first evening here the main course should be something English, for Harry's sake, so Egbert has produced a steak and kidney pie. I imagine it is a long time since you ate one.'

'Yes,' I lied, 'how thoughtful of you.'

Arthur took a glass of Cabernet Sauvignon with the steak and kidney, but I was pleased to see that he declined a refill.

At the end of the meal Mr Costas said, 'And now I have a little surprise for you. It was Katerina's idea, I must confess. I keep a small boat on the lake and I have an island about two kilometres from Lassita. I propose we set off around ten and that we have a picnic on my little retreat. Katerina has also arranged for fine weather!'

Mr Costas took the women for coffee in the conservatory, while Arthur and I moved to the snooker room. It was bizarre to be having a crucial conversation while playing snooker, a game I had not played since boozy evenings as an undergraduate. I knew little about the man, and had often wondered why his partnership with my father fell through. Since I may never have another chance of finding out, I asked him outright.

He did not reply and carried on playing, but I could see that my question had disoriented him. It must have caused him to fluff his attempt at a pot.

'Oh damn it', he said. 'Your shot, Harry.'

Perhaps because my mind was on other things, I succeeded in making a break which resulted in him conceding the frame. Samuel, the steward, had left a decanter and two glasses on the sideboard before we started the game, and I suggested we sit down to continue our conversation over a glass of port.

Arthur looked happier with a glass in his hand.

'You'll remember Alice Mtale I suppose, or were you too young?'

'I remember her well.'

'I was always fond of Alice. She worked for Sheila and me before your mother arrived. When Polly came out to join Henry, she needed someone to look after the baby and we agreed that Alice could move over to their place. Patrick was five and didn't need a nursemaid any longer.

I retired from the farm three years ago and Paddy runs it now. I'm sorry so many settlers got it wrong, there really was no reason to leave. We've had no problem keeping control of the place. I took the precaution of turning it into a limited company and we have local Kenyans on the board. If you come and stay with Katerina, I'll take you up to Eldoret to have a look. You and Paddy ought to get to know each other.'

Why on earth should we? I asked myself. And what had he just said? My mother arrived in Kenya with Barbara as a baby?

I said, 'Surely Barbara was born in Eldoret?'

'No, old chap, in Malta. That's how Henry managed to get demobbed so quickly --- that and because they had both served so long through all the pasting the poor island got. He came out with me to set up the farm, but your mother stayed until the baby was old enough to have her inoculations. Sorry, did you not know that?'

'I just assumed she was born in Kenya. But what happened after Alice
called you? You said earlier we should come in here so you could answer my questions. Please don't hold anything back. Can you tell me how they were found and where?'

FORTY-FIVE

Eldoret, 17 June 1962

Lying in bed, unable to sleep, Alice suddenly found the solution to her problem. She remembered the number. Tomorrow she would ring him on the telephone. Bwana Finnigan would know what to do.

Then she turned over and, at last, went to sleep.

*

'I set off as soon as I put the phone down', Arthur said. 'You may recall
there was no police station in Kisule, but I was friendly with Mc-Gregor, the Chief Super at Eldoret. He agreed to send a squad car up to Kisule. Then it retraced its tracks, driving slowly all the way to Nairobi, checking both sides of the road. They did all that could be asked of them, but no luck.

McGregor called me when they got back to Eldoret, to say he had called off the search.

'Is this woman Mtale to be trusted, Arthur? How do you know they didn't change their minds and shoot off on holiday?'

'I would trust Alice with my life. I've telephoned all the Nairobi hotels and I called in at Naivasha myself, on my way down to see the people at young Barbara's school. Has the old road been searched?'

'Every inch. On both sides, up past Molson's Point and as far as the junction. If it was a terrorist killing or a kidnap, we would have had some contact from them before now. In any case, things have been very quiet up there since the independence talks started. I honestly don't see what more we can do.

I think you'll have to agree to a missing-persons broadcast, Arthur, and perhaps an announcement in the Standard. I'm sorry, but I really can'na justify any further man hours until we do that.'

The port was at last beginning to have some effect on Arthur. His eyes were damp.

'There was no response to the newspaper announcement or the broadcast. It was another six days before Inspector McGregor telephoned again --- it must have been after five o'clock in the afternoon, because I remember that Sheila had to bring me in from the milking parlour to take the call.

Sorry to have dragged you away, but I thought you ought to know at once; we've found the car.

. . . . No. It was well off the road --- right off. Half-way down the escarpment below Molson's Point. According to what my sergeant said, you wouldn't be able to see it from above. Two Masai came into the District Office at Kisule early this morning to report they had found a car, but they didn't know what make it was. I sent some of my chaps along the valley track to take a look before we . . .

. . . . Hold on, keep your bloody temper. I purposely did'na ring you this morning. How was I to know it was their car? This could have been a false lead. I sent the RT sergeant with the search party and he has just radioed back ten minutes ago. It was a

Zephyr and it's them all right, or what's left of them, poor sods. I gave the chaps that photo the Mtale woman found for us--- it's definitely the Paines.

. . . . That's right. He must have chosen to take the old road. We have to draw our own conclusions as to why he went that way. I see no point in setting off now. It'll take my chappies four hours to get back to Kisule, so I told them to kip down for the night where they are and set off at first light. We should be up in Kisule well before they get there. Why don't you come down to the station around nine tomorrow morning?'

. . . . Yes, I agree. I don't imagine a chap like Paine has the sort of friends who would arrange a funeral. Would you ring the vicar at Kisule? Taylor, he's called; his number will be in the book. I think we ought to fix it a.s.a.p. as they've been lying there for over a week. When you speak to him, steer clear of the possible reason they went over, we don't want any talk of suicide. I gather Taylor is a bit of a hard liner on that sort of thing --- remember when old Stan Molson topped himself?

And I'll try not to get the coroner involved. I don't suppose he'll want to come all that way from Nairobi anyway, but I'll give him a ring when they bring the bodies in, just to check.

. . . . No, that's all taken care of. I gave my men three stretchers. I'll arrange to have some coffins ready for them in Kisule when they get back. By the way, I think we may have to have a whip-round for the funeral. I asked Jones at the bank to come in for a chat when we first started making enquiries.

No point in secrecy now, it's all going to come out in due course, but it seems he was up to his ears in debt. The bank will take everything. Maybe that's what drove him over the edge. Oh God, sorry! I didn't mean to put it like that. Isn't there a boy?

. . . . Is he? Poor little bugger, it's him we should feel sorry for; they are well out of it. Can you let his school know?

. . . . No, I don't suppose you do, but maybe Alice Mtale will be able

to find you their phone number. We will have to let her know what's happened, she was obviously very fond of them. Now you come to mention it, I do remember the laddie. Nice wee chap. What was his name?

. . . . That's it; Harry. He's the one we should feel sorry for. Poor Harry.

*

It was approaching midnight and I felt I could take no more. There was nothing I could think of to say, in response to what I had just heard. I found myself thanking Finnigan in a polite, detached manner, as though he had been relating something which had no direct bearing on me. Never in my most frightful nightmares had I imagined this outcome.

How could Dad have brought himself to commit murder? To take his own life, yes: bankruptcy could lead to that sort of desperation. And to take his wife with him? She had been unfaithful, that's true. But surely, she had expiated her sins a hundredfold by her devotion to him and her children; by willingly enduring the life he had inflicted on her. Her murder could possibly have seemed justified in the mind of such a troubled man. But an innocent child?

The cues were still on the snooker table and I rose to put them away. I managed to control myself sufficiently to bid Arthur a polite goodnight. Before I reached the door, he said,

'Hold on, son. I'm afraid that's not all.'

*

When I eventually left the snooker room, the light in the study was on. I looked in to see if Mr Costas was still up but everyone appeared to have gone to bed. The servants had probably gone home, so I turned off the light. I found the kitchen and poured myself a glass of milk from a jug in the fridge, then set off to take it up to my bedroom, but I saw Finnigan mounting the

250

stairs. I held back and watched him ascend with difficulty, supporting his weight with the banister.

My pyjamas were laid out on the pillow and the net had been
lowered. I drew open the curtains; the parterre was flooded in
moonlight, clouds were scudding across the moon. Mongoose
chased one another round the garden paths. I leaned out of the
window to watch them play-fighting and noticed the light was
still on next door.

When the milk was finished, I washed and put on my pyjamas.
After cleaning my teeth, I went over to get into bed but hesitated. I put on my dressing gown and went out quietly next door
to Mary's room. She was still awake, reading.

'I hoped you would come. Take this magazine and switch off the
light.' She opened the net. 'Get in. Shall I take my pyjamas off?'

'No, let's just talk.'

'Lie down here, then. What did you find out?'

There was no way to prepare her for what I had just been told.

'I have just met my father.'

FORTY-SIX

It was only seven-thirty when I was woken by a gong, early for
breakfast. I remembered this was Mary's bed. I crossed to look
in the bathroom, but she was not there. In a minute or so she
came in, wearing a bathrobe.

'You heard the wakeup gong, I see,' she said. 'Did you hear the
car go?'

'No, whose?'

'Arthur's. I saw him leaving a few minutes ago. You don't have to rush, by the way. The breakfast gong will be in half an hour. You were sleeping so soundly, I thought I'd better go next door, rather than send you packing.'

'Why?'

'Thought we'd better try to maintain some sort of respectability by pretending your bed had been slept in, though I'm sure old Martha will smell my perfume.'

'What reason did Arthur give for leaving so soon?'

'I haven't been down yet. No doubt he would have felt as awkward as you, going on this picnic pretending nothing had happened between you last night.'

It was a tremendous relief.

'OK darling', Mary said, 'Off you go next door and I'll pop in on my way down.'

Katerina and John were already at table when we reached the breakfast room.'

I'm sorry to say that Arthur Finnigan will not be joining us today,' John said. 'He remembered a prior engagement in Nairobi which he could not avoid, and he sent particular apologies to you, Harry, after what he said was a most interesting chat last night. He hopes to see you again very soon. Now, may I suggest a light breakfast. It is a long time since Egbert prepared a picnic and I fear he will have made it more of a feast.'

I was surprised to see that Mr Costas wearing a T-shirt and baggy khaki shorts. Katerina had on a long-sleeved cotton sundress and matching scarf. Mary had come down in a blue blouse, cotton slacks and loafers, so after breakfast I excused myself and made a quick change into more- or-less what John was wearing.

We seldom had a family picnic in Kenya; those I could remember were roadside breaks on the way to our rare holidays.

When I went downstairs there was a huge hamper in the hall. Egbert and two other servants carried it to an old Rolls Royce, whose driver was waiting to strap it onto the tailgate. I was even more surprised when Egbert went to the garage and drove out a Land Rover. The other two servants got in and they followed us. We travelled no more than about three-quarters of a mile, through the hotel grounds and down a bumpy track to the lake shore.

The 'small boat', to which John had referred the night before, lay outside a large boathouse. It seemed big enough to be seagoing, and old enough to have been owned by Heinz Lassiter. The tall smokestack issued steam. I stood beside Mary while the hamper was unloaded and transferred to the vessel.

'You might have warned me,' I said. 'I had expected a cabin cruiser, not a liner.'

'Daddy will be telling you about *Argo*,' she said.

I could just make out the name on a plaque below the funnel. There was an elderly man on deck, wearing a peaked cap with an extravagant amount of gold braid. Egbert and his two colleagues climbed aboard. Did we need a captain and a crew of three? For a half-mile sail? A private picnic for the four of us began to look unlikely.

'Everybody ready, then?' said Mr Costas.

We stepped up the gangplank and followed John into the cabin. Once inside, even I had no need to bend my head. It was not unlike the bedroom I had just left, with slightly older fittings and a lot more panelling. Katerina filled a kettle and lit the gas stove in a galley alcove.

'Coffee all right for everyone, or do you prefer tea, Harry?'

'He'll have coffee,' Mary decided for me. 'Now Daddy, I left it to you to tell him about the *Argo*.'

John explained that the vessel had been put on the lake in 1923 by Heinz Lassiter's son. It was built in Bremen, in what we would nowadays call 'kit form'. From Mombasa it went by train to Nairobi, before beginning a long and laborious journey to the plateau, taken on the final stage as head-loads by an army of porters.

'I have been told to scrap it and get something more modern, but I suspect Harry will appreciate why I think it must be preserved at all costs; and cost is indeed a major factor. I have been asked to make it available to hotel guests, but the insurance would prohibitive.'

'What about fuel?' I asked. 'It looks as though it's designed to run on coal.'

'No, even worse, Harry. Phillip Lassiter used wood. Can you conceive how many trees would have to be felled to get this vessel up and down the lake even for this short visit to my island? I now use coke, which has to come from Zambia, so you can understand why the old lady doesn't have many outings these days. Let's take our coffees up on deck.'

This was just the sort of outing to clear my mind of the turbulence I had felt during my fitful sleep. When we reached the island, I found that our picnic was not to be *sur l'herbe* but in a pavilion rather like the gazebo in John's garden. Trestle tables were carried from Argo and covered by damask tablecloths; then they were laden with an array of delicious offerings, such as Inge would never have imagined for one of her smorgasbords.

Meursault and canned lager had been transported in cold boxes, but the cans remained untouched. I had never drunk meursault but vowed it would henceforth be my white wine of choice. We four had, of course, no hope of finishing what had been set before us, which I am sure Egbert had intended. When we left for our tour of the island, what remained would find a hearty reception.

There was not a great deal to see on 'Isla Costas', and the midges were a nuisance, but John assured us there was no danger of snakes. Katerina took my hand and deliberately held back, until John and Mary were out of earshot.

'I had a brief word with Arthur before he set off.'

Surely he had not told her? She put my mind at rest.

'Of course, I don't know what took place between you last night, but I could see he was highly disturbed, and I have studied your face this morning. All I wish to say, Harry, is that I still very much want you and Mary to come to see me in Malindi. But, unless you tell me otherwise, I shall not have you meeting Arthur again.'

I could have kissed her. 'I am most grateful, Katerina. I hope you will forgive me if I don't explain.'

'Of course, my dear, but may I say one thing more. I have had nothing like the suffering you've already experienced in your young life, but there is one huge disappointment that I still live with. I have loved one man since I was a child. I can now be near him, but not truly with him. I suspect I need say no more.'

'I understand,' I said.

'So, if it is of any use to you, may I use an overworked cliché? Time is great healer.'

Now I did kiss her on the cheek.

'Thank you,' I said, 'let's catch up.'

Before our return journey, John and I clambered down to see the 'engine room', a title which seemed over generous for the cramped area amidships, where the two servants who had only recently been dressed in immaculate whites while they served us food and drinks, were now bare-chested, shovelling coke into the hungry furnace. Mr Costas had appeared to be one of the 'old school' employers I remembered from my Kisule childhood, but I was pleased to see that the hidden purpose of this visit was that we could thank the two young fellows for their efforts. We then went up to talk to the 'Captain' who, John made clear, was a superannuated chauffeur whose sole job was now to look after the ancient vessel.

My brief conversation with Katerina had, to some extent, cleared my mind of last night's trauma. With Mary close by me, I thoroughly enjoyed our slow journey back, along the shore of Lake Lassita to the waiting Rolls.

With Katerina's moussaka to look forward to and the welcome absence of Finnigan, this would be a memorable end to my penultimate week in Bandari.

FORTY-SEVEN

Since I was leaving on a Saturday, Mary warned me there would be a crowd at the airport to say goodbye. They all seemed to be there, the many friends I had made during those busy two years. All except Inge.

The computer tape of my final report had been dispatched a week ago to Haskins and Ede by courier post; the printout was in my airline bag. I kept tight hold of it, as I shook hands with the group who were already in the airport bar --- Peter Larsen, Albert Foch who had the apartment above me, Potty Potgeiter with Euphemia. When Euphie gave me a kiss, her breath indicated that the four of them had probably been there since lunchtime.

I was going out in style. When my latest bank statement arrived from Guernsey, I decided I could well afford to upgrade my ticket. Nobody else was at the first-class check-in. Mary went to see if the steward in the 'Top Traveller' lounge would let us bring the party guests in there.

'Sorry everybody,' she said when she returned. 'Couldn't even bribe him. I told him we would pay for the drinks, but he insists that four guests are the maximum. Anyway, that's no place for riff raff like us; let's settle down here. Right then, Peter. This is one of those occasions for some serious drinking - -- mine's a large vodka and tonic. I can see we are way behind you lot.'

It had been an emotional parting from Inge. Despite my assur- ances, she had made up her mind that I would not be coming back to Bandari.

I had my cases packed by eleven in the morning and Musa car- ried them down to the hall to await Mary's arrival, so I was up in Inge's apartment before twelve. She had invited me to spend the last few hours with her and prepared one of her smorgas- bords for lunch, but I was not at all hungry. The look on her face was enough to make me sorry I had agreed to this exten- ded leave-taking.

'Cheer up,' I said. 'This is not the 'Last Supper'. All being well, I should be back in a few months. You won't forget to take my motor-bike out for a run now and then, will you? I promise to write, and you must let me know how you are getting on.'

'No, Harry. What you are saying is not true. I shall never see you again, I know it. That is why I am sad today, because you are my favourite man. I told you that a long time ago, didn't I?'

She seemed determined to look on the dark side

'Why not come to the airport with us. Mary says all the beach house gang are going to be there; that should cheer you up.'

'No, I want to remember you as you are now, here in my apart- ment. I shall walk with you down the stairs and then watch you drive away and know that I have lost my English gentleman. You must not write to me because that will only make me wish that I had never met you.'

She made some of the herbal tea that I pretended I liked, and then took me round the table to fill my plate. I took only enough to avoid seeming impolite. Inge's depression was infectious. At the back of my mind I feared she may be right, I may never return to Bandari. Despite all the offers that had been made to me, everything still hinged on whether WAFCO would implement my proposals.

I hoped that by now she knew my feelings for her, but the words had not yet been spoken. Now was the time to tell her.

'I love you, Inge.'

She held me in her arms and put her head on my shoulder. I could not see her face but could hear her quietly sobbing.

When she had calmed herself, she said, 'Mary will not be here for two hours, so we have plenty of time. I would like you to fuck me. I will never get married, but I would like to have a baby. Maybe I would be lucky, and you will give me yours --- please.'

Her sweet face implored me. Her lovely eyes, wet with tears, tore at my heart. What would have happened if this had been last week, and not this brief precious time before we said good-bye?

'No, my darling,' I said. 'Not now; not like this.'

She picked up the glass paperweight I had given her and kissed it.

'Every night before I go to sleep, I shall kiss this and think of you. So please kiss me now, so that I can remember the feel of your lips on mine.'

*

Everybody wanted to buy me a drink. Final check-in time was

not for another hour. If I started now, I would not even be able to walk to the plane, and I was looking forward to the free BOAC champagne.

Despite what Mary had said, after her first vodka she also went onto tonic water. Around three o'clock another group of beach house regulars arrived. Terry Canham and his wife came, but they did not fit in with the crowd and left after one drink.

The last to arrive were Mercy and George, with the twins.

'I come here all the time, with Daddy,' said Poppet.

Pipit pointed to the first-class lounge. 'Me too, but Daddy says you are travelling first class. We have never been in there.'

'Come on then, you shall be my special VIP guests.'

I took a twin in each hand. Mary and their parents followed, and I signed them into the guest book. We grown-ups took a table. The twins went to sit on high stools at the bar and asked the barman for Cokes. George had a beer and the heavily pregnant Mercy wanted only water,

'So, this is it, my friend,' George said. I hoped this was not going to be another tearful farewell, and was relieved when he added, 'for now at least. But don't forget the christening. Our son will be named after you and you are going to be his godfather. Give us a firm date as soon as you can. We will delay it if necessary, won't we, Mercy?'

She smiled lovingly at her husband. 'I keep telling him not to count his chickens, as they say. He will insist it is going to be a boy. What is the female for Harry?'

'I suppose the nearest would be Henrietta but for goodness sake don't saddle the little mite with an old-fashioned name. Call her Mercy or Mary, something like that.'

'No danger of another girl,' said George. 'My cousin is sure.

259

George Harry Bwalya', that's who he will be.'

After they had finished their drinks, George said to Mercy, 'Come along dear, Mary and Harry will want to talk.' He called to the twins, who were still joking with the barman. 'All right girls, thank the gentleman and come along. Let's go up to the roof and I will show you Uncle's aeroplane.'

There was no doubt in Mary's mind that I would be back so no danger of tears. Nevertheless, it was a sad parting even for a few months. We talked of practical matters.

'I've left quite a few of my belongings with George and told him you'd send them on to me, if necessary.'

'I refuse even to consider it,' said Mary, 'but when you do come back the Umoja apartments will all be taken. I have another block almost as nice further down the coast, not far from Magoulas. I'll make sure to keep one empty for you.'

'All right but a proper rent next time. I'm not a charity case.'

'If you insist. By the way, I had a word with Daddy before we left Lassita. You know he likes you. Well, would you believe he suggested that you should move in with me? Not the sort of thing a parent usually suggests, I suspect he fancies you as a son-in-law.'

There was now nobody in the world closer to me than Mary; the awful secrets we shared ensured that, and our love for Barbara. If only I could love Mary as I was now sure I loved Inge. As I had loved Gaynor and Kitty. A relationship with Mary could never be like that. I needed a few months in a different environment: I needed time to stand aside from my emotions.

Mary and I were preparing to go back to re-join the party when Festus Kasonde poked his head round the door of the lounge. I had not seen him, but Mary asked him to come in. 'Congratulations Minister,' she said. 'Are you still deigning to talk to mere mortals like us?'

Mary excused herself to go and keep the others entertained. I asked the steward to bring a beer for my guest.

'My new appointment is not going to make any difference to our plans', he said. 'I came to tell you that.' He patted the airline bag on the seat beside me. 'Is this it?'

'Do you also have X-ray eyes?' I said. 'Yes, that is the printout, although my bosses should already be working on the tape I sent them. We just cross our fingers from now on, but just in case it doesn't happen, may I keep in touch? I shall always be interested to know how you get on.'

'I insist that you do,' he said. 'Now, though, we ought to take our drinks through to the bar. Your friends will be missing you.'

After its long take-off up the western runway, the VC 10 circled, to assume a northerly course, taking us over the airport build-ings. As I looked down over the car park, I could see a couple walking towards a pale blue taxi, each holding by the hand a small girl wearing a Marks and Spencer dress.

I didn't know this was to be my last view of Bandari for more than twenty years.

FORTY-EIGHT

Brough Farm, Matlock.

'Come down Dad.'

'I'm busy. What do you want.'

'The second post has just arrived and there's a letter from Zambia. It's addressed in Mercy's handwriting. May I open it?'

'Give it to your mother.'

261

'She told you at breakfast she was going shopping and I could tell you weren't listening. You spend all your time thinking about your precious hydroponics these days.'

'Don't be cheeky. All right then, open it.'

She runs upstairs to the library, a mirror image of her mother. My heart warms to her, even after she has irritated me.

'I haven't looked at the letter yet-- it's about six pages, but just take a look at this.'

She hands me an invitation card I never expected to get.

'The District Governor and elders of the Chikundu
request the pleasure of the company of

Dr and Mrs Harry Paine and family

at the installation of Mr George Bwalya
as Chief of the Chikundu
on Friday, 2nd July 1998 at Chikundu Boma.

RSVP. PO BOX 1, Chikundu, Zambia

'Isn't that super Dad? Did you know George's father?'

'No, he never came up to Bandari while I was there.'

'We *can* go can't we?'

'Don't you remember darling? We shall be in Malta in July.'

'We can go to Buenvista any time and it's so hot there in July. Gran and Grandpa can take it, or Mrs Fothergill can easily let it again. This isn't for another three months so you'll have plenty of time to organise things. You promised me and Mum we could have a safari holiday soon, and its ages since George and Mercy came over here. I was only ten then and . . .

'Shut up for a bit, will you, darling. Give me time to think. We'll talk about it when your Mum comes back. Go away and let me finish this draft.'

'You're such a crosspatch; I don't know why I love you.'

But she does go downstairs and leaves me alone with my thoughts.

Barbara has certainly matured since going to Castleberg. I was in two minds about them going co-educational but it meant we could send our daughter there. She is now hockey captain although still in the fifth form. We have high hopes she may get to Erasmus if she keeps on as she is. History seems her best bet.

There was mist over the High Tor when I got up, but now the view is clear. I can make out the ruins of Corbetts Farm, which always evokes happy memories. We are having a dry day for a change and, looking out over the fields, I can see Bill Palmer coming. He is walking slowly, but much more easily since he had the hip operation. He has taken the long way through the 'set aside' land, now covered with spring flowers. I've not seen them in such profusion since I was a small boy. Next weekend will be Easter and it is not difficult to guess what the basket contains.

So old Mr Bwalya is dead. He must have been eighty-five, maybe more; time just seems to slip by. Both twins are married now, and Mercy's Harry must be -- my God! Little Harry *twenty-two*.

It's Mary who keeps us all in touch. The friendships made in that couple of years in East Africa have survived largely due to Mary. That reminds me, I owe her a letter.

I often wonder what might have happened if WAFCO had appointed Haskins and Ede to implement my proposals and I had gone back for a second contract in Bandari. My proposals <u>were</u> implemented, but it was an American consultancy that got the job. Festus wrote to urge me to apply to join them, but I suspected there would be no long-term future if I did.

Festus's ethanol project never got off the ground. It was too ambitious for a little country like Bandari.

Mrs Miller turned out to be right about Hans Morgenthau. By 1975 he was in the middle of a messy divorce. He and Gaynor never got custody of his children, but they had two of their own. How Mary finds all this out I don't know.

Now it's time to tell you about my 'conspiracy theory'.

Did you ever hear about Langwa becoming the new Cape Canaveral? Nor did I. But you may remember that John Costas hoped for a dollar 'nest egg' for Mary, and for the refurbishment of 'Knossos'? Well, although 'Knossos' never became a satellite tracking station, some dollars changed hands. The American consultants used the estate as their headquarters and, according to Festus, the old house was improved substantially.

And Kasonde's plan for an agricultural marketing organisation <u>did</u> materialise. This lasted until Bandari joined the Commonwealth and their privatisation programme took off.

Ken Pereira stayed on for another four years before he and his family eventually left for Vancouver.

When the Americans left, the old house was taken over as 'State Lodge'. Heads of State stayed there when Bandari hosted the OAU conference.

Is all this coincidence? I leave it to you.

When John Costas died Mary and Inge were able to leave Bandari. They settled in Copenhagen and seem happy together, though I've no doubt they still have the odd row. The 'Inge Costas' fashion business is becoming quite famous. She got what she wanted, after all. A couple of months ago I saw a feature about her in one of the colour supplements, when they opened the boutique in Dublin. There was a photograph of the two of them, taken at their blessing ceremony. I was pleased to see from the photographs that Mary never had her 'nose job', but I didn't like the snide references to their relationship.

There was certainly no need to bring young Harry into the story. He is old enough to take it, though, and I suppose that sort of publicity does no harm if you are an actor. In fact, it probably helps as things go these days.

In case you are wondering, he is called *John Henry Andreas* Costas, so I have never been quite sure I am the father. In my defence, I didn't know about little Harry until the boy was seven. I was already married by then. In the photograph he did look like me, though. He would have blond hair if he were Potty's, or red like Mary's. But unless the colour was all wrong in the magazine, he certainly looked dark and very handsome. (Maybe I ought not to have said that last bit). I gather he speaks three languages fluently, four if you count Kiswahili.

You already know about me and my dreams. Well, sometimes there is this nightmare. He and Barbara meet somewhere, fall in love, and consider getting married. It is ironic to think that I am now in a similar position to Brown and Finnigan, but I did agree never to get in touch with Harry Costas.

No use thinking of what might have been; what might have become of those young countries if they had taken a different course. The world rolls on, and it becomes the responsibility of people like Festus to sort out the mess. I kept in touch with him for a few years before we began to run out of subjects of common interest. I sent congratulations when he became President and he wrote back insisting we all go over to see him sometime.

By the way, Potty married Euphemia in 1979. They moved to Zimbabwe but got out just in time. They are now the managers of a game park lodge in Natal.

I never saw Finnigan again after that night in Lassita. Arthur seemed to have gained the impression that some great change had occurred in our relationship. Why should he suddenly expect to be treated as a father, having been a stranger throughout my formative years? A chance remark made to him by Katerina Voyantzis was what led to me discovering something I would rather not have known. For the next three years he sent a Christmas card to me at Brough Farm. Kitty handed them to Richard Butterworth, who forwarded them to me in Nepal. But I never replied.

It was while I was in Nepal that the dear old man whom I called 'Grandpa' died. One of my greatest regrets is that I missed his funeral, but I was then living in a village half a day's walk from the nearest telephone. As usual, Richard coped magnificently, and Kitty arranged the funeral. I still miss him though.

Inge and Mary see Peter Larsen quite often. He is headmaster of a school in Odense and never got married --- still carrying a torch for Inge, perhaps. Surely, he must realise by now that neither of us ever stood a chance.

Those were happy days, when we were all young and full of hope. Please don't get me wrong, let me hasten to add that I am happy now. Couldn't be happier, but running my own consultancy is a struggle. Sylvester warned me it would be, when I resigned from the partnership. However, all that commuting to Cambridge was getting me down. Working alone is a tie and I'm aware that we don't get on holiday anything like as often as we should.

Suppose I get Mary to arrange for us all to meet for George's do? I'm sure she will already have accepted her invitation. If I fly to Kenya on the way to Zambia, I could push that proposal for a hydroponics project. Then, after George's installation, we could all go on safari together.

Why not to Natal?   Seeing Potty and Euphie would make it a 'full house'! We might even call on Festus. That *would* be a feather in Barbara's cap when she got back to school, having met a President.

Looking at these volumes in our library always makes me nostalgic.
I remember sitting with Tommy in Villa Buenvista, attempting to catalogue them. Poor Doris, twice widowed, but still battling with her arthritis and seemingly indestructible. Tommy dying so suddenly was a shock, but they did have nine happy years together.

There were times when I have been tempted to sell some of these books to help business cash flow, but I promised myself never to break up the collection. Barbara must have it when I am gone, I'm sure that is what Brown would have wanted.

I hear the Range Rover is crunching the gravel. Barbara has run out. 'Oh Mum, we've got a *wonderful* letter from Mercy and George with an invitation to go to his chiefing or whatever it's called. Mum, you've *got* to make Dad take us. You keep telling him he's working too hard and he promised you a safari holiday and Malta is unbearably hot in July. Mercy would be heartbroken if Dad wasn't there and . . .'

'Do stop talking for a minute, child. Let me put this shopping down. Go and open the kitchen door for your grandfather. He says his boots are too muddy to come in the front. He's brought us some Easter eggs.'

Yes, we will go. I'll show them the place where I was born. We will visit the peak and look out over that bleak landscape.   But this time I will have by my side a woman who has given me greater happiness than I could ever have deserved.

Barbara will see her Aunt's grave. ---Then I'll order a proper headstone.

Printed in Great Britain
by Amazon

70702075R00153